RAVEN

Stormy Souls MC Book 2

BY

Payton Hunter

This is a work of fiction. Names, characters, places, and incidents either are the product of the author's imagination or are used fictitiously. Any resemblance to actual persons, living or dead, events, or locales is entirely coincidental.

First eBook edition October 2023

Cover design by joetherasakdhi
Editor Nicola Thorpe,
PA: Tammy Carney

Paperback ISBN: 978-1-7385414-3-0

www.paytonhunterauthor.com

ABOUT THE BOOK

This is the book I always wanted to write but never dared to. It is a pure work of fiction, featuring what I love most: Bad Ass Bikes and the Sexy Men that ride them!

All people, places, institutions, and businesses are a work of my imagination, and similarities to real life are unintentional.

ACKNOWLEDGMENTS AND THANKS

Thank you to Tammy Carney for her endless patience and encouragement. To my editor Nicola, I would not have been able to do this without you.

I would like to thank my family and friends. Thank you to Nicky, Pete, Caroline, and Lola Wright for your encouragement.

If you would like to get in touch with comments, suggestions or just to chat

Email or find me on my Facebook page, or readers' group. I'll try to answer every message.

paytonhunter.author@gmail.com

DEDICATION

This book is dedicated to Caroline and Pete.

You are the best friends anyone could ever wish for.

Also to my amazing daughter.

Love and miss you always

xxx

CHARACTER LIST STORMY SOULS MC

Road Name	Rank	Name	Old Lady
Raven	President	James Saunders (Jamie)	Chloe
Rusty	Vice President	William Greenwood (Bill)	sister Ellie
Slender	Sergeant at Arms	David Brewer (Dave)	
Pennywise	Enforcer	Noah Nixom	
Spen	Treasurer	Spencer Dalington	Debs
Dawg	Secretary	Pete Cooker	Caroline
Clusseaud	Road Captain / event planner	Robert/Bobby Buck	Theresa/Terrie
Ferret	I.T. Guy	Zack Owens	
Vegas	Member / VP later	Vincent Albright (Vince)	Ashley
Moggy	Member	Craig Parkers	
Sparks	Member	Jason White	Ally/ Rainbow
Ratchet	Member	Ryder Gleeson	
Zippy	Member	Caden Giles	
Dougal	Member	Simon Baker	Sarah
Halfpint	Member	Dave Green	
Striker	Member	Eli Waters	
Greg	Prospect	Greg Brown	
Caleb	Prospect	Caleb Hayes	
Mom	Club mother, mother to Pennywise,		Helen Nixom

Others

Karen	Barmaid / Manager		
Neil	Bar Manager		
Fury	President Restless Slayers MC		daughter Meghan
Ghoul	Vice President Restless Slayers MC		
Masher	Sergeant at Arms Restless Slayers MC		daughter Tanya

Former

Flakey	Member	Carl Staunton	RIP in book 1

TABLE OF CONTENTS

1 — CHLOE

I'm sitting on my bed, head in hands as devastation rolls over me, paying the price for breaking my rules. Despite knowing better, I allowed myself to get close to Carl Staunton, a patient, and member of the Stormy Souls MC. Regardless of being two very different personalities, we developed a friendship.

His death left a gaping hole inside me. Every time I close my eyes, I see his face. Sometimes he smiles, sometimes he grimaces in pain, and sometimes he sulks, but he's always here with me. You can glean a surprising amount about someone in just a couple of hours, if you pay attention.

While it's heartbreaking to witness a once robust MC member, adored by those close to him, deteriorate and vanish from your existence. Even more frustrating is the fact that I'd been too busy to sit with him when his time came. Too busy to hold his hand, too busy to offer comfort.

These twelve-hour shifts are exhausting, often turning into fifteen hours, without breaks, the ability to have a drink, or use the toilet. The constant noise of call bells going puts us under enormous stress, especially since the pandemic. We've had almost two years of working flat out, leaving no time to get to know someone, nor build a therapeutic relationship. I've watched more directed to an open field to park. From the bottom of the small hill, we watch as bike after bike parks single file on either side of the path, forming an honor guard.

There are so many people! Some greeting each other; some just milling around. I survey my surroundings with curiosity and notice an exceedingly pallid Ashley, visibly grappling with her composure, as Vegas earnestly tries to provide support. The woman they affectionately refer to as 'Mom' stands by their side.

Raven and other members of the club walk toward the hearse, lifting the casket with the utmost of care, before carrying their brother to his final resting place. The silence, as everyone follows the casket and gathers at the graveside, is deafening. The minister gives a brief sermon as Carl's MC brothers carefully lower the casket into the ground. Once the sermon has concluded, I step forward with everyone else, white carnation in hand. With as much reverence as I can muster, I throw it onto the coffin, followed by a handful of dirt, saying my silent goodbye, unable to stop the tears from falling.

Once the crowd gradually disperses, I follow people walking down to the clubhouse. Since my invite includes the wake, I'll stay for a drink.

A tall brunette with glasses greets me as I walk inside.

"Hello, lovely lady, it's great to see you!" She smiles brightly at me. I realize I've seen her before, but my capacity for remembering names is zero. My confusion must show on my face as she explains. "I'm Caroline. I visited Flakey and Ashley when they were both laid up in hospital." Now I remember, the crazy woman who slapped Carl's ass! I grin at her.

"Hi, Caroline, I apologize. My brain isn't fully functioning. Of course, I remember you. My name is Chloe, as you know." I rush out my explanation.

"I know, lovely. You don't know many people here, so stick with me. I'll introduce you around. And please, smile. We're mourning, but we are celebrating his life. It's what he would've wanted," Caroline advises me, and I nod my head in agreement. He'd have hated a morbid affair.

I follow Caroline around for a bit, with Ally tagging along. They are a hoot, same goes for Ally's husband, Sparks. We chat away, and it feels as though we've known each other for years.

I love Caroline and her husband, Dawg. He's just as crazy and funny as she is. Above all, with both couples, love radiates out. You can tell they are as close as can be and love each other fiercely.

With the playful party mood, lots of laughter, and reminiscence, time flies. Though as the night wears on I start to feel like I'm intruding, an interloper in their private grief, so I decide to make my exit. As I rise to go, Caroline pulls me back to my seat.

"You can't leave yet. Stay and watch the show later." She smirks.

"What show?" I can't help but sound intrigued.

Caroline doesn't answer, just grins wickedly, winks, and taps the side of her nose. Ally comes back with another round of drinks—nonalcoholic for me—sets them on the table while nudging Caroline, who turns around, an evil smile gracing her face, gets up, and walks towards a ruffled looking Ashley and Vegas.

She stumbles right into Ashley, and Ashley struggles to keep her upright.

Caroline returns as quickly as she left, exchanging a conspiratorial smile with Ally.

Did she just stick her hand in Ashley's cut pocket? What the ever-loving hell?

I don't get to ask because I'm too distracted by Raven jumping on top of the bar. After greeting and thanking everyone for coming, he makes a brief speech. Glasses raise everywhere, and "To Flakey!" reverberates around the room.

What follows next has everyone hooting, hollering, and catcalling. Raven hands over to Vegas, who goes onto one knee in front of Ashley and proposes in the sweetest way. Of course, she says yes. And I'm the one whooping loudest.

2 — RAVEN

The last few weeks have been tough, probably the toughest of my life.

My private and work life turned into a constant roller coaster, and I don't know whether I'm coming or going. I took some serious blows when I discovered my VP bad-mouthing me, interfering in business, and threatening my sister. Furious, I'd like to kill him with my own bare hands, but everything was put on the back burner when Flakey ended up in hospital, and consequently died.

I ordered Rusty not to come back for the funeral. I wouldn't have been able to stop myself from beating the fucker to a pulp.

Flakey's death decimated us. He was a long-time brother and one of the best people you'd ever meet. We're reeling from his sudden death.

To top everything off, Vegas proposed to my sister, and tomorrow we must attend the Restless Slayer MC rally. We're going because they're our dominant club, meaning we are affiliated with them. We maintain a great relationship, and I've known Fury, their Prez, Ghoul, his VP, and Masher, their Sergeant at Arms for years.

It's therefore nothing personal, but we could all do without having to travel for hours. Fuck, we should be trying to gather our thoughts and deal with our grief.

Fury appears next to me, claps me hard on the shoulder, and says, "It never gets easier, brother, does it?"

I look at him and nod. I've seen lots of death in my time, inflicted it, watched it come for us, and it's wearing on me now. Despite us running the club legit, there's no letup.

Leaving Fury at the bar, I make my way through the room to the outside, and as I pass the old ladies' table, I clock Chloe, wiping her eyes. Such a sweet, loving chick, and so out of place amongst us jaded bikers. Her capacity for empathy is something else.

What I first noticed about her was her shining hazel eyes, her long, blonde hair, streaked with a red shimmer, and her beautiful face. I make a note to myself to speak to her before she leaves. I hold little hope, but maybe she'll agree to still help with the donor drive, and man the stall already set up for us at the Slayer's rally. Nodding at the girls, I walk past and outside, desperate for time to think and a deep long breath of fresh evening air to clear my pounding head. I find myself a picnic table to sit on and light up. I know smoking kills you, but hell, the devil will get you one way or the other, and it calms my nerves.

My peace doesn't last long. I groan, watching Slender and Pennywise walking over with intent.

"No rest for the wicked, Prez," Slender starts. "We need to talk." He is my SAA, and I respect him for his dedication.

"What's on your mind?" I ask Slender. He looks at Pennywise and unspoken communication passes between them.

"Rusty. He can't keep getting away with this. I've spoken to Ferret, who followed up on the banking inconsistencies, and guess who banked the money? Rusty did. Just like Karen said. Ferret hacked into the ATM camera, and you can clearly see Rusty walking into the bank around the time of the deposits." Slender takes a deep breath.

Pennywise, our Enforcer, who works closely with Slender, picks up the slack.

"Not all club members are aware of Rusty threatening Ashley, but they know what he's like with women. They witnessed the Saragate at the party and a lot of them are champing at the bit to get a punch in, Prez. We need to make a plan, otherwise, this thing will blow up real fast, sending us up shit creek without a paddle," he explains.

I hear them, I'm listening, but the blood pounding in my ears and the raw fury running through my veins drowns out their voices.

"He... is... mine!" I growl at them. "He'll pay for this, all of it. I'll kill the rat bastard myself!" My anger is boundless and a bit of the old Raven—the violent man who shoots first and doesn't bother asking questions—comes to the fore.

"Prez, you need to keep a handle on this. You know it's gotta go through the table. We can ask for him to be out bad," Slender tries to placate me.

"I fucking hate this!" I hiss at them. "I want him dead, not out bad!"

"What's the plan, boss?" Pennywise's question seeps through my rage. Taking a deep breath, exhaling slowly, trying to control my fury, I stare at my boots. When I raise my head to look them in the eyes, an icy calm settles over me.

"We don't take this shit to the Slayer's rally. I know he'll be there, but we do...

not... make it general knowledge. We cannot afford to lose face like that, and sure as

shit, not in public," I grate at them and both nod in agreement.

"Here's the plan," I decree. "We keep a close eye on him at the rally. No one's

to let on anything is wrong. Once we get home, we go straight to church, where first

he'll be stripped of his tape. That fat fuck is no longer VP. For now, he only wears the

tape for organizational reasons. The bad-mouthing and Sarah incident serves as reason

for this decision. We collect all our evidence, then there'll be an open meeting,

presenting the facts. Then, we'll vote. He'll go in the bunker after, and I'll leave the

removal of his tattoos up to you boys. If I get involved, he'll be dead, not out bad."

Both Slender and Pennywise nod.

"I'll get Ferret to gather the evidence we have, plus the statements from the club

girls and old ladies," Slender states, crossing his arms over his chest. I nod and both of

them leave, my head a hurricane of emotions and none of them positive ones.

Rusty's been my VP since I took over, and my father's VP for years before that.

I trusted him with my life, so have the brothers. It's a struggle to believe that

he'd be so devious, not to mention heinous where my family is concerned. He was my

13

father's best friend, yet he fucked my stepmother, and after being discovered, threatened my sister with the vilest repercussions if she talked.

She kept his secret for sixteen years and me in the dark, hence I continued to put my trust in him, considering his contributions and regularly seeking his advice. The depth of betrayal I feel is bottomless. If I was my father, or even the old Raven, I would wrap Rusty in chicken wire and throw him in the deepest lake to rot in the bottom so he'd no longer pollute the air everyone breathes. But I worked too hard to turn this club around and am unwilling to risk it all for that shithead. His time is running out, and his punishment will be severe.

Enjoying the cool night air for a moment longer, I light up another cigarette and let the momentary quiet soothe me. Chloe walks out of the clubhouse ready to leave, accompanied by Ally. They're walking towards me, heading for the parking lot a few yards behind me in the open field, failing to notice me, deep in talk.

"Hey, you two, wait up!" I call over to them, moving my ass off the table. Ally looks around and grins as she spots me.

"Raven, to what do we owe the honor?" Her curious and intelligent eyes weighing me up.

14

"I wanted to have a quick chat with Chloe, if that is okay with your majesty?" I bow and wink at Ally, who bursts out laughing.

"What can I do for you, Raven?" Chloe answers, shooting me a curious look.

"Remember we discussed the bone marrow donor drive and the stand at the rally? We're still doing that in Flakey's honor. The Restless Slayers have everything set up. Apologies for it being such short notice, I understand if you've made other plans. But if you're free, would you still be able to help?" I hope my question isn't too forward. She's done a lot for us already. Her eyebrows rise in surprise.

"With Carl gone, I didn't think the club would want to take part. I really admire you for wanting to continue with this!" she exclaims. "Sure, I can do that. Just give me the details. When would I have to be there?" Chloe smiles as she asks.

"Could you manage tomorrow afternoon? Ally has all the details. Do you own a tent? Or do we need to book you a motel room somewhere close?" I need to know what arrangements to make.

"Oh no, it's fine. I've got my camping gear, so a motel room is unnecessary. The brochures and all different types of information materials, banners, etc. are in the back of my car already. Got stuff last week, before things with Carl happened, in preparation. I'm ready to go," she tells me, then turns to Ally to ask, "Could you text me the details? Or even better, could I follow you and your ladies to the site?"

Ally responds instantly, "Sure you can. Meet me and the girls tomorrow at lunchtime here in the parking lot. You either can follow us in your car, or you can ride with one of us. I'm sure Raven won't mind if your gear goes with the support vehicle. You can set up your tent with us." Her enthusiasm that her new mate will join us is obvious.

Chloe's grin is blinding and makes me realize just how stunning she is.

"Really? I could ride with you? Oh my God, that'd be fantastic! I'll gladly accept a ride with you. If it's okay with Raven to take my stuff, that is?" Her eyes glint with excitement as she looks at me.

"Sure, no problem. Just make sure you are early, so we can throw your stuff in the support vehicle without Clusseaud having a coronary." I smirk.

"You ever been on the back of a bike and ridden any distance?" I question Chloe, curious to know whether she'd make the four-hour ride without falling off the bike at the end. I'd pick her up alright.

She winks at me and retorts, "Don't you worry about me. I'll be fine. I even own a helmet and bike shoes!" Her devious smile has me wondering what's going on in her head, but I keep my trap shut and just nod.

Ally and Chloe wave and walk off, chatting about tomorrow and their plans.

Chloe waves as she drives past in what I can only describe as a rust bucket. I can't even make out the model. Shaking my head, I chuckle to myself; could be a fun weekend, if it wasn't for dick face. You never know, I might get lucky and an eighteen-wheeler flattens him on the way. That would save all of us a lot of trouble.

Ally sneaks up, scaring the shit out of me.

"Raven, Raven, Raven, was that a look I saw?" She winks mockingly.

"What the fuck are you going on about? I need to tell Sparks to tan your ass more often, woman. No looks here, other than a normal one and distinct astonishment at how that heap of shit of a car of hers is still rolling," I volley back.

Ally, Spark's old lady and manager of the diner, is good people.

She runs her own club. The Wild Pixies are hilarious and are a national club. Women, who grouped together to form an MC, hold meetings at parties, rallies, or pre-organized ride-outs. They've been going for a few years and when they get together,

of Bud and a bottle of JD to my cart, pay the clerk, head to my car, shove everything in the trunk, and fly toward the clubhouse.

The parking lot is swarming with activity. Members milling around everywhere, loading vans, checking over bikes, gas tanks, and tires. To an outsider like me, it looks like mass chaos, but everyone has a job and they're executing them perfectly. Once I located Raven, he directs me towards Clusseaud, who points me towards the prospects, who transfer my stuff into the support van.

Ally, Caroline, Greta, and some other girls I've never met before are already there, prepping their own bikes. After hugging Ally, we move inside, share some laughs, have a drink, and just relax until Clusseaud gives 'the ten minutes until go time' signal. Heading into the ladies' I change into my bike gear, stuff jeans and sneakers into my backpack, grab my jacket and helmet, leaving the restroom ready to meet Ally outside.

Caroline stares at me, aghast.

"Wow," is all she has to say. I smirk, always nice to leave someone speechless. Ally looks me up and down.

"Oh boy, I can't wait to see Raven's face," she cackles. We are at the end of the convoy, with just the van, prospects, and Clusseaud behind us. Raven, who's on the first bike, revs his engine and lifts his left arm, circles it over his head, and starts rolling out of the gate.

I climb on behind Ally, get comfy, lean forward, and hold on. We ride out in double file formation and will stay like that for the duration of the ride. Once we hit the interstate, I relax a little more and let go of Ally, trusting her. Just watching the scenery go by chills me out. Before we headed out, I'd set up my Bluetooth headset so I could listen to my audiobook. It keeps the boredom at bay, and hell, nothing wrong with a hot, sexy book boyfriend.

Two hours in, we stop for gas and a comfort break, then quickly saddle back up to get on the road again. The sun is sinking lower, and the temperature is dropping as we leave the interstate. Only half an hour to go and we'll be there.

Once we arrive, we're greeted by the Restless Slayers MC, the host MC, and are shown to our camp spaces. To my surprise, a large marquee sits centrally between the Pixies and the Souls, which are bordering one another. Inside are tables and chairs, a hot water urn, and electricity connections. Not too shabby at all!

Everyone drops their kickstands, and you can hear the groans of everyone getting off their bikes, flexing and stretching their sore muscles. I rush to find the restroom, pleasantly surprised about how many decent chemical toilets there are in our area. After sanitizing my hands, I open the door, stumble, and lose my balance, my fall only being stopped by a broad chest. I look up and straight into a huge biker's eyes. His cut states he is the Slayers' VP, Ghoul.

"Well, if this isn't a pleasant surprise, having a beautiful woman almost falling at my feet." He grins. "I know I'm a babe magnet, but never had a chick accost me outside the toilets!" he quips.

"I'm so sorry. Thanks for the catch. I'm Chloe. I'll be manning the bone marrow donor stall. Nice to meet you, Ghoul." I wink at him.

"I'll make sure I'll drop in later after everyone's set up and pay you a visit," he answers. Wow, he has a gorgeous smile. Gotta love a guy that is stereotypical biker, beard and coiffed back blond hair and all those muscles! I walk off, but keep turning around, hoping to catch another glimpse.

By the time I get back to the campsite, the support vehicle's unloaded and everyone's busy putting up their tents. It takes me about twenty minutes to set up mine by Ally's and Caroline's tents, throwing joking insults back and forth.

Laying out my air mattress, sleeping bag, and the rest of my gear, I grab a six-pack, crouch out of my tent, and offer beers to the Pixies. Drinking our beers, we stand around, teasing the Souls for taking forever to set up.

Ally nods over to Raven. "He hasn't stopped staring at you since you've taken your helmet off!" she chortles. "If he had laser eyes, your ass would have two large holes burned through your leathers!"

"Oh, really?" I ask. "Maybe I should've put on a bit more of a show then." I wink at Ally. "He's a fine specimen after all, with that dark long wavy hair and the three-day stubble. And God, I just want to lick his biceps!" I joke, leaving Caroline and Ally open-mouthed and Greta laughing like a hyena.

"Interesting!" exclaims Caroline.

"Yes, very," Ally says, agreeing with her.

"Hey, chicas, can you point me toward where the stall might be?" I ask, hating to spoil their fun, but I really need to get set up for tomorrow.

Ally drums the Pixies together and off we go, stall hunting.

Finally, we're pointed in the right direction. A nice pop-up marquee with several tables and a couple of chairs is waiting for us. Ally makes a call to the prospects, and within five minutes, they're lugging all my materials up to us.

We get busy arranging leaflets, sign-up forms, donor cards, and collection tins for money. I look up as Raven walks toward us, holding a large cardboard tube. "This is for the stall, thought it might help."

Oh dear, he's as grumpy as ever. I smile at him, holding my hand out to receive the tube. As I open it and pull out its content, I gasp.

A huge-ass picture of a smiling Carl looks at me, his cut in place with a beer in his hand and a black stripe printed across the corner of the poster. The next one is a club photo. Four members, with their back to the camera, showing off their cuts, displaying the Stormy Souls patch proudly.

The third one is another one of Carl, but this time on his bike. I swallow hard, tears clouding my vision. Prospects are mounting a club flag on the back wall, and Ally leans towards Raven, hugging him and kissing both his cheeks, her eyes as glassy as mine.

We put up the posters around the sidewalls of the stall and stack leaflets and forms on the tables. Ghoul walks up and places two beer glasses in front of me, filled with Restless Slayers MC pens. He grabs one and fills out a form and puts a twenty in the donation box, nodding at Raven. He also hands a program to us, so we know the event order.

As Raven, the prospects, Ally, and the rest of the girls, apart from Caroline, leave, Caroline rips the program out of my hand.

"Oh my God, Chloe, this is going to be so much fun! Looks like they put a lot of prep and thought into this!"

Caroline bounces up and down in front of me, like a hyperactive puppy. "Look at this," she giggles. "They've got games tomorrow: Slow Race, Balloon Toss, and Weenie Bites!"

25

I look at her, utterly stumped. She may as well have spoken in Chinese because I have no clue what she's talking about.

"What the hell is Weenie Bites?" I ask, not sure I really want to know.

"It's a rally game, played by a rider on a bike and someone teaming up with him/her, standing on the passenger pegs, riding towards a sausage hanging off a string. The passenger must bite the sausage to get a winning point. You get three runs. Highest score wins," Caroline explains.

Now, that actually sounds like fun.

"Let me see that." I snatch the program out of her hands, start reading, and immediately burst out laughing.

"Dirty Karaoke? What the hell?" I laugh my ass off. "Looks like we're in for a treat tonight," I snort.

"Who should we sign up?" Caroline smirks. We share an evil grin and make our way to the main tent, where we find the sign-up sheet. We flick through the music list and rub our hands together. Now, this *will* be good.

We add several names to the list, including mine, then roam back to the tents. It's getting late and I'm dying for a drink.

Ally grabs hold of my arm and warns me, "Don't go anywhere near the marquee, hun, they're having a meeting. Stay here with us."

I wondered where all the guys had disappeared to. Ashley, Debs, and Sarah sit with us. We light the oil drum firepit and sit around it for over an hour, trying to ignore the shouting and ruckus coming from the marquee. Ashley sits with hunched shoulders, leaning on Ally. Even Caroline is quiet for a change. Ally looks at me and asks me to tell them a bit about myself.

"Okay, so you all know my name and that I'm a nurse on the Oncology floor. I'm thirty-six, an only child of a single mother, and took my bike test in secret," I say, laying my finger over my mouth secretively.

Watching Ally grin at me, I continue, "I live in an apartment near the hospital. I've always been a little rebellious, and my mom is super conservative. She'd have a heart attack if she knew where I am." I wink at the girls. "I love rock music, bikes, and a bad boy just does it for me. Mind you, I've been single for the last five years now and I'm not looking for a relationship either. The last guy was a schmuck, so I'm just pleasing myself at the moment, and happy with that." I add, "Anything else you want to know? Just ask." I stand, take a bow, and sit back down.

The noises from the marquee are getting louder and I'm trying hard not to eavesdrop. Ally pulls Ashley back into her seat as she tries to get up. We can easily hear angry raised voices without a clue who the target is, I'm just glad it isn't me.

4 — RAVEN

We reached the rally site without incident, not that I expected one. It took some time setting up. However, the marquee the Slayers' crew provided us with came as a welcome surprise. Since it has tables and chairs, it will serve as a common area.

Cold fury is coursing through my veins just thinking about Rusty, my so-called VP. His stealing money from the club is enough to throw him out bad with a severe beating. But threatening my sister for years, fucking my father's old lady—my stepmother—and holding it over Ashley's head? She was a kid, ten years old, for fuck's sake. I also have my suspicions that he was the driving force behind Karen spiking Ashley's drink. My head is about to explode with all the information I have received in the past week. It'll be tough to hold church and not beat the shit out of him right now! The brothers are giving me a wide berth. The stress of the last few weeks, including Flakey's death and funeral, is leaving its mark on my disposition. I am normally a grumpy motherfucker anyway, but all of this is pulling me into an evil place, a place I never thought I would venture down again.

Feeling like a failure is not something I expected to hit me. I didn't protect my sister, had no clue about what was going on, and couldn't help a brother. In short, it makes me feel like the shittiest person on the planet. Yet I'm still having to deal with all the other club shit, like being robbed blind by my VP, the bunnies complaining about how rough he handles them, my sister's

28

best friend being embarrassed as fuck by his childish, disrespectful antics, plus about a million other things.

I gave Rusty a long leash since he's been at the table longer than me. Obviously, too long of a leash and too long at the table. This all changes on Sunday. Slender and Pennywise are well aware. Ferret has his portable IT gear with him, just in case the need arises to bring Sunday's church forward. We need to be ready for anything that could be thrown at us from Rusty's side. Slender and Pennywise are on the lookout for his trike, and Rusty messaged me saying he's about forty-five minutes out.

Now, to make the troops aware. I grab my beer, unzip my tent, walk out, and call a quick meeting in the marquee for all to attend, including the Pixies for now, just to make sure that they are aware of our church meeting, and to speak to Ally and explain what needs explaining.

◊◊◊

The officers are standing in the front of the marquee, with everyone grabbing chairs and taking a seat.

"This is just a quick meeting to let everyone know that we'll have church in a few and a mandatory church meeting on Sunday, when we're back. As unusual as it is, it is absolutely necessary. All Stormy Souls members are to attend. Prospects are to secure the property. Only patched members are permitted inside the clubhouse. Make sure no girls are brought back. Club members only!" I yell across the marquee, leaving no room for anyone to misinterpret my instructions. My orders are crystal clear. They reflect the importance and seriousness of the event. The brothers are subdued for once. I close the meeting, but nod at Ally to stay behind. Once everyone else leaves, we take a seat.

"What's up Raven, need my help?" she asks, looking me straight in the eye. She's a straight shooter, our Ally, which only increases the respect and love I have for her. As President of her own club, as an employee, and my brother's old lady.

"Rainbow, you know about the shit going on with Rusty. You've been Ashley's confidante and I'm grateful to you. You were there for her when I couldn't. So, I'm giving you the courtesy heads-up now, trusting that you'll keep my sister away from the clubhouse on Sunday. I'll need a written statement from Sarah about the incident with Rusty the other week. Could you get that for me?" Her eyes are on mine as she nods her agreement.

"I can do better than that, Raven, I can get you statements from both Sarah and Ashley, if that'd help you?" Ally deserves my respect and I'm utterly grateful for her understanding and help with this delicate matter.

"I know I don't have to ask for your silence about this, so I won't waste my breath," I tell her with a small smile.

"It'll be judgment day for Rusty, and several votes will take place. You know the score, Rainbow." I watch her nod in a serious demeanor.

"Yup, I do. I hope the fucker gets what he deserves!" she hisses, her eyes alight with hate. "Don't worry, I'll make sure the Pixies, old ladies, and Ash are busy Sunday with a girly pampering evening at mine. Though promise me, you'll ask for help if you need it. I'd like to castrate that dick myself." She's as cool as a cucumber when she spits out the last sentence, making me grin. I love this girl! She'd grab the nearest blunt instrument and go straight for Rusty's balls.

"I want the marquee for an hour later. We need to have our church meeting here if that's okay with you?" she queries.

"Sure, have at it, once we're done, Prez." I smirk at her.

"Thanks, Prez, appreciated." She salutes and clicks her shitkicker heels, which has me laughing. It looks so ridiculous.

Ally's WMC works differently than typical MCs. The Pixies are a national club with, last I heard, about forty members all over the U.S. of A.

Some mistake the Wild Pixies WMC as a party club, but it is far from that.

They take the sisterhood as seriously as we take the brotherhood, and they'd fight tooth and nail for each other. Ally only surrounds herself with worthy people, resulting in loyalty and respect in her club being second to none. Ally's job is tough, uniting forty unique personalities, spread all over the country, but somehow, she manages and does it well.

I watch her fire off what I assume to be a group message, and make herself comfortable at the table, before I stalk out, running my hand through my hair, concerned about what is coming.

◇◇◇

My phone blips.

Slender: Spoke to Masher. As soon as Rusty rides up, the Slayers' prospects will escort him up.

Me: Thanks, man. Sunday we've got to get Halfpint and Eli patched in first. We'll need them in for the vote.

Slender: Why not have church here and vote them in today?

Me: Good idea, let everyone know to be ready at six pm.

My reply is short and sweet, as I struggle to not project my anger and my itching fist.

31

About sixty minutes later, I hear Rusty's pissed-off voice as he's being escorted to the Souls' campsite. He's not happy.

The Pixies' meeting has finished and most of our members are already in the marquee, having beers.

"Rusty, great to see you, you've arrived just in time for church." I slap his back, wishing I had a knife to jam into it. But I can't let on just yet, got to keep my cool for just a little longer. Soon though. I take a deep breath, trying to calm my inner beast.

"What the fuck, Raven? I'm being escorted?" he splutters at me, his face red, eyes blazing.

"Just thought it'd be easier than trying to weave your trike through, and we have a church meeting, so it was imperative that you make your way here as quickly as possible," I lie and smile at him, gritting my teeth. It's taking everything not to smash his teeth in, right this very second.

Rusty's eyes tell me all I need to know. The clear derision and contempt in his stare speak louder than words.

"Let's get on with it then, *Prez*." His tone dripping with disrespect.

My fists clench involuntarily. Slender watches me with an unobtrusive shake of the head, trying to keep me calm.

The meeting begins like most others. Spen does his business thing. We bring the *VP* up to date with the closure of Stormy and its refurb, but not in any detail. Then it's Dawg's turn to speak.

"I think it's time to patch Halfpint in, and Eli too, they more than earned it. Two awesome prospects, who can't wait to be brothers. They'll do us proud!" I'm in complete

32

agreement with Dawg. He's spot on. They've never wavered. Not even with the shittiest jobs we gave them.

I kick off the vote, and it's unanimous. Pennywise gets up and walks out of the marquee. He returns, dragging Eli and Halfpint behind him with a slapped-ass look on his face. They are left standing at the end of the marquee, heads bowed, looking flustered, worried they fucked up.

I stand.

"You two halfwits got anything to say for yourselves?" My tone is extra harsh. I look from one to the other.

"Nothing? Sorry, assholes, I'll have to take your prospect patches!" I roar at them. Halfpint and Eli look as though they're ready to spew in the middle of the marquee, especially as Pennywise drags them by the arm right in front of the officers' table.

"What the fuck?" a now furious Eli mutters. "I've done nothing wrong, so why the fuck?" he grunts through clenched teeth.

"Well, you can't have your full patches with the prospect ones on, can you?" I smirk, throwing them their full sets. "Get sewing, assholes!" Applause, hoots, and hollers break out as both men grin from ear to ear. Everyone can see the pride on their faces.

"Patch in party!" hollers Sparks, and everyone bangs their bottles on the tables in agreement while Halfpint and Eli find a seat.

5 — CHLOE

Deciding to ignore the goings on in the marquee, I take a walk around the site.

There are plenty of vendor stalls. Leatherwear, patch makers, all sorts of biker jewelry, even a stall selling "F*cking Hot Sauce" chili sauce in many sizes and variation. You don't need imagination to work out just how hot "Ass Buster" is going to be. Makes me giggle. There's a first aid tent, multiple bars, and several large-scale marquees with different stages set up. The biggest marquee holds the largest stage and has two poles installed. It's a biker's paradise. I mosey on through the bike show, which is filling up with beautiful bikes. I love a nice bobber.

As I'm gawking at the bikes, Ghoul appears by my side.

"Hey, pretty lady, we have to stop meeting like this or people'll start talking!" He winks at me showing me his best smile.

"Not your best pickup line, biker, I think you need to practice on someone who falls for those." I tease him. He throws his head back and laughs.

"I like you, straight out, no BS, that's refreshing."

Taking that as my cue, I respond, "Talk about refreshing. It's time you bought me a beer!" Batting my eyelashes for all they are worth. He roars with laughter, grabs my elbow, and leads me to the main marquee, where the bar is manned by Restless Slayer MC members and prospects. He orders two beers, and we turn around, chatting about nothing in particular. Bikes mainly, and what my ideal bobber would look like, while we watch the first band set up.

The first band plays that loud screamo music no one can understand. Definitely not my taste, so I wave and dawdle back to my tent. Caroline, Sarah, Ally, and some other girls are still sitting around the oil drum fire. Ashley is notably absent, as is Vegas, but a few tents away, their growls are clear for everyone to hear.

"Watch out, it's bear mating season, and a couple found their way into Vegas's tent!" Sarah shouts, a few decibels below fighter jet noise, causing the whole place to erupt into laughter. Ally nudges me, grinning from ear to ear.

"What?" I ask innocently.

All she replies is, "Caroline confessed!"

I can't help giggling like a school kid in her first sex ed class.

When I ask Ally, "Is it time yet?" She looks at her watch and nods at me with a conspiring grin.

She stands, cups her hand to her mouth and shouts, "Last one in the beer tent is buying!"

All we see is a cloud of dust as she hustles towards the main rally area, closely followed by Slender, Pennywise, Caroline, Dawg, Sparks, Raven, Dougal, and the rest of both clubs.

We all know who's round it is, by the noises from Vegas's tent. Once there, we have to get our own beers, since Vegas and Ashley are absent for the time being. I just hope they'll turn up soon. Caroline and I have plans for them.

◊◊◊

We keep the main event a secret, not sure how, but we do. Between all of us, we have several beers, tequilas, whiskey; you name it, we consume it in large quantities. Raven loosens

35

up after the second whiskey and is actually smirking at me right now. That's when the announcer grabs the microphone and welcomes us all to Dirty Karaoke, before the first person is called up on stage.

Masher, the SAA of the Restless Souls, gives a rousing rendition of ZZ Top's, *"Pearl Necklace"*. He receives a standing ovation and thunderous applause. That guy can sing!

Next up is Ally, with a special version of *"I Will Survive"*.

She starts with a quiet voice.

"First I was afraid, I was petrified. When you said you had ten inches, Lord, when you said you'd stick it inside, I nearly died…" All the while looking and pointing straight at Sparks, making vulgar hand motions. The room is erupting with shouts, hollers, wolf whistles, and laughter. "…Go on now go! Walk out the door. Don't you promise me ten inches, then turn up with only four…"

I'm laughing so hard, tears are streaming down my face, especially when Slender and Pennywise grab Sparks under the arms and carry him up onto the stage. Ally makes a proper show of him. I can't even listen anymore. I cough, splutter, and lose my breath, laughing. Caroline is on the floor now; Sarah is wolf whistling and screaming.

"Woohoo, show me your four inches baby!" I try to swallow my Bud but all I do is inhale it, causing me to cough my lungs up, while still laughing.

Raven walks up, slaps me on the back, shouting, "Are you okay there?" right in my ear. I grin at him and nod.

Just as Ally breaks out with, "…Last time I saw a prick that small was Gladstone's running naked ass…"

Both Raven and I burst into howling laughter, watching Ally and Sparks making a real comedy duo out of themselves. The applause is deafening as they act out the last note and take a bow.

Next are a few other guys from different clubs. We get to hear "*Big Balls, S.E.X, Give the Dog a Bone*" and many others, then it's Vegas and Ashley's turn.

"*Pour Some Sugar On Me*" takes a whole new meaning, and the marquee suddenly seems very steamy.

Caroline reappears in front of me with an evil grin. A feeling of impending doom creeps over me. Raven, still standing next to me, moving with the music, looks at Caroline and suddenly looks sobered by her evil smirk.

The announcer shouts, "Next up is a nomination from the Stormy Souls' MC, who put forward their Prez. Raven, get your ass up here!"

Oh my God… I hadn't put his name down.

This is gonna be fun.

Raven knows he can't chicken out but points a menacing finger at the guys while he climbs up on stage. The music starts. The first notes of Kings of Leon pump through the speaker. I almost pass out when Raven opens his mouth and the sexiest rough voice I've ever heard starts singing. His voice makes my pussy clench and, as if he knows, he looks straight at me when he belts out, "*You. Your sex is on fire!*" Our eyes meet and a bolt of electricity hits me while his eyes hold me captive. Even with hundreds of people here, it feels as though he's singing only to me. My legs turn to jelly, my lower body fills with heat and my sex is on fire! Wow, I'm melting and gonna have to change my panties.

My heart is thundering in my chest, and my mouth is as dry as the Arizona desert. His gaze has me hypnotized and frozen to the spot. I hear Caroline snort, but it doesn't really reach me. I dig my fingernails into the palms of my hands to stop myself from moaning. My alcohol intake has been rather high tonight, yet I don't feel drunk. Just hot, so hot I want to go on the stage, rip his jeans off, sink to my knees, and take him into my mouth! Oh God, I am drunk. Very drunk. I must be, because I feel like a horny teenager. The song finishes and his eyes are still on me as he makes his way back to my side while everyone around him whistles and offers backslaps.

"Next up, naughty nurse! Chloe Sanders, get up here!"

I am in shock. I look at Caroline, who rubs her hands in glee. The bitch! I'll make her pay for this. I'll coat her with honey and leave her in a bear's den!

Raven smirks. "Go on, or are you chicken?"

"Chloe, come on up here!" the announcer repeats, so I trudge my way to the stage. My legs feel leaden. I look at the card the announcer guy shows me. Oh man, seriously? Caroline is dead meat! Yes, as I stand up here looking at this card, I am planning her murder.

The music plays and my cue board at the bottom of the stage shows me the words. I decide to give them a show, one that will rival Ally's, so, on the spur of the moment, I change the lyrics. I look at Raven. Okay, two can play this game. I smile sweetly at him and start singing. No one knows I used to sing in the church choir, but that's a bonus now. Being drunk also helps.

"Baby, take off your shirt real slow… And take off your boots… I'll take off your socks… Baby, take off your jeans…Yes, yes, yes!" I sing with my huskiest, sexiest voice, moving my body slowly and seductively on the stage, keeping my eyes locked on Raven's.

"You can leave your cut on…You can leave your cut on…You can leave your cut on!"

The room is stomping their feet to the beat of Joe Cocker's *"Leave Your Hat On"*. I walk to the edge of the stage, take my braid down, shake my hair out and accept a bottle of Bud that Ghoul holds out to me, smirking. I wink at him to thank him, then I return to my cue board.

"Go over there…Turn on the lights… All the lights… Come over here… Stand on that chair… Yeah, that's right… Let me lick you right there!"

The room is boiling, and the crowd is going wild. Raven's eyes hold mine and they are almost black with heat. It's like the rest of the room has faded away and there is only us. Hot, and turned the hell on.

"Now give me a reason to lick… You give me a reason to lick… You give me a reason to lick… sweet darling… you can leave your cut on!" I finish strong and take my bow to suggestive hip thrusts, offers of lickable dicks, wolf whistles, and thundering applause. Mother, I am gonna burn in hell for this!

Ghoul is standing by the side of the stage, waiting to escort me to the bar. I'm glad he is with me, as the crowd is getting rowdy. We are standing at the bar, chatting, when I'm grabbed and spun around to face a tense Raven.

He looks at Ghoul and tells him in a terse tone, "Go away, asshole!"

I am confused. What was that about? Raven puts his hand on my hip, yanks me to him, and kisses me into next week.

My legs buckle and I resort to grabbing hold of Raven to keep me upright. His tongue is plundering my mouth, like he owns it. I'm instantly soaked. Nothing makes me hotter than a toe-curling kiss. It's almost as though he's fucking my mouth with his tongue. He pulls me flush against him, and I can feel his hard on pressing into me, making my eyes roll back in pleasure.

I'm panting and moaning into his mouth, which has him groaning. He drags me out of the marquee and leans me against one of the posts, grinding himself into me. I swear I could come there and then, just by the delicious friction he exerts on my throbbing clit. I want to climb him like a tree.

He lifts his mouth from mine. "We have to stop, Chloe, otherwise I'll fuck you right here!" he groans. "You were so damn hot on that stage. I needed to feel you, just couldn't help myself."

I pull his head back down to mine, not ready for this to end, kissing the side of his neck and nibbling with my teeth, lightly nipping, placing kisses on his jaw and finally his lips. Tracing them with my tongue until he opens to me.

I kiss him slowly and deeply until he takes control of the kiss and turns up the heat, frying my brain until it's a melted, steaming pile of goo. He groans, lifts me, and instinctively I wrap my legs around his waist, as he walks us to the campsite.

No hesitation when he undoes the zipper on his tent. He puts me on my feet. We rip our clothes off, drunk and on fire for each other, burning with need. I take off everything but my light blue lace thong, standing in front of him, fondling my breasts, lifting them, and twisting my nipples. His eyes turn almost black with need.

"You're wet for me, aren't you?" he states. "I can smell you from here. I bet if I touch you, I'll find you soaked." His voice is rough, but feels like a caress. It elicits a deep moan from me.

I watch him take off his jeans and boxers. His spectacular erection points north, bobbing against his chiseled, muscular body. That man has a six-pack I just want to lick, and his tribal tattoos suit him, making him look dark and mysterious. He helps me lower myself onto the mattress on the floor as he pushes me backwards. There is no stopping now. I look up at him and giggle.

"What?" He smirks at me. "A lady's wish is my command!"

I run my hands over his cut, which is the only thing he's left on, then under it, needing to touch his taut, hot skin, exploring the muscles in his back and chest.

"Before we go there, stud, I'm on birth control and clean. What about you?" I ask him, curious to see what his response will be. I don't mind casual sex, but safety first.

He continues to duel with my tongue, and I can't help but lift my hips toward his, grinding my still panty-clad mound against his impressive erection. His fingers work their way into my drenched folds.

"Not been with anyone in a year. So I'm clean. Can suit up though if you want me to?" He looks at me questioningly. "You are so wet for me, soaked!" he groans as he strokes my folds and my clit. If he carries on, it'll all be over in seconds. He pumps his finger into me, and I can feel myself clamping around him. It's been over a year since I last had sex and B.O.B. doesn't count. I want to taste him; my mouth is watering at the thought of his rock-hard dick. Pushing him off, I straddle him, placing my throbbing, hot entrance over his pulsing dick and slowly rub my heat and wetness against him.

"No glove, I trust you," I whimper, sliding further down until I'm between his legs. I take a moment to admire his gorgeous cock. Long, thick, and slightly bent upwards. I lean down and run my tongue over the tip. He throws his head back and moans. That sound is music to my ears. It makes me feel powerful and sexy. Wrapping my hand around his root, I lick all the way up his shaft, lapping up the drops of pre-cum collecting at the head. Teasing, I run my tongue around it, before closing my lips and moving my mouth down his shaft, sucking tight.

41

"Jesus," he groans, making a hissing sound. "Fuck yeah, just like that!"

He loves me blowing him as much as I love tasting him.

"Meghan!" Suddenly there are voices all around the tent. "Meghan, where are you?" We both stop and stare at each other. The frantic voices are like a bucket of ice being dumped over our heads.

"Fuck!" Raven swears and gets dressed, so I follow his lead. It sounds serious. We can finish this later. It's more important to find out what's going on.

As we make our way out of the tent, several Restless Slayers are wandering about, calling for "Meghan." Raven talks to them and it turns out that Meghan is the eighteen-year-old daughter of Fury, the Slayers Prez and she hasn't been seen for a couple of hours. It's her first rally and her disappearance sparks concerns. We join the search, and luckily, after about an hour, they find Meghan. Her friend Tanya, the Slayers SAA's daughter, found her and led her to their tent. She seems to be okay.

Raven and I split up during the search, so I do not know where he is. By now I feel embarrassed about what happened in the heat of the moment. I can still taste him. Behaving like a slut is not my style, so I blame it on the alcohol, make my way to my tent, take some ibuprofen, and drink a bottle of water before I crawl into my sleeping bag. The tent seems to spin a little, but nothing too bad.

6 — RAVEN

For fuck's sake, can there not be one drama free evening in my life? I knew we had to stop when I heard frantic voices calling for Fury's daughter. I met both of them earlier, to pay my respects, and Ghoul, the VP, Masher, the SAA, with Tanya, his daughter. God, Chloe is hot! That mouth of hers nearly exploded my mind, never mind my cock. Two hours later and I'm still semi hard.

I want nothing more than to taste her, then bury my dick deep inside her. But business before pleasure, I sigh. I'm glad they found Meghan. It's not normal for a young girl to disappear at a bike rally. Highly unusual. Guards and security are everywhere. Along with the site being gated, she would not have been able to leave unseen. Being Fury's daughter, she'd know her way around well, and she wears a Princess cut so everyone knows she's untouchable. Glad to hear Tanya found her. My guess is, she'd had a few too many underage drinks and didn't want to face her dad. Fury is no fool and realizes that kids will be kids, just like we were at eighteen. I wouldn't wanna be the person who served her tonight, though. The thought makes me wince for the poor bastard who did.

When I get back to the tents, I can hear soft snoring coming from Chloe's. Smiling, I shake my head and make my way back up to the party area and the brothers. As much as I want to fuck Chloe until she begs for mercy, we're here until Sunday, so I have plenty of time to work into her pants.

As I walk into the main marquee to watch the band, a sheepish Caroline hides behind Dawg, who apologizes for his old lady.

"Sorry, Prez, when there is drunk mischievousness to be had, she can't help herself. Didn't realize you had such a great voice, though."

"Weird apology, man," I chuckle. "None needed anyway. It was a fun night. How do you put up with your old lady? She's a handful." I smirk at Dawg. He just shrugs his shoulders.

"Caroline's worth it. She's my lover, partner, strength, and has an iron backbone. Hell, she'd take a bullet for me and I'd take one for her. Best thing that ever happened to me was meeting this one." He affectionately pulls Caroline to his side and kisses her cheek.

I'm happy for them, but looking at this picture of biker domesticated bliss, I can't see that for myself. I've never wanted an old lady. Nowadays I prefer to bang the same easy woman but found that I am no good at relationships. Not that I cheat, I wouldn't. I'm man enough to tell them to get lost well before then, but club business usually scares them away before that happens. The reality of dating a biker, a Prez at that, differs vastly from the romanticized version a lot of women dream about.

It takes a special person to put up with our lifestyle. Especially since I am the President of my club. A lot of responsibility rests on my shoulders. My woman would need to be independent. There's little time for me to spend handholding. If I was even entertaining the idea of getting an old lady, well, let's be honest, that's not very high on my agenda, it's not a position for a weak chick. There're a lot of expectations that come with being a Prez's old lady.

If you think being Prez is hard, being the Prez's old lady isn't glamourous either. With the expectation to lead the other old ladies, take club bunnies in hand, when necessary, oversee the domestic side of the clubhouse, organize shit like family parties and special occasions, not to mention being there for the brothers and the other old ladies when required, it's involved. I can't think of any woman valuing her sanity, who'd want to become a Prez's old lady

I enjoy my own company as much as the brothers', and often keep to myself. The last few months, things haven't been running as smoothly as I'd have liked, and I hate Rusty still hanging around. The next few months are gonna be tough. He's gonna lose his shit for sure on Sunday.

A lot of hard work is coming my way. Most importantly, we need to find another VP and the club has to be renovated and vetted out. Vegas and my sister are getting married. Because we patched in Halfpint and Eli, we need numbers, meaning a recruitment drive. Being down to just one prospect, Greg, is not acceptable. Plus, I'm mulling over how we could expand our businesses. The tattoo studio will go a long way towards that.

The music drones and gets on my nerves. My head is pounding, so I grab a bottle of water from the prospect behind the bar and make my way back to the campsite. When I get to our marquee, I see lights flickering and walk in to find Ferret staring at his laptop.

"What ya doing, bro? You should be out partying," I ask him. He jumps about six feet. Obviously, he didn't hear me approach. That makes me chuckle.

"Jeez, Raven, you just took ten years of my life!" Ferret huffs. Still chuckling, I shuffle around his back to look over his shoulder, watching a moving dot on a map.

"Rusty?" I guess. Ferret nods.

"Yup, looks like he's fucked off again. Did you know?"

I shake my head. "I had no clue, Ferret. He didn't speak to me at all after the meeting. Think he smells a rat?" I raise my eyebrows at him.

"Maybe, Prez, I guess we'll find out Sunday," he says as he closes his laptop. "Gonna make a move, was a tiring day, Prez. Hey, awesome voice by the way. Got a video of the karaoke from the Slayers." He smirks at me.

It makes me groan. I know exactly what will happen. It'll be on play at every club party for years, and distributed far and wide. Whatever! I don't give a fuck. Getting grumpy is a sure sign that it's time to take some pain relievers, drink my bottle of water, and put my head down. Dawn will come soon enough, and tomorrow's gonna to be another long ass day.

As predicted, the damn birds wake me up around five in the morning, leaving me feeling hungover and as though I've not slept for days. Rolling over in my sleeping bag, I try to get back to sleep for a few hours. After I moved myself back onto my mattress, which, of course, I rolled off during the night, I rummage through my bag, grab some more painkillers, and down them with what is left in my water bottle. Then I punch my pillow for more comfort, close my eyes and pray for a just a few more hours of uninterrupted sleep.

Minutes later, at least that's what it feels like, the zipper opens, Slender steps in, kicks my feet and grumbles with a serious face, "Get up, man, we have a problem."

Groaning, I chuck on my clothes. Within a minute or two, I'm out of my tent and in the marquee. "What's up? Tell me where we're at and what needs sorting." Slender and Pennywise sit at a table shoveling scrambled eggs, bacon, and toast into their mouth, grinning at me.

"Prez, sorry, but it's urgent. The Pixies have cooked breakfast. Made too much bacon, eggs, and sausage. We need your help to demolish it, preventing food waste and all that…"

46

Pennywise grins at me with a full mouth. I walk over, grin at him, and slap the back of his head, NCIS Gibbs style.

"Bastard!" I grumble at him, but grab a plate and a mug, make my way to the Pixies' kitchen setup and smile sweetly at Ally, who is manning the cookers.

She plates up a mountain of bacon, eggs, sausages, adds two pieces of toast, and fills my mug with steaming hot black coffee. I lean over and kiss her cheek.

"Thanks, Ally, you are a lifesaver!" I mutter. She just smiles and waves me off.

I return to Slender and Pennywise, sit down at their table and start loading my fork. The food is delicious. Must make sure Ally gets a donation for her club funds and we pay for the extra food. We shovel in silence for a while, filling our guts.

Slender is the first to break the silence.

"Prez, I thought about our VP issue. As in the issue that we won't have after Sunday. Pennywise had a thought and I think it could work, but before making a table suggestion, we thought we'd discuss it with you informally first."

I nod, swallow my egg and bacon, sip my coffee, look at them, and wait. I've been working with these two assholes for years and understand they wouldn't approach me with half-cocked shit too ridiculous to consider.

Pennywise looks at me and blurts out, "Vegas."

"Come again? Have you lost your ever-loving fucking mind?" I ask, thinking I must have misheard him.

"Vegas. I know he's not your favorite right now, but he'd suit the post and puts the club way before himself. He's loyal, knows the brothers, supports you still, even after having taken

47

your beating, despite it wasn't being strictly required. He respects the fuck out of you and loves this club. I think it could work," Pennywise elaborates.

"Just give it some thought," Slender adds.

Just because Vegas and my sister are an item, doesn't mean I don't hate that he went against my '*don't touch my sister*' order. Although I must admit, he came through where the bar was concerned, and certainly for Flakey. I know he'd take a bullet for Ashley, me, or any of the club brothers and their families. Far be it from me to question his loyalty and devotion to the club. He's a good man to have at your back. But as my VP? That's not something I ever considered.

I nod at Slender and Pen.

"I'll think about it and talk it over with Dawg, Spen, and Ferret as well. See what their opinions are." It'd be stupid to dismiss their suggestion off-hand and realistically, I can't see anyone else wanting the position. Some are brilliant brothers, but they're not leaders.

◊◊◊

I take the day to wander around with the brothers, have a look at the bike show, shoot the shit with Fury, Ghoul, and Masher and catch up with people I haven't seen in more than a year. I enjoy the rally atmosphere but am always on my guard. Sitting with the Slayers and chatting, I overhear Ghoul telling a brother,

"Man, I met this sexy-ass chick yesterday. She's with the Pixies, into bikes, likes a bobber." He smirks before continuing, "Apparently rides herself, though hasn't got a bike at the moment."

Oh, looks like another one will bite the dust. Where they find these chicks?

"Hey, Ghoul, who's the broad you're so eager about? Don't think Ally has any new girls?" I ask, trying to figure out who he's on about.

"No, dipshit, not a club member! I'm talking about the skirt you brought to do the stall for the bone marrow drive, Chloe! Man, she's hotter than Hades, knows about bikes and doesn't scare easy. Wouldn't mind getting me some of that."

My head shoots around to Ghoul. No fucking way! Oh hell to the no! I have first dibs on Chloe, and no other man is getting in there!

"Ghoul, fuck off and leave her alone," I growl at him.

He looks me up and down. "Is she yours then?"

"No, she's not, but she's a friend of the club," I reply.

"Well, if she's not yours, she's free to make up her own mind, isn't she? She sure was okay to flirt with me last night," Ghoul mocks.

"Stay away, Ghoul!" I growl at him, get up and stomp off to the sound of the Slayers' laughter following me.

What the fuck? She flirted with Ghoul? I shake my head to rid myself of the thoughts. She has every right to flirt with whomever she sees fit. So, why does it piss me off so much? Not that we went all the way last night, more like heavy second base. Yet still, it annoys the fuck out of me. We definitely had a few moments there, and even though I'm not up for an old lady, a steady lay would be nice. Looks as though I either have to up my game or admit defeat to Ghoul. Fuck that, it ain't happening. Not on my watch. Fuming, I stride over to the stalls and find Chloe's. With the sizeable crowd of people in front of the table, it's easy to spot. Chloe, Caroline, and Greta are behind the stall. I'm not sure what to make of Greta. Used to be a guy but changed into a female. Fair enough, she was a slight guy, so doesn't look mannish now, but the thought of taking hormones, being demeaned for years, and then having my dick taken off makes me cringe. Greta is funny and has an awesome personality, but that kind of shit is not for

49

me. Not everyone is aware of her sex change, and those who know don't talk about it. I only know because I met her years ago when she was still a he. I promised not to broadcast my knowledge, so I won't. Don't know how to act around her sometimes but I don't dislike her.

As I approach the table, it becomes obvious the ladies are run off their asses, taking names, handing out forms, returning completed ones to boxes, and taking money for the collection.

Caroline pleads with me, sounding exhausted, "Raven, so glad you showed up. Could you step in for me for a second? Need to use the restroom and take the collection box to Spen. Grab a new one."

I lift the box and it's heavy. Looks like everyone has flashed their cash, which is great news for the cause.

"Sure, hon, go do what you need to do," I reply, stepping inside the stall. Chloe smiles, nods at me and for the next couple of hours, we work side by side, talking to people, bikers, and citizens alike, drumming up support for Leukemia sufferers, handing out leaflets and pointing folks into the right direction of how best to help. It sure is no hardship, but we don't get the chance to talk and get to know each other either.

Once the crowd thins, my stomach growls.

"Where is Caroline? I need some food," Greta complains, and I've got to agree.

"Go, take a break, get some food. I was gonna bring some to Caroline, but she's nowhere to be found," Ally says as she walks up, pulling Debs behind her.

"Probably doing her usual, getting distracted by Dawg and the bands," Debs sniggers. Debs and Ally get behind the stall as Greta, Chloe and I walk away and towards the food stalls. Greta splits off to the vegetarian stall while Chloe and I head to the BBQ.

"Man, I'm starving!" she sighs.

"That makes two of us, then." I grin at her. "How's the head?" I smirk.

"Fine, thanks, I felt funny last night so went to bed. Took some painkillers and had a bottle of water before I went to sleep. That sorted me out. Not to mention Ally's mega hangover breakfast," she babbles as she struggles to look at me, embarrassment radiating through her flushed cheeks.

I struggle to get the picture of her naked body on top of me, rubbing herself on my dick like a cat in heat, out of my mind. The way her mouth felt around me has my dick standing to attention.

"What would you like?" I ask her. "My treat."

She chooses ribs and fries, while I ask for steak and fries. Once we have our food, we take a seat at one of the picnic tables and dive in. She groans with delight, taking a bite of her rib. I struggle to keep my dick under control and not jump over the table to lick the meat juices off her lips. I have to turn away and clear my throat before I'm able to speak rather than drool. Just as I am about to tell her we will revisit last night, Ghoul pops up behind her, notices us and plonks himself on the seat next to her.

"Hey, beautiful, how's your day going? Saw your stall was pulling in the crowds. Well done." He smiles at her.

"Yes, thanks, it's been a successful day so far. Everyone has been generous, and lots of people have signed up to get registered and tested. This is gonna make a real difference," Chloe replies. Ghoul nods.

"Hey, Chloe, we've got a spare bike with us, and I'd happily lend it to you. Fancy signing up for the Slow Race later? I'll be racing, and so will be quite a few others," Ghoul asks with hope in his eyes.

"Wow, that is so nice of you! Yes, thank you, I'd love to! When does it start?" Chloe jumps up, claps her hands in excitement, and hugs Ghoul.

"In just over an hour, darlin'. I'll have prospects drop the bike at the Pixies pitch, so you can come over on it and do a few practice laps since you've not been riding for a while." Ghoul smiles at her.

The burning need to plant my fist in Ghoul's face hits me and has me struggling to remain calm.

"Put my name on the list too, Ghoul!" I interject, barely able to contain my... what is it I am trying to contain? It's not jealousy, that's for sure. I just know she could do better than that asshat.

7 — CHLOE

Smirking, I look from Ghoul to Raven. Clearly, there is some sort of rivalry going on. Not sure what that's about? Excitement pulses through my veins. The bike loan is such an unexpected perk to the weekend.

My heart thumps with excitement, and my cheeks ache from smiling so hard. I throw my arms around Ghoul and give him a resounding kiss on the cheek.

"You are my hero!" I announce, bouncing up and down. He just laughs, pulls out his phone and makes the call. Raven looks like he swallowed a lemon. Not impressed, huh? Do I care? Nope! I get to ride, so he can suck it up, buttercup.

A growl emanates from Raven, making me chuckle. Not sure why he's in such a mood. Not as though he has any rights. I finish my ribs, grab my drink, and head towards the bike to check it out, leaving the two alpha bikers to it. I can't be doing with this pissing contest shit. That's teenage stuff and does nothing for me.

Raven follows behind me. Even though I don't turn around to check, I can feel his eyes on me, burning holes in my back. Back at the tents, I squeal in excitement. A beautiful, deep red Street Bob is sitting there, right in front of our marquee with the keys in the ignition.

I can't help myself, so I run to my tent, jump into my bike gear, and mount the Street Bob, helmet in hand, turn the key and let her growl to life. Man, I love the rumble and vibrations of a Harley. Shoving my helmet and gloves on, I kick down into first and roll towards a gap in the surrounding club bikes. This bike feels amazing. Within seconds, another bike appears right behind me on the path heading off site. I inspect my mirror and it looks like Raven's bike. What the hell? I pull to a stop before I get to the gates.

He pulls up next to me and leans towards me.

"Coming with you, you don't know the area, don't want you getting lost."

I nod at him. He has a point. I've no clue where I am, so I appreciate the gesture, and motion for him to take the lead as we pull out of the site.

The feeling of freedom and peace that flows through me and roots itself deep in my veins and soul is indescribable. For the first time in ages, I can breathe. My mind drains of all worries and thoughts until only the bike and the road exist. The sun warms my face, the wind in my hair despite the helmet, and the roads Raven is taking me on are amazing. Long sweeping bends, beautiful scenery and not too much traffic. I let out a scream of happiness.

I check my mirrors, look ahead, open my throttle, and shoot past Vegas as though he's standing still. My adrenaline junky side has come out to play. Increasing the speed, I lean the Street Bob as low as she'll go into the corners, shifting my position, and just enjoy a few high-speed cornering miles. In my mirror, Raven is right behind me. I clock a sign for a rest area and pull in.

Switching the bike off, I dismount and walk to one of the picnic tables overlooking an amazing landscape. You can see for miles in every direction. As my ass hits the top of the table and my feet hit the bench, a fuming biker appears next to me.

"What the ever-loving fuck was that?" he yells at me, hand on hip.

"Calm down, you'll give yourself a stroke and gray hair. Won't suit you." I smirk at him.

Looking at him, standing there, with his hands on his hips, and his face beet red with anger, causes me to giggle. What can I say? Inappropriate laughter is how I roll. Nothing and no one is taking my high away from me, especially misguided macho alpha male behavior. That doesn't fly with me. At all. My mother brought me up to be independent in every way and I'm grateful for that. Not having to depend on anyone but myself is a gift. No woman should ever have to rely on a man, nor should any man have to rely on a woman.

"What you did was reckless. You could have wiped out and ended up in hospital, or worse." He's like a dog with a bone and it's getting on my nerves. I've had enough of his whining. Since he's stood right in front of me, I know exactly how to shut him up. Still vibrating from my spectacular ride and a little hot for this man as well, I lean forward, grab his hips, pull him toward me, and plant my lips on his. I can feel the quick tense of surprise before he leans in and tries to take control of the kiss. A battle of lips and tongues ensues. A duel, a scorching duel of tongues that has me drenched in an instant. He pushes his hands in my hair and holds my head still while he explores my mouth. This is the hottest, most passion filled, bone-melting kiss I've ever had. I can't help but moan in his mouth, which has him groaning. After a few minutes, we pull back. My chest heaving, I'm panting for breath, feeling dizzy. Jeez, that man has skills. He needs to get his mouth licensed as a lethal weapon.

"You damn crazy woman!" he admonishes me, with no heat to his words. "No doubt you know how to ride. It was hot as fuck knowing you were behind me, but hell, watching you overtake, move on and pass me… that was something else!" he states with a grin, readjusting himself, his erection clearly outlined in his jeans has my mouth watering.

With a smile, I let him know my thoughts.

"Glad you enjoyed the view, though I guarantee you didn't enjoy the view as much as I did the ride. Now, let's just get one thing clear here. You're not the boss of me. You don't tell me how I ride, who I talk to, or what to do. I ain't one of your brothers or minions. If I want to talk, or spend time with Ghoul, I damn well will, and your input is not required. He's a good guy, and I like him. I wouldn't suck face with him, but I like him.

"Second, neither you nor anyone will ever tell me how to ride. I'm who I am. That's the only person I'll ever be. You don't like it? Piss off then," I proclaim. With that, I stand from the table, lean in, and kiss Raven's stubbled cheek. He just stands there, gawking, surprise marking his face as much as the respect I see in his eyes.

The view draws me in and has me walking to the edge of the rest area, which is on top of a small hill. The views of the fields and countryside are just spectacular, especially with the glimmer of the river in the sun meandering through the valley below. Throwing a glance over my shoulder, I notice Raven has taken my place on the table and is watching me intently. He looks deep in thought, and gorgeous. With his long dark wavy hair, his wraparound sunglasses, and three-day stubble, he's easily the sexiest specimen of man I've ever come across, and he has my pussy doing a rain dance with just one look.

My physical and mental reaction to him is very intense. I can sense him walking in the room, and can feel when his eyes are on me. Nothing similar has ever happened to me before. If circumstances were different, I'd work my ass off to get to know him better, to see where this attraction leads. But he is a biker and a President at that. My mother's warnings and disgust ring through my ears like a big-ass bell. I love riding, being on a bike, and don't discriminate, evidenced by me even being here. I love the scene, the rallies, the music, and the free-living mentality. But getting involved with an MC Prez is a whole different ball game. Being thirty-six, not sixteen, sweet and innocent with rose-colored glasses on, I know how the world works. I've always been a sucker for a bad boy and it bit me in the ass each time I got involved with one. The last time was about five years ago, when I dated a guy I met in a club. He was the definition of a strong male alpha with the typical rugged good looks and rebel persona. Everything went great until he put his hands on me for the first time. First, it was just a shove. Then a harder shove, and then a slap across the face. Finally, after a punch sent me sailing down the stairs, I got myself out of the relationship. But not before I didn't pay him back with his own baseball bat. If I had a road name, it ought to be slugger.

I ran and ended up in Arnold, got a job at the hospital and stayed. That was four years ago, and I've kept myself to myself ever since. There are a few colleagues I socialize with, but that's about it. I'm past the point of messing around.

Raven walks up to me, stands by my side.

"What is it you want, Chloe?" he asks, looking straight ahead, not at me. "The chemistry between us is off the scales, and it's obvious I want you. I want to fuck you, do all the dirty things your mind only dreams of, but relationship material… not sure I am built for that. I am not a manwhore anymore, prefer to share my bed with the same woman for as long as we both want to, but I'm not looking for an old lady. I need someone who is independent, doesn't need to hang off me, and doesn't need to be babysat. Got no time or patience for that kind of crap."

Smiling at him, I lean over and nudge his shoulder.

"Well, Prez, that's quite a speech. Since honesty is what we're doing right now, I'll return the favor."

I take a deep breath and begin explaining myself. "Not sure I want or can deal with relationships stuff, either. Let's face it, I'm thirty-six and single for a reason. I'm too used to doing my own thing and keeping myself safe. Yes, safe, as I've had terrible experiences with your type of guy."

I stop for a moment, gathering my thoughts.

"You're right, the chemistry is astonishing, and I struggle to keep my hands off you. There's no hiding that I want you, Raven, but I am wary at the same time."

Taking a deep breath, I pull up my big girl pants and continue. "I don't really know what I want, Raven, I have no expectations. Let's just take it a moment at a time, enjoy each other's company, and not tag a label to this."

He turns me towards him, his eyes searching mine as if to determine whether I'm being honest or not.

"I can do that, Chloe. While we do that, we're exclusive, though. I don't share and I wouldn't expect you to have to either. Let's see how the chemistry pans out and enjoy it while it lasts."

He pulls me into his hard body, hands on my ass, and his lips come down to kiss me. This is an altogether different kiss, overwhelming my senses with its slow sweetness. The sensual movement of his lips against mine sends shivers down my spine and makes me break out in goose bumps all over as much as it spreads lava-hot desire all through my lady bits.

I lift my arms around his neck and run my hands through his hair, rubbing his scalp tenderly. The slow, deep, and sweet kiss lasts for eternity, it seems, and melts me into a pile of goo. I'm breathless and hot as hell when it ends.

"Hmmm... that was worth waiting for." Raven smiles at me. "Let's get back so I can beat your ass at slow racing!" He chuckles, causing me to smack his arm, which I don't think he even felt.

"Neanderthal," I mutter, following him back to the bikes, getting on and letting him lead us back to the site, feeling as if a thousand-pound weight has dropped off my shoulders. One I didn't even know I was carrying. It feels like my smile will freeze on my face and I'm singing to myself the whole ride back. I'm ready to see where this goes.

◊◊◊

Standing in a long line of waiting bikes, slow racing, Vegas, Raven, Ally, Caroline, Ratchet, and some others are in a group with me. Apparently, there's a prize for first, second and third. Three groups of ten start and only the top three go through to the next round.

Closing my eyes, I take a deep breath to calm myself and concentrate. This is not my first rodeo. Slow speed control is something I practiced in advanced rider training and am great at. The engine rumbles underneath me, causing the vibrations to snake their way through my body. That's where my full focus is. Becoming one with the bike.

The signal to start comes, and I roll off, keeping a slow speed. Slipping the clutch with my foot on the brake, I reduce my speed to a very slow crawl. I don't focus on anyone else but me and the bike, feeling instinctively for the center of gravity and working out how far I can push it. My speed reduces and reduces, now sitting at a very slow walking speed. Some bikes have gone past me, some are behind me. I increase the revs, pull the clutch in a touch more and control the speed with the back brake. I am now crawling. Shit, that wobble almost had my foot down, but I caught it at the last moment. A few yards before the finish line, I'm almost at a standstill, balancing the bike with the brake and my body position. Another bike wobbles past me.

When I roll over the finish line, a round of applause and hooting breaks out from the Slayers watching their bikes come in, and the Souls and Pixies for me coming in third, followed by Raven second, and a Slayer in first. Ally makes fourth, joint with Caroline. Vegas is sixth, and I'm not sure what happened to the others. We wait for the other heats to finish. Now there are nine of us left. The first five go through to the final heat. I make my run and again finish third. Here we go again. Raven, me, Fury, and two others who are not club bikers, so I don't know their names, end up making it to the final heat.

The signal sounds, and we set off at a super slow pace. Unfortunately, the first non-club rider makes a mistake. He lets the clutch out. With the high revs and back brake, it causes him to wheelie and bounce his front wheel twice before he loses it and ends up in the dirt with his bike on top of him. A huge "Ohhh!" explodes from the crowd. Everyone stops and runs over to help. Luckily, he's not injured, other than his bent out of shape pride. Four of us left and we seem to all move in a line, reducing speed almost in sync. I have to do better if I wanna win this.

Raven and Fury are acing this. On the last ten yards I slow it down to alternate moving and stopping, standing on the pegs to balance the bike when still.

"You gotta be fucking kidding me!" Ghoul growls as he passes me.

"Fuck my life!" Raven isn't any happier than Ghoul as he rolls past.

It takes all my skill and concentration to keep the bike upright and balance my way into the finish line. I won! I've gone and won on a borrowed bike. My face is going to crack with me smiling. I lower the kickstand, turn the engine off and jump off the bike, performing a victory dance. It might be childish, but I include sticking my tongue out at Fury and Raven, pulling funny faces at them, with the crowd laughing and clapping a beat to my dance.

Masher pulls us all up on the makeshift stage. He hands Fury and Raven each a twenty and a small plastic trophy, congratulating them on their skill. Then he walks up to me, microphone in hand. He grins, hands me an envelope, a larger trophy, and someone shoves something else in his hand.

"Now then, Chloe, it's been some time since I've seen that much skill. The judges have decided," I wait with bated breath for him to continue, "to officially crown you the Restless Slayer Rally Slow Rider Queen!" He steps up and places an obviously homemade crown, made from electric and soldering wire, on my head. Blushing with pride, I feel touched by the recognition and a lot of embarrassment.

Taking the microphone from Masher, I face the crowd. "I want to thank my fellow competitors, even though they are losers." I make the big L gesture on my forehead before I continue, "Thank you to the Restless Slayers MC for lending me this beautiful bike to take part, and thanks to the Stormy Souls MC and Wild Pixies MC for supporting me.
Further thanks go to my agent, my mother, the father I've never known…" I jokingly list about a hundred more people, imaginary and real. Masher takes the mic off me, wrenching it out of my hand.

I go along, pretending to fight him for it, under the hooting, hollering, and laughter of the crowd. He turns me around and gently pushes me off the stage, waving his hand at me as if to shoo a fly away, shaking his head, raising his shoulders as if to say, *Women, what can I do?*

Pouting, I put my hands on my hips, and stomp away from the laughter and clapping of the crowd, loving my life, opening my envelope as I walk away, crown on my head and trophy in hand. I've just made a quick hundred bucks.

8 — RAVEN

Fury and I look at each other with consternation. Oh, the bitter pill of defeat, even if administered in a sexy, sassy package, is still hard to swallow. How the hell did we sink so low to be put in our place like that? We shrug shoulders and retreat to our own corners. I'm not pissed or anything, just amazed at the astonishing control that woman has when riding.

Chloe sits by the oil drum fire, counting her winnings when I park my bike. Watching her smile, I feel instantly lighter. As I stride up to her, she smirks and waves. I lean down and kiss her silly, to hollering and whistling from Ally, Sparks, and some others by the tents.

"See? Told you there was a look," Ally gleefully tells anyone, whether they want to know or not. I smile against Chloe's mouth.

She whispers against mine, "We're drawing a crowd." Giggling against my lips. I love that sound on her. Honestly? I couldn't care less whether we are. My dick is throbbing behind my jeans, and all I want is to drag her into my tent like a caveman. The need to be inside her is almost painful. I readjust myself, pull her up, sit in her chair, and drop her into my lap. It feels intimate and somehow right.

"Congratulations, my queen!" Dawg and Dougal are taking a knee, bowing before her, making her burst out laughing. Dawg lifts her hand and places a kiss on it.

"Hey, asshole, less of that, capisce? Or else I'll have to remove your balls, and what would your old lady say about that?" I threaten Dawg.

Caroline pipes up from behind us. "Help yourself, Raven, not that he knows how to use them, anyway," she teases. Dawg is on his feet in a split second and chasing after his laughing and screeching old lady.

"I'll tan your ass for that, woman!" he mock threatens.

Howling with laughter, we watch him trip on the uneven ground, chasing her until she's laying on the floor, thumping on the ground, rolling around laughing as Dawg hobbles towards her. He sits down, draws Caroline over his knee and spanks her ass in full view of everyone. Those two are crazy, just crazy, but they belong together.

I hear a throat clearing behind me, and as I turn, Ferret stands there. From his stance, it's obvious he wants a word, so I playfully smack Chloe's butt and lift her off me. She just grins at me as I walk off to the marquee with him.

"What do you need, Ferret?" He wouldn't seek me out if it wasn't important, not his MO.

"I checked the tracker on our VP. He hasn't gone straight to the clubhouse. It tracked him to Ellie's. I'll monitor it, and if he's not moving from there within the next hour, I'll make some calls," Ferret reports.

"Okay, do what you think is necessary." I nod at him.

My anger resurfaces, and my mood takes a nosedive. I stay in the marquee, despite everyone else on their way to watch the Balloon Toss and Wiener Bites. On impulse, I take out my phone and call Ellie. She takes her time answering.

"Hi, Raven, what can I do for you?" her muted voice reaches me. Suspicion crosses my mind. She is not normally the quiet type.

"Is Rusty with you?" I ask her straight out.

"Yes, and he is in a foul mood. He came in, ordering me around. I don't know what went on, Raven, but he's nasty. Threatening me that if I told anyone he's been here, I'd not like the consequences. Something's snapped in his brain. Raven, he is scaring me. Rusty wasn't right last time he was here, but today? He's just evil."

That makes me sit up straight. He's threatening his own sister?

"Ellie, listen to me. I realize you can't talk. If he gets physical or hurts you, text me and call 9-1-1. We will come for you. You are one of ours and we'll protect you, honey. Promise you'll call if you need us, or call if you need anything. Anything, okay? We're trying to get a handle on him and keep you out of the line of fire," I explain the best I can without giving away our plans.

"Thanks, Raven, I will. I'll try to get rid of him as soon as possible, and I promise I'll call. Gotta go now. I'm in the bathroom and don't want him to get suspicious," she replies and disconnects the call.

Ellie has me worried. She's an awesome girl and doesn't deserve his wrath. The only one deserving of wrath is Rusty. He's got himself to blame, and can count himself a lucky fucker to have gotten off lightly for now. As if I summoned them, Slender and Pennywise walk in.

"Rusty is at Ellie's, threatening her and up to no good."

They're none too happy when they hear what I've to report.

Slender balls his fists by his side.

"I'll kill him if he touches her," he hisses. He and Ellie had a thing a long time ago. She moved away, and it took Slender quite a while to recover. Ever since, he has not been in a relationship with anyone. He's turned professional manwhore with his Viking looks. He's a hit it and quit it kinda guy. His visceral reaction surprises me.

"I swear, Prez, I'll kill the bastard if he goes anywhere near her!" he grates out, and I believe him. "I hate the bastard!" he spits.

"Don't worry, he will get his in the end," I reply with a hand on his shoulder, knowing how he feels.

"We'll just have to give him enough rope, he'll hang himself. Sunday will be here soon," Pennywise adds.

Pennywise is an old soul. He is much wiser and more mature than his age lets you believe.

◊◊◊

After a full day with games and ride-outs, we're all sitting around the oil drum fires, talking, listening to music, and chilling. We brought some grates to put over the drums and are using them as makeshift BBQ grills. The atmosphere is very mellow. Again, Ashley and Vegas are absent with snores rattling their tent walls, making all of us grin.

Ally, being the evil witch she is, gets hold of Vegas's beer mug. She fills it with flat beer, takes a Mars bar out of her pocket, warms it up, squishes it a bit, removes the wrapper, and drops it in. It looks like a turd floating in piss. Everyone watching sniggers. She creeps to Vegas and Ashley's tent and places the turd-floater directly in front of their entrance. Rubbing her hands gleefully, evil grin firmly in place, she returns to her seat. Chloe, sitting on my lap, is shaking with suppressed laughter. Ratchet gets up and kicks their tent. No reaction. Sparks starts shaking their tent… still the snoring continues. Moggy and Spen walk round the tent, remove the pegs and guy ropes, making the tent collapse on top of them. Vegas must still be the one snoring, because we can hear Ashley now.

"Vegas, wake up!"

We are all sniggering by this time. Dougal walks over to the tent now that Vegas has stopped snoring.

"Come on, you horn dog, food is ready!"

For a second, there's silence. Then: "Fuck off, Dougal, I have a hard on and I'm not afraid to use it!"

That sets us off howling with laughter, and we can clearly hear Ashley groan, the sound of a smack, and Vegas shouting, "Ow, what was that for?"

"Because you're an ass!" Ashley grates as she opens the zip and tries to extract herself from the collapsed tent. She knocks over the turd floater, screeches in disgust, and we can hear Vegas screaming like a girl as the fake turd and piss, looking very realistic, run into his tent and pool around his feet.

"You dirty bastards. Who did this? You sick fucks!" Vegas shouts, as he is trying to extract himself, having more problems though because of his size and being caught up in his sleeping bag. Ashley looks around, eyes squinting. Since we're all laughing our asses off, they figure out someone has pranked them. She shakes her head at us, grins, grabs a steak from the BBQ and starts eating, while Vegas appears, one foot still trapped in the sleeping bag, hopping around in his boxers. Gotta love my club!

◊◊◊

A few of us stayed around the fires, while most others have gone to watch the bands and have a beer, or two, or five. I snuggle Chloe on my lap, and Slender is sitting with us, his brows furrowed and subdued. He is worried about Ellie, his thoughts dark. I try to talk to him, but he shuts me down. Caroline and Dawg are with us, too. Pennywise grabs his guitar and sits across from us. He strums, and we are all dumbstruck by how good he is. Chloe and Caroline sing along to *'Tennessee Whiskey'*. Unable to help myself, I join in. We don't notice Caroline stopping, nor Slender watching us open-mouthed. We all get carried away in the moment.

"Wow!" Caroline exclaims. "You sound amazing together." Clapping her hands together. "Do another one!" We settle on Foo Fighters *'Skin and Bone'* and afterwards Pearl Jam's *'Breathe'*.

Caroline and Dawg slip away unnoticed, leaving for their tent. We remain oblivious to anyone else leaving. In the end, it's just Pennywise and us.

"Right, folks, time for me to hit the hay," Pennywise yawns at us. We nod at him and after he leaves, Chloe stands and walks towards her tent. Oh no, not again! I am ready to go after her when she emerges with her mat, sleeping bag and pillow, takes it to my tent, and places it next to mine. Now, that I can get on board with. When she returns, we sit for a moment longer, just cuddling and enjoying the chill time. I never thought I was a big cuddler, but tonight has changed my mind. Just to hold her close makes me feel at peace, and inhaling her clean scent calms my senses.

She turns her head towards me and gently kisses my lips. The kiss is sweet, sensual, and slow burning, but I can feel it turning into an inferno. It feels like we connected on some deeper level, which is one part scary and one part amazing, as I never thought I'd feel this way. The softness of her hair on my face, her soft warm fingers touching my cheek, tenderly stroking it. Her sweet caress is driving me crazy with need. Need for a deeper connection, need to touch her, and taste her velvety smooth skin. She tastes of mint and sweetness, a taste I can't get enough of.

67

Needing more of her, more of this, I stand and carry her into the tent. Kneeling down with her nestled in my arms, I stretch us both out on the mattress. I don't notice the cool, hard floor underneath us. All I feel is her surrounding me. I lean over her, carrying my weight on my arms, which are flat on the floor next to her head, and lower my mouth to hers until our lips almost meet. Shivers run down my spine when she breathes in my breath and I breathe hers.

We give and take in equal measures; the intimacy rising a hundred-fold. Her soft hands finding their way under my T-shirt, kneading my back with a gentleness that has me completely relaxing, while causing the hairs on my arms to stand and goose bumps to run all over me.

My lips trace her forehead, her nose, and trail along her mouth and neck, where they rest and nibble. I cannot get enough of the sweet taste of her skin, her warmth, and silky softness. The intensity drives me on, shifting lower and slowly pulling up her shirt, exposing her soft curves. My fingers trace the lines of her bra, the red lace driving me crazy, looking sinful against her creamy skin. I pull down a cup and kiss her soft, pillowy breast, causing her to moan deep in her throat, pushing her head back into the pillow and arching her back towards me. My dick is as hard as steel and uncomfortable in my jeans.

As though she can sense it, her hands move down to my front, undo the button, and pull down the zipper, before her small hand finds her way into my boxers, stroking across my pulsing erection. I nearly lose it then and have to fight for control.

"You have to stop," I whisper in her ear. "Or this will be over before it has even begun." After kissing her thoroughly, I return to stroking and teasing her breast, her nipples are hard and pebbled, and the need to suckle them is overwhelming. My mouth finds her hard nub and sucks it deep into my mouth with her back arching and her pushing her nipple further into my mouth. She whimpers, her hands restless on my back, alternating between gripping me and stroking, then kneading me. As she moans, her nails rake down my back, making me shiver. I sit up, pull her shirt over her head, and undo her bra.

"Please, Raven, I need to feel your skin," she murmurs, her eyes dark with need. I rid myself of my shirt and run my fingertips over her torso. Paying special attention to her sensitive sides and the soft swell of her belly. Following my fingers with open-mouthed kisses.

My fingers undo her jeans, and my hands slide under her, pulling her jeans down and off. She's laid before me in just her red lacy thong, and she is stunning. The sight of her stirs something deep inside me, and when I lean over her to kiss her tender lips, a jolt of electricity courses through me.

"So beautiful," I whisper in her ear. "You are so gorgeous." Running my fingers through her hair, need and heat curling deep inside my abdomen, my heart beating like a drum. I kiss my way down her chest, paying attention to the other nipple, teasing it with the tips of my calloused fingers. Her chest is heaving, and it hypnotizes me. My mouth wanders lower, leaving her chest, moving across her abdomen. I place soft kisses on her hip, push my fingers inside her thong, and draw it down her legs. Her aroma hits me like a train, and I nearly come in my jeans, like a prepubescent teen, just from the smell of her arousal. My eyes lock on hers, which plead with me. I sit up to remove my jeans and boxers, my cock throbbing and standing proud. She reaches her hands out to me, beckoning me to her. As my knees rest between her gorgeous velvety soft thighs, my hard dick rests on her pubic bone. She grinds against me, driving me insane.

"Please, Raven, I need you inside me." Her pleading murmur is all I can take. I position myself. She reaches for me, and guides me into her hot, soaking wet entrance, her intense heat scorching me. I enter only the tip of my aching cock and have to stop for a moment to remain in control. She's moving restlessly underneath me, trying to get friction. I sink myself all the way into her in one slow stroke. Her hot, wet pussy is strangling me, clenching around my cock.

"You are so tight," I groan, struggling to keep myself from coming. I grind my teeth and root myself deep inside her, not moving. After a few moments, I withdraw almost all the way before I push back into her, setting a slow, leisurely pace. Her gasps and whimpers spur me on, but I keep a languid rhythm, covering her lips with mine, devouring her.

This isn't the typical fuck. This is what everyone talks about, but you never know if you will experience. I am pretty damn sure this is making love. So intense, so connected, I can feel her deep in my soul. She's in every breath, every heartbeat, every touch. I'm connected to her with every fiber of my being. My emotions are all over the place, and I can feel something surge inside me. I can feel her flutter around me and her kissing me back more frantically. It makes my balls draw up and I feel a tingle move from the base of my spine upwards. I push into her deeper and with more intensity, causing more friction to her clit, and that is all it takes for her to go over the edge. As she spasms around me, milking me, I can feel myself release and root deep inside her, only making the smallest movements. This orgasm is so intense I see stars and my vision goes hazy. The waves go on and on forever. When they finally calm, I roll us onto our side, still inside her, and pull her close. Her breath tickles my chest, and no words are spoken.

9 — CHLOE

I cannot believe what I just experienced. I'm still recovering from the intense, blinding orgasm I just had. Something happened between us, something special. I can't quite put my finger on it, but it definitely happened. Never have I felt so connected to anyone, nor had sex with this intensity in my entire life. As my breath and heartbeat calm, I can feel a connection left behind, like a ribbon, attached to my innermost self. He's still inside me and I love it.

Opening my eyes, I stare into his deep brown ones, and know he feels the same. His eyes reflect how moved he is. I feel a tear leaving my eye, running down my cheek. It's a happy tear. My smile reflects his as he wipes my tear away. My eyes close and I scoot closer to him. I wish I could climb inside him. I feel safe in his arms, falling asleep within seconds.

◊◊◊

My eyes open to bright daylight and Ally standing behind our tent with a pan and spoon, banging both relentlessly together, calling folks up for breakfast. I groan and stretch my aching body. After a night with not much sleep but plenty of orgasms, I wonder how I'll manage the four-hour ride back today. Raven's standing over me, fully dressed, grinning down.

"Don't look so smug, it's all you fault," I groan, grabbing my clothes, and getting dressed. He holds his hairbrush out to me and I realize I have bed hair. It takes forever to untangle the rat's nest on my head, but at last, I manage. Walking out of the tent together, they tease us mercilessly. Not that I care. I expected that.

Vegas and Ashley are waving at Ally, busy laughing and pointing at the tent behind her. I take a seat and turn to see what they find so amusing. Sarah is coming out of Dougal's tent, her face bright red. Everyone is heckling and applauding her walk of shame. She turns and disappears into her own tent. Dougal meanwhile comes out of his, grinning like the cat that got

71

the cream, no pun intended. Dawg slaps him on the back, as do most of his brothers. A very sheepish Sarah makes her way to the tables and sits in a free seat next to Greta at the other end.

"Don't think you can hide, Sarah. We all saw you! I'll get my claws into you later and make you spill, don't you worry," Ashley shouts across the table, teasing her. Sarah's face is almost the color of her hair.

"I hate you so much right now!" She points her finger at Ashley, sticking her tongue out at her, causing everyone to burst out laughing.

The rest of breakfast is a calm affair. Everyone helps to wash up and tidy, then we all start packing up and loading the support vehicle. After double-checking the site and saying our goodbyes to our hosts, we saddle up. I'm behind Ally again, grateful for the helmets and wind noise, making it impossible for her to pepper me with questions.

After a few gas stops, it is late afternoon by the time we roll up to the clubhouse perimeter. We help unload and stow things away, and after a quick drink, I say my goodbyes. I try to catch Raven, but he is busy.

"Church in an hour!" he hollers. Taking that as my cue, I drag my gear to my car, load up, and make my way home. I'm desperate for a nice hot bath and an early night. We collected so many forms over the weekend that the folder is bulging, and I am dying to know how much money we raised. But I guess that will all have to wait until tomorrow. I'm glad I still have another week off. The way I feel right now, I don't want to go back to work at all.

Just as I sit back and relax in my bath, Budweiser in one hand, kindle in the other, my phone resting on the side of the bath, it buzzes. I sigh, put my bottle and kindle down and reach for my phone.

Raven: Hey, beautiful, you left without saying goodbye?

Me: You were busy, so I thought I'd give you space.

Raven: Really not necessary. Rather wrap you in my arms right now.

Me: Aww, you are so sweet :)

Me: I'm sitting in the bathtub, with my friend Bud and am just chillaxing. My muscles are sore from when you attacked me last night and refused to let me sleep!

Raven: Are you complaining? Didn't hear you complain last night unless you were moaning at me 'cause you needed your sleep? LOL.

Me: No complaints here. Loved every second.

Raven: When are you back at work?

Me: Got another week off. Not sure I wanna go back at all. That's a decision for another day though.

Raven: Okay, beautiful, I've got to get ready for church and sort this shit show out. Want to meet up tomorrow for lunch?

Me: Sure, love to. Come to my place, I'll cook.

Raven: Look forward to it, beautiful, see you then xxx Sleep well, sweet dreams

Me: XXX

10 — RAVEN

This weekend wiped me out. The depth of Rusty's betrayals burden me as the question keeps going around in my head. *How did I not see this?* Well, no point beating myself up after the fact, no way to change it now. How did I become so conditioned by my dad to put blind trust in people without questioning their motives? It makes me feel like shit. Like a failure. Not only did I fail my club, but I failed my blood family even worse. Not that they did not warn me. Ashley, Vegas, and lots of other people warned me. Did I listen though?

Like a shithead, I listened, and dismissed them off-hand. Not a mistake I'll repeat. It also made me gain a newfound respect for Vegas. He warned me straight up, told me to watch my back. Looks like I underestimated him, my mistrust and stubbornness hindering my judgment.

Annoyed, I look at my phone, which hasn't stopped ringing all day. Just not by the person I *want* to speak to, Chloe. She's been on my mind all day. The ride back to the clubhouse dragged ass, and I kicked myself for letting her ride with Ally instead of on the back of my bike. But it would've given the impression she's my old lady when she's not.

Ellie's name flashing on my caller display shakes me out of my thoughts.

"Hey, Ellie, are you okay?" Her call drops my gut through the floor. Ellie rarely, and rarely, with a capital R, calls me. That she does now, not once, but twice, worries me sick.

"Raven, sorry to call you again. I'm scared. Rusty isn't himself. I mean, he's always been harsh and moody, but this weekend? This is something different. I wasn't supposed to tell you he came by my house, but he threatened me. He told me, *'If you open that trap of yours and tell anyone I was here, I'll make sure you'll regret it for the rest of your life. I'll come for you, Ellie, make no mistake about that!'* Raven, his eyes were dead. I didn't recognize my own brother," she explains, so upset that I can hear her voice wobbling.

Clenching my jaw, I try to sound calm and reassuring, while rubbing my tired eyes. "Ellie, I've no clue what's going on with him. He certainly won't hear from me that you called. But I have a feeling that he's about to lose his shit. Ellie, do you trust me? Do you trust the club?" I hear her breathing, and wait while she thinks this over.

"Yes, Raven, I do. Sadly, I don't trust Rusty, though," she responds. That makes me listen up.

"What happened, Ellie? Did he touch you? Put hands on you?" I swallow hard, fighting to keep my fury under control, certain I already know what her answer is gonna be.

"He hit me, Raven. I had to waste a good steak on my face, and am now sporting a shiner," Ellie says, trying to lighten the mood.

My anger rips through me like a tornado. Struggling to keep the oncoming explosion under wraps and my voice from croaking, I clear my throat.

"Ellie, can you do me a favor and trust me? Pack a bag for a few days. Come and stay with us for a while. You can stay with Ashley and Vegas. They won't mind. We're having church in a few minutes. I'll discuss it with the brothers."

I hear her sigh.

75

"Okay, I'll pack a bag and drive over. Just let me know when Vegas and Ash have agreed, and I'll be on my way." I can hear her packing in the background.

"What about your job? Do you have to take vacation days?"

Ellie's laugh is entirely without mirth.

"I am in between jobs, Raven, lost mine last week. Need some help? I'm multi-skilled," she says, no humor left in her voice.

"We'll talk about the details later, Ellie. I gotta shoot now. I'll call you after church." With that, I disconnect the call. What the ever-loving, sideways cactus fuck?

I am the first to walk into church and look at this massive table, a leftover relic of Stone's day, and wonder if I have to burn this damn thing before the last ghost of Stone is exorcised. The brothers are making their way in, taking their places, the one on my right taken by Rusty. For now. I give them five minutes, then we'll get this show on the road.

◊◊◊

"Right, boys, settle down!" I call above the noise of chatter, waiting for silence so we can get started.

"Settle down, let's get this over with!" Rusty shouts into the room. As one, all eyes turn on him. I spot Vegas clenching his fists and Sparks putting his hand on Vegas's arm in warning. I know precisely how he feels, struggling to keep my cool.

Instead, I stare at Rusty, Slender and the other officers and tell them with a smile,

"Yes, let's get started, shall we?"

"Spen and Ferret, the floor is yours." I point at Ferret, inviting him to start up his projector.

Spen stands.

"As you are aware, the club is losing money on Stormy's and we currently shut it down for renovations. I checked last year's accounts and couldn't work out where the money went missing," he explains.

While Spen talks I closely observe Rusty, as do Slender and Penny. Vegas stares at the table.

"So, after checking all the books, I had to presume that the losses were because of Karen's tardiness." This line we agreed on. Rusty's eyes first go wide, blood draining from his face, before he shifts further back into his chair. Little does he know.

"Karen had signed all the accounts payable and receivables which didn't tally with the deposits. Don't worry, we have dealt with her."

Spen takes a moment to pause when Rusty speaks up. "Excellent." Rusty just can't help himself.

Spen continues, "Imagine my surprise when I saw the security camera footage Ferret got ahold of." He nods at Ferret, who starts the projector, sharing a video clip, clear as day showing Rusty entering the bank, walking up to the counter, handing paper and money over to the clerk before leaving.

"So, the question is, Rusty, where is the money you stole from the club?" Slender asks as Ferret points at Rusty. Slender and Pennywise are getting out of their seats and go to stand behind Rusty. There's no chance of getting away. He dug his own hole, and we'll bury him in it.

"What the fuck? You can't do this. I never stole any money!" Rusty blusters.

"No." Ferret looks him in the eye before he states calmly, "You set Karen up to take the fall for you, which is even worse."

Rusty *must* know what is coming. He's been in the MC long enough to know what consequences will be waiting for him. He tries to stand, but Slender and Pen shove him right back into his seat. I shoot an icy glare his way.

"We ain't finished, not by a long shot," I growl at Rusty.

I hold up pieces of paper, written statements from Sarah and Ashley. My sister talking about how she suffered his sneers, threats, and blackmail tactics for years. Sarah detailing his harassment of her.

Vegas stands, so do I.

"You thought you could threaten my sister, fuck my stepmother behind Stone's back, and I wouldn't eventually find out? Let me tell you something. I bet my ass that if we got Karen in here right the fuck now, she'd tell us *you* put her up to spiking Ashley's drink that night. *You* ordered the beer to be watered down, *You* ruined the bar's reputation, *You* stole the money, *You* fucked Stone's old lady and threatened his daughter, my sister!" Punctuating each *you* with my finger stabbing his flabby chest. I am rabid now.

Sparks can't hold on to Vegas any longer. Vegas jumps across the table and punches Rusty right in his face. The satisfying crunch of Rusty's nose breaking makes me feel a tad better, but jealous that Vegas got the first shot in. Rusty slumps over in his seat, holding his nose and split lip. Pen shoves Vegas into a chair before he can do any more damage. I remain standing.

"We have sufficient evidence, Rusty, and I'm now asking the members for a vote. Your position in the club is untenable." I get my knife out, smile when I see the dickhead flinch, and unceremoniously cut his VP patch off.

78

"You are no longer VP. Now we are going to vote on you being out bad. I need a hundred percent vote on this." I look around at all the brothers. This is serious shit and absolute silence reigns at the table. With deep satisfaction, I take out my lighter and burn his VP patch in front of everyone.

Out bad, for our club, means you get kicked out, with a major beating and have your tattoos burned off your skin with an iron or a blowtorch. You are not welcome inside the club's territory at all, and no other clubs will touch you. There've been cases in the past where we voted to send the member to Satan, but that's not happened for many years.

"Everyone for kicking Rusty out bad, say aye!" I kick the vote off. "It's aye from me!"

"Aye." Comes simultaneously from Pennywise and Slender. As we go around the table, everyone votes aye, until it gets to Moggy. He and Rusty joined more or less together and Moggy struggles with his conscience.

I can't believe he looks at me and says, "Nay!" The rest of the brothers jump up. Vegas grabs Moggy by the throat and punches him. Pandemonium is about to break out.

"Sit your asses down, right the fuck now!" I roar into the fray. Slowly, order returns and the brothers are holding Vegas in check. Although I don't blame him, I'd like to do the same, however I have to deal with this shitstorm appropriately, whether I like it or not.

"Dawg, please record the vote. I propose we vote on demotion to prospect level, loss of full patch and a fine of $50,000, plus reparations to Ashley and a beatdown. Eighty percent vote will be adequate for this," I growl.

Again, we go round the table and all vote, "Aye". Slender and Pennywise drag Rusty to his feet. I run the knife under his patches, removing them all, walk over to Spen, grab some old prospect patches, and stick them in Rusty's top pocket with a smile.

With deep satisfaction, I draw back my arm and land several punches to his face, gut, and ribs. Rusty knows better than to hit back. By the time it's Vegas's turn, Rusty is in a fetal position on the floor, covering his abdomen and head. Vegas kneels next to him.

"This is for threatening my old lady!" he tells Rusty, before he punches him in the head, then stands and kicks him in the back and groin.

I lean down to issue my own warning, "You ever go anywhere near my sister again, I will fucking kill you. This is not a threat; it's a promise, you piece of scum sucking shit!"

"Halfpint, Eli, get two others to help you show the prospect the door please," Ferret chips in. Halfpint and Eli duly drag him outside. Once they return, they do so with arms full of beer bottles, which are very welcome at this point.

"Without further ado, let's get cracking. First, we need to elect a new VP. Is anyone volunteering?" I look around the table, not expecting anyone to raise their hand, and hence I'm not disappointed when it doesn't happen. "Any nominations?" I ask, knowing I can count on Slender and Pennywise.

Slender stands. "I nominate Vegas!" The look on Vegas's face is priceless. Pure shock and panic. If it wasn't such a serious situation, I'd laugh.

"Anyone seconding this?" I ask.

Pennywise stands and confirms, "I second." No surprise there.

"Let's vote. I need an eighty percent vote on this, boys," I say as I look around the room. Slender and Pennywise vote aye, no surprise there. We continue round the table. Vegas is a nay, but that's not a problem, I expected that from him. Everyone else follows Slender and Pennywise.

"Vegas, do you accept?" I ask him, not missing Pen's encouraging nod.

"I'm stunned, but since you all seem to think I can do it, I accept." Vegas's face tells us how serious and proud he is.

Spen throws a new Vice President patch towards Vegas with a smirk and yells, "Happy sewing!" Watching Vegas, it's clear how moved he is by the amount of trust shown to him, making me glad I listened to Pen and Slender.

"We are all aware of what went on with Rusty. Today I received a phone call from his sister, Ellie, who most of you know." I relay the phone conversation and can tell by the grim faces and tensed fists that the brothers aren't happy. Not at all.

"I asked her to pack up some stuff for a few days and come here," I explain. "Vegas, could she stay with you and Ashley? Rusty wouldn't go to your place, nor will he expect Ellie to be there. Somehow, I feel we need to keep her safe."

Vegas nods and replies, "Sure, can't see a problem there. I'll discuss with Ashley, but yeah, sure, no problem. She shouldn't stay on club property, and definitely needs to stay out of his way."

"I'll send her a message with your address and tell her to head there. She could be here in under two hours," I add, raising my eyebrow towards Vegas in question.

"Yeah, that works. We'll be expecting her." He nods.

Ferret looks at his laptop.

"Not a moment too soon. The tracker I installed on his trike shows he's on the move, and it looks like he's going in that direction." I nod, appreciating his input.

"Any other business?" I look up and down the table.

"Is Vegas paying for the first round?" Ratchet pipes up. *"As ifs"* sound all around the table.

Dougal raises his hand.

"Go on, Doug, the floor is yours," I encourage him.

He stands, looks around, takes a deep breath, and growls out, "I'm claiming Sarah."

The entire table erupts to cheering, and hands are thumping on the table. I am one of the main table drummers. I've known Dougal most of my life, and although he is a little older than some, he's the best brother any of us could ever wish for. He deserves a good woman. A strong woman, who can give as good as she gets and is wholeheartedly behind him. It's obvious they are into each other. Since returning from the rally, Dougal's been like a Rottweiler who peed against an electric fence where Sarah has been concerned. Fierce and in a rotten mood if anyone so much as looked at her.

"We'll make this a quick vote, Doug." I smirk at him. "Anyone against?" No veto comes, and with that, the meeting closes.

Everyone disperses, apart from Vegas and me.

"Thanks, Prez," Vegas starts. "I'll work hard not to let you or the brothers down."

I nod, certain he'll give his all to the club. He always has.

Vegas takes out his phone, calls my sister and lets her know about the houseguest while I text Ellie the details. Vegas waits for me to finish. Curiosity radiating from him.

"What are we going to do about Rusty? You and I both know that something fishy is going on with him. So do Slender, Pen and Ferret. I can't believe Moggy voted against the out bad."

Internally I couldn't agree more with him, but don't show it on the outside.

"A vote's a vote, whether or not we like it. All we can do now is hope the bastard leaves on his own and with no trouble. Though I admit, I have very low expectations," I state with a sigh. "It worries me he's smacking Ellie around and is threatening her. It's almost as though he's losing a grip on reality these days. Who the fuck knows? And I can't say I'm over eager to find out what is going on with him. I supported him for years and he stabbed me in the back, like the conniving snake he is."

I pull a bottle of JD out of the drawer under my end of the table, take a deep swig and offer the bottle to Vegas, who declines. The burn settles my frayed nerves.

"We'll get there, Raven. I've got your back." Vegas stands, slaps my shoulder, and walks out of church, having a home and a woman to get back to.

I stretch my tired bones, rub my eyes, grab the bottle of JD and walk to my house behind the clubhouse, just out of sight but within a five-minute walk. I altered a cabin to my taste and moved in after the old house burned down. It has two decent sized rooms. A living room with a couch and TV, a small coffee table and my record player. I prefer vinyl over CD or streaming every time. A small divider hides a small kitchenette with a door leading to the bathroom. The other room is my bedroom. I portioned the bedroom and bathroom off so I could make a kitchen. Big enough for my king-size bed, chest of drawers, a small desk with a small tv sitting on it, so I can watch TV in bed if I feel the need. It's small, but mine, and that counts for something.

I drop onto the couch, JD bottle in my hand, and drink straight from the bottle. What a weekend. Refusing to think any more about Rusty, I instead choose to think about what happened with Chloe. Since I am no longer a manwhore, I don't use club pussy and prefer being with the same woman more than once. However, the visceral reaction I've had to Chloe is unusual, even for me. When she's near me, I want to howl at the moon to let anyone and everyone know she's mine. I've never been the possessive type before; I can't even say I've ever fallen in love. In the past, my relationships were based on not despising the other person and having physical compatibility, so possessiveness has never been an issue.

It's different with Chloe. I've not been able to stop thinking about her since she first appeared at Carl's bedside, threatening him with a wire brush and disinfectant. She makes me laugh, and I like her no BS attitude. Finding out she rides, just threw a switch for me. I wanted to hang a massive sign around her neck saying "mine" with an arrow pointing towards me. Jealousy shot through me with furious intensity when Ghoul made moves to impress her. Her reading me the riot act was just the sexiest thing ever. She couldn't have made me harder if she had been naked. She stays calm and collected, has a great sense of humor and her laughter has something soothing about it. Shaking my head at myself, the thought, *look at me all poetic and sentimental,* is at the forefront of my mind. I know I'm easy on the eyes. Women have always liked me. Rarely have I ever had to try. Yet, with Chloe, I want to.

The sex was off the charts, and I can honestly say I've never had sex quite like that. With such bone melting intensity. I'm more the hard fucking kinda guy. Not this time, though. The experience left me rattled at the time, and still rattles me now. I want Chloe to be mine; I know that. She's the one for me. The big question is, does she feel the same? This is all unfamiliar territory. I'm in dangerous water here. Chloe could tie me into knots and own me. She makes me vulnerable, something I've never experienced before. Not sure I'm enjoying this particular feeling, but I am falling hard and fast for her and am honest enough to admit it to myself. She has more power over me than anyone ever should.

Vulnerability is not a good look on a Prez. The wisdom I'm so in need of eludes me. So, all I can do for now is to go with the flow, see where it leads and keep up some barriers, while trying to lower others without looking weak. The only thing I know for certain is that something has changed, and I don't wanna continue living the way I have. My life needs to include and encompass Chloe. Yes, I know how crazy this sounds. Her scent, her smile, her taste, her touch. Like a crack addict, I'm hooked. We've only been apart for a few hours and I am already going through withdrawal.

Taking a hot shower doesn't help, neither does the half bottle of JD I drink during my epiphanies. I am pretty loaded. Probably best to just fall into bed and sleep it off.

11 — CHLOE

Forcing my eyes to open, I roll over in my comfy bed and check to see my clock showing ten a.m. Who doesn't love vacation days? Especially after a fabulous weekend, knowing that you still get to sleep in. Plus, I can't wait to see Raven. Raven, ah, just thinking about him makes me hot and bothered. Shit, it's ten a.m., he'll be here around one and I ain't even dressed yet. Gotta get a move on, grocery shopping and cooking are on the agenda. That thought has me jumping out of bed and into the shower. It takes another five minutes to throw on some acceptable clothes for shopping and I'm out the door.

Parking my car at Walmart, I grab my phone, which has rung several times along the way. Whoever it is, shows persistence. When I look, I recognize the number from the hospital. What on earth do they want? They know I am on vacation.

Annoyed, I call back. It's the administrator with the bone marrow department.

"Hey, Chloe, sorry to disturb you on your days off. It's Elsie. I know you were planning on distributing some information about bone marrow donors and possibly finding more interested parties to come forward. Did you have any luck? Hate to ask you for a favor while you are on vacation, but we have several people that could really benefit from a donor sooner rather than later."

"Sure, I'll come by after I finish shopping. Just to warn you, there is a ton. I can't believe the response we received. We couldn't help Flakey but hopefully we can help someone else," I say with sincerity.

"Thank you so much, Chloe! Again, I am so sorry to bother you while you are on vacation," Elsie apologizes.

"That's fine, Elsie, I'll drop off the forms I collected over the weekend. Hopefully, we can save someone's life," I tell her.

"That's fantastic! Okay, Chloe, see you in a bit then," she replies.

I hang up and make my way inside the store. Basket in hand, I throw in everything I need for a seafood risotto, side salad, and freshly baked bread, rush through checkout, and am parking at the hospital within ten minutes.

Grabbing the massive box with the signature forms under my arm, I walk to the donor registration office, shove through the door and drop the box on the desk.

"Wow, that was fast," Elsie says, looking a little stunned. "Are you kidding me? Please tell me that box is not full of forms." She looks a little scared.

"Yup, I was very persuasive this weekend. It should give the donor base a nice boost," I answer.

◊◊◊

After leaving the hospital, it's around eleven-thirty. Raven will be here in about an hour and a half. He texted earlier, letting me know he's gonna be late. The risotto is just about finished, so is the salad and the bread is sitting next to the oven, ready to go in the warmer for a few minutes before we eat.

Now that I have some free time left, I fire up my old rickety laptop. Months and months ago, I finally succumbed to peer pressure and joined the Ancestry DNA brigade. Never got round to checking my results. My eyebrows hit my hairline when I sign into the site and see how many results there are. Apparently, I have lots of distant relatives all over Europe, with the bulk in Scandinavian countries. Ha, *that's* where my blonde hair comes from. Smiling to myself, I scour the results, look at family trees, where fifth cousins, twice removed, feature heavily.

The last notification states that there's a close relative match. I groan. Mom must have done a DNA kit as well, can't wait to get my ear chewed off when she sees I'm on here and have flagged. Reluctantly, I open the notification. Yup, this has to be my mom, as it clearly states possible relationship, parent-child. But why are there two entries? Going hot and cold, I start feeling a little dizzy. As I look closer, one of the icons is blue, the other red. I click on the red one. Yup, that's my mom, Theresa Sanders. So, who in the hell is in the blue icon? Have I got a brother or something? Has mom kept things from me? My heart is thundering. It feels like it's beating double its normal speed, and I'm overwhelmed by a sinking feeling as I open the icon. *What the fuck?* "No way, no fucking way!" I shout before everything goes dark.

◊◊◊

I wake with a groan, dazed and disorientated, wondering what the fuck I'm doing laying on the carpet, with a huge egg-sized lump on my head, and a headache from hell. Feeling still dizzy and extremely weak, I slowly try to sit up and get my bearings. I lean my back against the desk and try to take some deep breaths until the noisy, dull hum in my ears recedes, and my eyes can focus without it feeling like I'm on the spinning teacup ride in an amusement park. After the dizziness and nausea pass, I manage to get on my knees and pull myself up, sitting down on my desk chair. Unfortunately, that's when it all comes back to me. When I look at my laptop, the tab

88

remains open. Best match, probable parent: Robert Buck. This can't be right. When my mom spoke about my father, which was almost never, it sounded as though he was dead. Not that she ever told me he was, but that's what I presumed. Jesus, this can't be right. Surely she must have received similar notifications? She wouldn't have kept this from me for all these years. Fair enough, I didn't submit the test because I wanted to find relatives; it was a joke really. Someone from work bought me the test as a present and after being pestered for weeks, I completed and submitted it.

Never in a million years did I think it would bring anything like this up. My mind is racing and my thoughts a jumbled mess. I'm gonna phone Mom. No, better yet, I'm gonna go and see her. She can't wiggle her way out of this now. I need answers!

I decide I better message Raven. This is more important and I need to deal with it now.

Me: Sorry, something came up. I've gotta go see my mother. Can we postpone until later?

Raven: Sure, you alright? Is your mom okay?

Me: Bit of a family emergency thing. I need to speak to her now, face-to-face. I'll explain later. Is six okay?

Raven: Sure, I'll see you then. Call me if you need me, Chloe, promise!

Me: I promise. See you later xx.

◊◊◊

Pulling the car into mom's drive, the gravity of the situation hits me like a dump truck. Unsure which emotion claws at me more: the gut-wrenching disappointment in my mother for leading me to believe I had no father, sadness to have missed out on something I could have had, or the fury about her having kept this from me for so long. My emotions are raging uncontrolled right now, and this is before I've even gotten out of the car. I feel so betrayed. Why? Why would she do this to me?

I walk to the door, which flies open, and Mom throws herself at me, hugging me tight. "Hey, love, I wasn't expecting you! It is so good to see you. Come in, come in." Her smile is beaming. Finding it hard to look at her right now, I walk past her in silence and straight into the front room, where I plop myself on the couch. The place where I used to curl up with a book and a quilt in the corner, the place I always felt safe.

Mom putters about in the kitchen then comes back, carrying a tray with coffee and home-made cookies. I grab a cup of coffee, ignoring the sweets. She takes a seat in the chair opposite me.

"What's up, honey? You look serious, and you don't often just drop in on me. What's on your mind?" She smiles at me.

"Well, Mom, I've had an interesting day today. You remember Elsie at work?" I ask. "Oh yes, how is she? She still working admin?" mom replies.

"Yup, she is. A few months ago, she gave me an ancestry DNA kit. I got some interesting result back," I tell her. To say my tone is glacial is the understatement of the century. I'm fresh out of empathy with her, as I watch her face pale.

"What?" she whispers, looking at me in complete shock.

"Name of Robert Buck mean anything to you?" My tone is as icy as I feel inside.

Her hands clap over her mouth, but she can't contain the audible gasp. For a few moments, it looks as though she'll pass out, but against all odds, she composes herself. I watch her get up from her chair and go into the kitchen. When she returns, she has two glasses of amber liquid in her shaking hands. Holding one out for me, she sits back in her chair and throws back her drink in one shot, closes her eyes while experiencing the burn, and waits for me to follow

suit. So, I do. Appreciating the warmth and burn the rum leaves in my throat.

Mom looks at me, her eyes cloudy with regret.

"I'm sorry, Chloe. I hope you can forgive me. There's not much to tell, but I will tell you

what I can, and hope you'll understand." Nodding at her, I decide I owe it to her to listen.

"I met Rob—Robert—otherwise known as Bobby, when I turned twenty. I was so

impressed by his motorcycle and couldn't believe that he was interested in me. He was so

handsome. Black straight long hair, olive skin tone, very native looking, without actually being

native. Strong arms, muscular body, with a small scar on his cheek, where he'd gotten into a

fight." She takes a sip of her coffee, appearing lost in her memories.

"We dated for several months. I felt so grown up with him and loved him so much. I

thought we wanted the same thing, but apparently not. When I went to a party he and his friends

threw, I caught him having sex with some trashy girl. He saw me and smirked, didn't stop, just

smirked at me. I turned and ran, devastated. That's when I realized he didn't just ride a

motorcycle, but he was thinking about joining an MC. One of his biker friends confirmed it. I

knew then that he wouldn't be able to change and that I'd been just another notch on his bedpost.

A fling. Whereas for me it had been love. Otherwise, I'd have never let him near me. He took my

virginity, Chloe. I gave it willingly at the time and never regretted it. It was a special experience.

Turns out that after he got what he wanted, he wasn't interested anymore."

My fists are balling, and although she speaks without malice, I can feel my compassion

coming to the forefront for her and anger for that asshole who hurt her.

"I never saw him again, Chloe. There was no point. None. I heard later that he patched in

and got in with the wrong crowd. Even did some time in prison. To be honest, I was glad he wasn't in the picture, and I never told him I was pregnant either. I needed to put it behind me so I could get over it. I looked at him as a one-night stand. We only had sex that one time, honey, and I got a surprise gift. You. You've been the greatest gift in my life. I am so proud of you."

Her eyes are shining with tears. "I never considered how this might affect you. You have a right to know, but back then, I just wanted to protect you, Chloe. That's all I ever wanted." Tears are streaming down her face now. I jump off the couch and race to her, pull her up and wrap my arms around her. "I'm so sorry, Chloe, please forgive me!" she sobs into my neck. All I can do is nod, as tears are running down my face, my voice refusing to work.

We stand there embracing and crying for what seems like forever. When we finally compose ourselves and sit back down. Trying not squeak, I clear my throat.

"Mom, I understand a lot of things better now. Your hatred of anything related to motorcycles, your attitude towards bikers, your opinions, and concerns. I am grateful for being your daughter, for the way you brought me up. But that didn't give you the right to keep this from me for so long. I'm thirty-six years old and had to find out who my father is via a DNA test and accidental discovery. That's not right." I shake my head at her.

"You should have told me years ago when I was old enough to understand. You chose not to. That hurts, Mom, really hurts." My eyes are stinging with new tears. "I understand why you did what you did, but forgiveness? That will take time, Mother. I love you very much, but I don't particularly like you right now," I say as my silent tears fall.

"I understand," Mom replies. "All I can do is tell you how sorry I am. I never meant to hurt you. I wanted to protect you. Now I can see how wrong that was, but over the years, I convinced myself it was the right thing to do. Chloe, I am sorry, and I hope one day you'll be able to forgive me. You are my world, sweetheart, and I love you more than anything. I am so proud of the person you've become," she says as we both stand and hug again.

I have nothing else to say to her. I'm desperate for some time to myself to sort through my thoughts and feelings. Not wanting to hurt her or say anything, I might end up regretting because I'm furious. I say goodbye and leave, watching my mother's sad eyes disappear in the rearview mirror.

12 — RAVEN

The day drags on with all the normal, mundane things. Signing off on kitchen budgets with Mom, agreeing on the handling of the club bunnies, and discussing whether to hire a cleaner, is not my idea of fun. The whole day, I struggle to keep my mind on the topics at hand and not on Chloe. This morning the thought of her made me so hard I jacked off to memories of her magic lips around me. Sad, but true. I've got it bad, and I know it. It takes an enormous effort to keep my mind on the matters at hand and stop it from wandering to the girl with the long blonde, red streaked hair and expressive hazel eyes.

Clusseaud appears in my doorway.

"Got a moment, Prez? Just want to confirm the details for next week's Poker Run," he asks. I sigh and want to say no, but am wholly aware that I can't. We owe this fundraiser to Carl. I wave him in and he takes a seat.

"Okay, boss, the route, and the checkpoints are ready to go. Are we providing refreshments at the checkpoints?" he inquires.

"Yeah, but only soft drinks, and there'll be portable toilets available. They should arrive before the poker run starts," I confirm. "Poker card sets have arrived and the posters are printed.

The stage is reserved, and the band booked. I'm also gonna speak to Chloe about manning the stall again tonight," I tell him.

"Do we have anything else?" Clusseaud asks, going through his notes. "Might as well make the most of the fundraiser."

I have to agree. "I believe Ash is organizing raffle prizes from bike dealers, local businesses, etc., and there will be an auction. Ashley can plan that shit. She's good at it. Me? Not so much. Apparently, we owe her a fundraiser for the kids' home she works at. They need a new minibus."

Clusseaud taps his finger against his chin, deep in thought, before he speaks, "Actually, Raven, we could split the proceeds. The pre-planned events and raffle can go towards the hospital and any extra money, such as donations and whatever she has planned on stage, can go towards the minibus."

Damn, I knew I kept Clusseaud around for a reason. Why hadn't I thought about that myself?

"We could sell tickets for people who want to perform on stage, like an open mic, and to those that want to listen to the music, then donate all of those proceeds towards the minibus. Get the local community involved. In fact, we could donate a maintenance service from the repair shop." Clusseaud can be unstoppable when he gets going.

"Love the idea, man. We can do both without having to do two separate events. Maybe we could find out if there are any local bands for the open mic portion on stage?" I contribute, being swept along by Clusseaud's current. "I'll leave it in your capable hands, man. Great ideas. Can you liaise with Ashley and the hospital?"

He nods. "Sure thing, Raven, I'll sort it. Can you sort out a checkpoint schedule for the guys?"

"I'll get Vegas to do that, man. Anything else?" I look at him.

"Nope, that's all for now." He nods at me, before standing and leaving my office. Looking at my clock, I note it's almost five, time to get ready and head out.

As ridiculous as it seems, I have a pep in my step while I stroll to my place. Walking into the bathroom, I shuck off my clothes and take a shower. I consider shaving but then decide not to. Chloe seems to like my stubble, I think to myself, grinning, and my dick agrees. I grab a white T-shirt and worn black jeans, get dressed, shove my feet into my boots, throw my cut over my leather jacket, and stride out to my bike. Throwing my leg over, letting the old girl roar into life, I roll out, filtering into traffic at the main road. Stopping at a stall by the side of the road, I buy a bunch of wildflowers and stick them inside the front of my jacket. I want her to know that I'm not messing around. Never felt like I wanted to do something nice for a woman before, but for her I do.

It's five minutes to six when I roll to a stop outside her apartment block. Her car is in its allocated space, so I set my bike behind it. Making my way to the door, I pick her door number and ring. The buzzer sounds and I make my way up to her apartment. She smiles as she stands by the open door, however I can't help but feel something is off. Her smile does not reach her eyes, and she looks as though she's been crying. Within a millisecond, I'm on high alert.

"Hey, Raven," she greets me. I pull her to me, hold her tight, and kiss her hair.

"Hey, to you too, Chloe, missed you," I mumble into her hair, which smells of tropical flowers or some shit. With my finger under her chin, I lift it up and plant a chaste kiss on her

96

lips. She wraps her arms around me and melts against my body. That's better. Good to see her relax a little.

"Bad day, huh?" I ask, handing her the flowers as we walk inside.

"You can say that again," she huffs, the strain in her voice as clear as day.

"Thank you for these. They are beautiful. I love wildflowers." There's a slight smile playing around her lips. "Are you hungry?" She looks at me questioningly.

"Starving, darlin'. I could eat a horse." I smile down at her. She nods, sets out two plates, cutlery, removes a salad bowl from the fridge, and a small loaf of bread out of the oven. It doesn't look like she has a kitchen table, so she transfers it to the small living room table. Whatever is in the casserole dish, it smells amazing. When everything, including butter for the warm bread, is on the table, she waves her hand at me, indicating for me to sit on the couch, and brings over the casserole. She spoons seafood risotto onto my plate and my mouth waters. I help myself to some warm bread, butter it and complete my plate with some salad.

I wait for her to sit before eating. The taste is out of this world. My tastebuds are doing backflips with the deliciousness in my mouth. A loud groan of pleasure escapes me before I can stop it, making Chloe giggle. I love that sound. It makes me smile, even with my mouth being full.

"Wow, Chloe, this is amazing!" I tell her. "My new favorite meal!" I mumble out between two heaping spoons full of food. She just smiles and we continue to eat in comfortable silence. No need for words at the moment. But I place my left hand on her right knee and squeeze it, which earns me another smile. This time it reaches her eyes.

After we finish eating, we sit back. "Man, I am stuffed! Thank you, Chloe, this was absolutely fantastic! I love seafood, but this was something else."

97

"Glad you like it." She smirks. "I decided to let you do the dishes to show your gratitude." She winks at me.

"No problem. If you just show me where the sink is and where the soap and sponges are, I'll give it a shot!" I tease her. She playfully slaps my head as she collects all the dishes. I beat her to the sink, wash and dry while she puts everything away.

The tension radiates off her in great waves again. Not sure what's happened, but something did, that's for sure. And I'll be damned if I won't try to find out what has her wound so tight. I hate to see her this stressed and upset about something. If I can, I'll do anything possible to make things right for her.

"What would you like to do now?" I ask, looking into her hazel eyes.

"Honestly?" she replies. I nod. "Can we go for a ride?" she asks hesitantly.

"Sure, honey, grab your gear and we're off. Anywhere in particular?"

"Nope, just ride. I need to feel the wind in my hair, and just blow away the cobwebs. It's been a hellish day," she says, with no further explanation.

It only takes her a few moments to grab her jacket and helmet, put her boots on, and walk out the door. I appreciate her need for this. Riding clears my head, too. I get it.

I get on my bike, start it up, watch how Chloe puts down the passenger pegs, and feel her slide on behind me. She gets comfortable, wraps her arms close around me and nods at me in the mirror. I can honestly say I've never had any woman on the back of my bike, well, apart from Ashley, but this just feels one hundred percent right.

I love the feel of her warm, soft body behind me and the feel of her hands on my stomach. We pull out and start riding. It's as easy as breathing.

98

After a few moments she relaxes behind me, leaning into me and being one with me and the bike. It's a spectacular feeling, touching me to my core. Never have I felt so fulfilled and at peace before. It's erased any lingering doubts I had. This is the perfect woman for me. Now I just have to get her to realize that.

When I arrived tonight, she was so nervous, fragile almost. No idea what happened today, but I know I want to slay her dragons, keep her safe, protect her. The depth of that need surprises me, but I'll keep an open mind and go with it. I can acknowledge it for what it is. This woman seems to be my equal, and I have fallen hard for her.

I like she calls a spade a spade, recognizes the gray between all the black and white. Love that she knows what she wants and needs and is not afraid to show it. Her confidence is inspiring, and her ability to surprise me an unexpected bonus. She's independent and holds down a very demanding job in her everyday life. That alone makes me want to go into protective overdrive.

The way she dealt with Carl, Ash, me, and all the brothers, she deserves a medal. It must be tough on her to deal with that kind of life and death situation almost every day. I have nothing but the greatest admiration for her.

She rests her head on my back, and I know it's time to make our way home. We've been riding for forty-five minutes, and it'll take the same time to get back. The sun set a while ago. The calm darkness, countryside noises, and rumble of the engine have done their job to provide some much-needed relaxation.

Turning off the engine and watching her get off my bike, it's obvious that a different person takes off her helmet. Gone is the strain around the eyes and the wrinkled brows, instead replaced by a small smile on her lips.

She leans towards me and waits for me to remove my helmet, before she leans in, with her arms around my neck, her helmet bumping into my back, and kisses first my cheeks and then more enthusiastically my mouth, whispering, "Thank you, Raven," against my lips. It takes all of my control not to throw her over the bike and fuck her right there.

'Not the time, Raven, not the time!' I admonish myself and my rock-hard dick. Instead, I kiss her back softly and whisper, "You are welcome, Angel, anytime!" Before pulling her closer and holding her. We stand there for a moment, lost in each other, before she steps back and I'm able to get off the bike. In the fashion of ladies first, I let her lead me, but follow close behind. The need to protect her ever present.

As soon as we get inside her apartment, she wanders to the fridge, takes out a couple of beers and moves over to the living area. It's modest. She only has a couch, a low coffee table and an old comfy chair. She's mounted her television to the wall, freeing up space.

Chloe sits on the couch, snuggling one of her throw pillows, while I sit in the chair, take my beer from her and wait for what I know she is steeling herself to share with me. Leaning forward, I wait, holding my breath, hoping I don't have to kill anyone.

"Come on then, Angel, let's hear it," I encourage her.

"Sure you're ready for this?" Her slightly sarcastic tone makes me stiffen. I know it's not that she doesn't trust me, more that she might not be ready for this. I just look at her in silence, nodding at her to continue.

"So, I logged into my Ancestry account today. Months ago, I sent in a DNA test, just for fun. They found a match."

I am not sure what she is talking about. It sounds like some sort of genealogy thing. Didn't know she was into that.

"What does that mean, Chloe? I'm not sure I'm following you." She glances at me with a look I can only describe as having the entire weight of the world on her shoulders.

"Raven, they found a DNA match. A close one. They found the father I never knew I had." Wow, what a bombshell to have dropped on her. I struggle to come up with an appropriate thing to say.

"Chloe, I am not sure what to say. It doesn't seem like you're thrilled about it. How do you feel about the news?" I decide honesty is the best way forward.

She raises her hands in resignation before dropping them back into her lap, holding onto the cushion as though anchoring herself before answering. She is upset and I don't enjoy seeing her like this.

"I don't know what to feel, Raven. I am so confused! After finding out, I went to my mother's and confronted her. It was the shittiest situation ever. When she finally told me the truth, it all made sense. Her anti-motorcycle attitude is all based around my sperm donor. Can't call him father, as he never was one. He was a biker, Raven. Mom caught him cheating, never saw him again, and never told him she was pregnant. She always told me he wasn't around anymore, which I took as meaning he was dead, and it was too painful for her to talk about, so I never really dug deeper. Yet here I am, knowing I have a biological father who is alive and is clueless I even exist. What am I supposed to think? My thoughts waver from *dickhead biker,* to *I must have inherited the bike gene from him,* to *what does he look like, did he get married, does he have other children* and anything and everything in between. What do I even do with this information? I don't know!" Her voice is full of unshed tears, which has me jumping up and rushing to her side. Lifting her up, I sit down on the couch with her in my lap, holding her tight.

As expected, the tears come, and knowing better than to placate her, I just hold her tight and rub her back, whilst she cries her eyes out on my shoulder.

It takes a while for her to cry it all out and start calming down. I lean back, kissing her wet eyes.

"Angel, I wish there was something I could do to help you see things clearer, but other than being here for you when you need it, I don't think there is," I tell her while cuddling her close in my arms.

"Thanks, Raven, it's all I need right now. Thank you for being here and for being supportive," she hiccups.

"Just know if you ever want to find him, Angel. The club will help you. Ferret can get into records and do some research if you like."

"Thanks, Raven, not right now. I need to let this sink in first," she replies, sounding a little calmer.

We spend the rest of the night watching mindless movies, snuggled up on her couch, talking about this and that. Nothing important, just getting to know each other stuff. Suddenly, she sits up and looks at me.

"Hey, I just realized, I don't even know your real name!" She sounds perturbed, which is adorable. I laugh at her and kiss her nose.

"Sorry, Angel, how could I forget such an important detail," I tease her, "It's James Saunders, though my sis calls me Jamie."

She lets out a relieved sigh. "Thank God it's not Robert, Bobby, or Bob!"

Not sure where that came from, but I snicker anyway.

"Glad you don't object to James."

She looks a little contrite, which makes me chuckle even more.

"Oh, I like Jamie." She winks at me, biting her lower lip, making me instantly hard as steel.

"Care to show me how much?" My need ramps up tenfold as I watch her eyes hazing with desire. She closes the distance between us and claims my mouth with hers. This is no gentle kiss, it's a bone melting, instant boner, *I need to fuck you right now* kiss that has me standing up with her still in my arms and carrying her to the bedroom.

Dropping her onto the bed, she bounces, and we strip off our clothes. It's a race to who gets naked first. The need is overpowering. She scoots to the front of the bed and pulls me closer to her. She looks up at me, licks her lips and grabs my pulsing hard-on by the root. Her eyes never leave mine as she licks and teases it with her tongue from base to tip. I need to put my hands in her hair just to steady myself and not blow my load there and then. Her lust darkened eyes are almost black as she holds mine.

I watch her go down on me and take me deep into her throat, swallowing around me. Stone cold sober, this experience is even more intense than last time. I won't last. Her mouth is deadly and the best one ever to have graced my dick.

I could easily just let her blow my mind to completion within minutes, but I am a gentleman and ladies first has always been my attitude.

I push her back, flip her over, sit on the floor, and pull her down to my mouth. Tasting her is the most amazing aphrodisiac. Both sweet and tart flavors combine on my tongue, making my cock throb and a low groan escape my throat. I could stay here and drink her up forever. Her little noises of pleasure are driving me wild. Licking and sucking, placing small hickeys around her entrance, I let my desperation for her dictate my actions. My finger finds its way into her hot, tight pussy, stroking her from the inside. Her breath hitches as it finds the right spot. I know she's close, but if I don't get inside her now, I'll lose my mind. With a last lick and suck on her clit, I move away, grab her hips, and pull them up.

"Please, Jamie, I need you inside me! Fuck me, Jamie, please, now!" she begs.

Who am I to deny a lady? I line myself up at her entrance and push in with one long, deep stroke. Her heat and tightness overwhelm me, more so when I can feel her flutter around me, with such intensity I nearly lose it.

Holding her hips still, I mutter through gritted teeth,

"Angel, stay still for a minute, otherwise this will be over before we even really get started."

I try to clear my brain with stupid shit so I don't blow my load too soon. Moggy in underwear, an oil leak on my bike, anything to regain control. Eventually, I pull part of the way out.

"Please, Jamie, I need you to fuck me, hard!" Chloe groans. Not needing to be told twice, I start a punishing rhythm of almost complete withdrawal and hard hammering all the way deep inside her. She lowers her upper body and changes the angle, making me go even deeper. I can feel her muscles tense and hear her scream, "Jamie!" as she comes hard around me.

I bite my lip, clench my eyes shut, staving off my impending explosion. As she comes down from her orgasm, I reach around, pull her body up against me, fuck her hard and fast, one hand finding her nipple, twisting, and squeezing it, while the other finds her clit, pushing down hard. She throws her head back against my shoulder, and wails as she comes hard again. I can feel her flooding my dick and can't hold back any longer. Another push, my balls draw up and my muscles tense. I root deep inside her and explode. Pulse after pulse, seemingly never-ending reams of cum enter her, blowing my mind.

We sink onto the bed. I roll onto my side, pulling her into my arms, working the quilt over us. "Wow, that was…" she purrs, making me laugh.

"Go on, what was it?" I snigger.

"Bone melting!" comes her reply. She snuggles into my side with a relaxed smile on her face. We doze for a bit, reveling in a feeling of closeness and peace. But I know I have to leave soon. Tomorrow is a busy day with an early start.

It's after midnight by the time I extract myself from her arms and get dressed. She walks me to the door, kisses me goodbye, making me want to stay even more than I already do. At the last moment, I remember to ask.

"Hey, Angel, would you be willing to man another donor stall at the Poker Run on Saturday?"

"Sure, Jamie, no problem, I am still off this week, so yeah, no problem," she replies as I drag her to me.

Kissing her senseless, I murmur, "Thank you," against her lips before I turn and trudge to my bike.

13 — CHLOE

When I wake up, I feel like a freight train has hit me. Physically, I am deliciously sore from last night. Mentally, I am drained after yesterday's discoveries. It feels as though I need to sleep for a week, and even then, I am not sure it'll be enough.

It's unbelievable how things have been developing.

Raven... sorry, Jamie... seems intent on being with me. I am trying to work out what we are, other than brand new. Is he a manwhore? Can he change his ways? Could this be a relationship, or am I just a brief fling for him on the side? I just don't know.

What I *do* know is that I like him a lot. He's a fascinating man and so scorching hot to look at, that I could constantly fangirl about him. He seems so tough and mean on the outside, whereas at least with me, he's a big softy on the inside, making it easy for me to like and trust him. All the time spent with him seems worthwhile. There's so much depth to this man, who shoulders a mountain of responsibility.

I can't help but feel I'd like to provide him with the same peace he gives me. Be his soft place to land. I realize it's crazy because we've not known each other long at all, but it feels like a genuine connection is forming between us. Something deep, real and serious. Or am I the only one feeling it?

I almost asked him to stay last night, but didn't want to seem clingy or too forward. Guess we'll take it a day at a time and see where this leads.

Since I promised to manage another stall at the Poker Run, I fire up my laptop and Google Poker Run. I've never heard of such a thing, but what I read, I like. It's a fantastic idea to raise money.

I shoot a text to Raven.

Me: Hi, Jamie! Sorry to disturb you, hope you slept well and got home okay.

Me: Look, I have some questions regarding the stall setup for the poker run and the fundraising activities you are planning. Could you give me more info?

Raven: Hi, Angel, was just thinking about you. I got home fine and slept okay. Almost asked you whether I could stay but didn't want to crowd you. You had a stressful day.

Me: I almost asked you to stay. I enjoy being with you. xxx

Raven: Same here, Angel. Next time.

Raven: I'll give your number to Clusseaud if that's okay, he is in charge of all the planning, he'll be able to give you all the info you need. I'll get him to message you details.

Raven: There'll be stuff like a raffle, auction, open mic night etc. Be best if he sends you a program draft so you can look it over.

Me: Thanks, Jamie. Sorry, I feel like I am making more work for you. Just want to see if I can help.

Raven: No problem, Angel, I like you asked and that you want to help.

Raven: What are your plans for today, gorgeous?

Me: No plans, prepping for the weekend and a chill day. Wanna come over later?

Raven: I wish, beautiful. I am booked up today and tomorrow. Got a run today and a meeting tomorrow about the bar renovations. Sorry, darlin'. I could come over Thursday though? If you want me to?

Me: I'd love to see you Thursday. Gives me time to consider your offer to help me find my father. I'm still not sure if I actually want to, but if I decide to, I'd appreciate your help. Gonna go now and leave you to your busy day. See you Thursday. xxx

Raven: That's fine, honey, I'll be thinking about you. xxx

◊◊◊

The next two days drag like old knicker elastic. I receive several messages from Clusseaud about the Poker Run, and contact Ashley to see how I could help. The auction the girls are planning sounds bloody hilarious; it's gonna be fun! I agree to sell raffle tickets at the stall and set about emailing work, asking for prizes.

Gemma, one of my managers, is collecting prizes and even Elsie is involved. The Donor Registration Center collected money and bought a voucher for a lavish meal for two at a local steak house. So today, I'm making the rounds, collecting the donations, which I'll drop off at the clubhouse and meet Raven there. It's finally Thursday.

I've missed him, despite talking on the phone and several messages during the day. He chats about his day, funny things happening and the renovations of the bar. It sounds as if it's all falling into place and so far going smoothly. I don't miss the tiredness in his voice, though, realizing there are things he can't or won't talk to me about. I just wish I could be there for him, the way he's here for me. He makes me feel important. I want him to know that he's important to me, too.

Putting my kindle away, I get ready for the evening. My makeup is light and I decide to opt for a dress that hugs my curves, making them look fantastic. Sliding into my high heels, I'm ready to face the world. My first stop is at the hospital. I am stunned by the number of donated prizes and struggle to fit them all into the car. From plushies, to a brand-new coffee maker and even a chocolate bouquet. It's humbling to see how many people contributed and how high quality the items are. Expecting unwanted or re-gifted items, it comes as a pleasant surprise.

After I picked up the restaurant voucher from Elsie, I make my way to the clubhouse, where Clusseaud is waiting in the parking lot with Raven. Clusseaud must have been stunning to look at once upon a time. He has broad shoulders and muscles everywhere. The man obviously looks after himself. His hair is gray, short and his five o'clock shadow makes him look hot for his age. He's at least six foot six, the same height as Raven, making me feel dwarfish, being five foot eight, which is not short for a woman. Yet, they both tower over me.

As I step out of the car, Raven's chin drops. His eyes meander over me and the heat in his eyes almost scorches me. I smile as I walk towards him. Within seconds, he is on me, pulling me into his body, kissing me soundly. He devours my mouth, my knees almost buckle, and I am panting by the time he releases my lips. "Wow, you look stunning!" he breathes into my ear, sending shivers down my spine.

"You are not so bad yourself!"

He's stunning in his dark tight jeans, white tight-as-hell T-shirt showing off his muscular arms, biceps popping with his cut, only enhancing his raw beauty. He takes my breath away, and I wonder if being sexy and handsome is a requirement to be a member of the MC. Most of the men are hot as hell.

After having regained my equilibrium, I open the car doors and trunk. Clusseaud whistles.

"That is a lot of stuff you amassed there," he says with admiration in his voice.

We unload the raffle items into the clubhouse. There's a mountain of stuff. Ashley, Sarah, Debs, and Ally are sorting them into categories. I spoke to Ash earlier and offered to help, so I jump right in. Some items we can bundle together, like signed books from authors Ashley knows, Car/bike care kits, and from the local grocery store, we paired sundried fruits with infused oils. Even a makeup basket comes together. There's something here for everyone. We decide to have a kid's raffle, as we're bulging at the seams with plushies, chocolates, jigsaw puzzles, roller skates, and even a bicycle.

Ashley and Ally lean towards me.

"Make sure you bring a big purse, with lots of money, for the auction!" They grin at me.

"Hell yes! I need that in my life!" I cackle.

"What are you ladies so happy about?" a suspicious Sparks asks from behind us, making all of us jump, looking slightly guilty.

"Nothing, dear," Ally replies. "Just your mere presence is making us happy! Is that so difficult to believe?" She bats her eyelashes at him. I nearly pee myself laughing.

It takes a couple of hours, but we've everything sorted. Finally, Raven grabs my arm and drags me away, much to the amusement of everyone else. We make our way out of the clubhouse. When I say make, what I mean is he drags me behind him, and I try not to face-plant in my high heels. Luckily, it's not far. No sooner have we walked through the door that I am shoved against it and caged by his body. I breathe in his all-male scent, making me instantly wet,

110

while he is kissing the life out of me. *Yay, it looks like I'll get door sex*, is my last conscious thought before he makes me crazy with need.

"You are driving me insane in that dress," he grumbles. Just the reaction I was going for.

"I am going to fuck you, Angel, with nothing but your high heels on!" he groans into my ear, making me moan. The loud growl of my stomach interrupts us. He lifts his head, looks at me with disbelief, and starts laughing.

"Looks like I have to feed you first, though. You might end up withering away on me!" he snorts.

He orders a Chinese delivery, and we put some music on while we wait for the food to arrive. I am impressed by his eclectic vinyl collection. I flip through and start laughing as I hand him a record.

"Seriously?" he asks me. I just nod in fits of giggles. He puts the record on and within seconds Jerry Reed's "*Bird Medley*" fills the room, causing me to snort and Jamie to shake his head at me. I love rock music, but country is my guilty glee.

It takes less than twenty minutes until Jamie opens the door to the prospect carrying our food. We sit down and dig in. Once we cleaned up our mess, we settle on his couch and snuggle up.

"How are you, Angel? Are you okay?" His voice dripping with concern.

Here goes nothing.

"I'm fine, Jamie. Are you still up for helping me find my father? I need to know where I come from. It's as if a part of my identity is missing," I tell him, looking into his eyes.

He nods.

"I get that. Have you got any details you can give me?"

As I nod at him, he takes out his phone and makes a call.

"Hey, Ferret, could you come over for a sec? Not club related, but Chloe has a problem, and I'd like you to help if you can… Aha, see you in a few."

"He's coming over. You can give him the details and he can start searching for you."

"Thank you, as I don't even know where to start. This is a bit beyond me."

A few minutes later, Ferret knocks on the door and steps in, laptop in hand.

"Hey, Chloe, what can I do for you?" He smiles at me. I like Ferret. He's another one of these hunky men with a blinding smile and phenomenal physique. I sit back, whilst Raven explains the situation to Ferret. Raven offers Ferret a beer and they both sit down to discuss the best way forward.

"Okay, Chloe, let's hear what information you have," he encourages me.

"It's not much. I spoke to my mom, who said he was a biker. He cheated, and she left. Never saw him again and never told him she was pregnant with me."

"Do you have a name? A date of birth?"

"Nope, no date of birth. He must be in his late fifties though, given my age and my mom's age at the time she got pregnant. I have a name, Robert. Robert Buck," I say, feeling like we have absolutely nothing really to go on except for a name. There must be hundreds of Robert Bucks out there. This will be like trying to find a needle in a haystack.

"Come again?" Raven asks me, wide eyed, and Ferret looks very uncomfortable.

"Robert Buck, why? Do you know him?" I ask, suddenly on high alert.

Ferret clears his throat, closes his laptop, gets up, and looks over at Raven, and says, "I'll leave this one to you, Prez," before walking out the door.

All I can do is stare after him. What the hell is going on? Raven has his head in his hands. When he looks up at me, he slowly shakes his head.

"This has to be a joke," he mutters. "Are you sure you got the name right? Robert Buck? And he's an MC member?"

"Absolutely, my mother even confirmed it," I answer him. He sighs, gets up, and walks over to me. He kneels in front of me, his hands on my knees.

"Angel, I not only know Robert Buck, but so do you." That news has me reeling.

"What? How?" I can't figure out what to ask first. I'm stunned. In a million years, I wouldn't have seen this coming.

"Angel, listen, I know the man very well. He is clueless as to your existence. How do you want to play this? Do you want to meet him in person? Or just start with a phone call? What are your thoughts?" His gentle voice reaches me, drawing me out of my confusion.

"I haven't really thought about it, Jamie. I thought I would have lots of time until I found him. Now I'm not so sure. How do you know him?" I ask. Stunned, I am struggling to process this revelation.

"He's a biker and a great friend of mine, Angel." Raven speaks to me quietly. A gazillion thoughts race through my mind. In no particular order.

"I can call him and ask him to come over, if you like?" Raven offers.

I take a moment to think.

"Will you stay with me, please? I don't think I can do this on my own." I feel like a small child begging, but Raven just pulls me close and wraps me in his arms.

His heat and strength infusing into me.

113

"I promise I won't leave your side, Angel," he says with a gentle kiss to my lips. I nod at him, still confused and a lot anxious, watching him take out his phone and make the call.

"Hey, man, have you got a few minutes? Yes, sorry, I know you are busy, but this is kinda urgent. Can you come to my place and help me with something? Thanks, man, appreciate it." The call disconnects and Raven looks at me.

"He'll be here in ten minutes. Are you sure you want to go ahead with this, Chloe? I'm right behind you, whatever you wanna do, honey. Regardless of whether you want to see him or have a relationship with him."

I swallow hard.

"Yes, I need to find out. Thanks, Jamie, for being here with me." I lean my head onto his shoulder, feeling like the proverbial lamb being taken to slaughter.

A few minutes pass and there's a knock on the door.

"Come in!" Raven calls. The door opens, and a disgruntled Clusseaud steps in. I look behind him, thinking, *'how inconvenient, I don't want to discuss the Poker Run right now, I am nervous enough as it is,'* but only Clusseaud enters.

"What's the big emergency that you needed to see me right now?" he grouches. I look at Raven, then at Clusseaud and back at Raven. Suddenly, the reality sinks into my scattered brain.

Raven looks at me, clasping my hand as though he's scared, I'll jump up and run. And honestly? The thought crosses my mind. I can't breathe, my chest feels tight. I get up, walk to the window, open it, breathing in the clear night air, trying not to lose it.

"Clusseaud, sit for a moment. Chloe has some questions for you, I think. It'll explain why I asked you here. Just try to be patient." I hear Raven. My voice is giving out, and I clear my throat several times.

I turn to face them.

"Do you…" I squeak, not in command of my voice, making Raven come over to me. He stands behind me and wraps his arms around me.

"It's okay, honey, I am here, I've got you," he murmurs in my ear.

I try again.

"Do you know someone named Theresa? Theresa Sanders?" I look at Clusseaud, trying to decipher his facial expression.

"Not that I can recall," he answers. "Why do you ask?"

"A little over thirty-six years ago, Theresa Sanders dated a biker. She caught him sleeping with someone else, walked away and never saw him again." My eyes never leave his.

Suddenly, he pales.

"Theresa? As in Terrie?" he stammers.

"Yes, Theresa, Terrie Sanders," I confirm, waiting for his reaction.

"Haven't heard that name in a long, long time. That was back when I was a stupid youngster. I loved Terrie, but wasn't ready to admit it to myself. She walked in on us after I left with a club bunny. She never made a scene, just walked out. Tried to find her for months, but never could." He sighs, regret radiating out from him. "How do you know her? Do you know where she is?"

Raven squeezes me tight and pulls me closer against him.

"Yes, I know her, and know where she is, but I don't think she wants to see you," I answer his question with a calmness I don't feel. "Theresa Sanders is my mother."

Clusseaud's mouth gapes open. Shock marring his face. A riot of emotions playing across his features. Regret, sadness, anger, something akin to hope, pain, and disbelief.

"Why are you telling me this? I'm not into living in the past and torturing myself about past mistakes!" he snarls.

"Because you are looking your *past mistake* right in the eye, Father!" My temper gets the better of me, anger shaking me to the core.

"Is this a sick joke? I don't have any kids!" he yells at me.

Snatching the piece of paper from the Ancestry DNA results up from the table, where I dropped them when Ferret left, I shove them at Clusseaud.

"You're not? This begs to differ!" I hiss at him.

He takes the document, collapses onto the armchair, and reads.

"This has to be a mistake!" he states, deep in denial.

Raven walks to the kitchenette, gets out a glass and fills it with JD, handing it to Clusseaud, who downs it in one shot.

This is not how I wanted to spend the evening with Raven. Now regretting my actions, I wish I'd just let him fuck me against the door instead of unleashing chaos. I drop my ass on the couch, shaking like a leaf.

116

14 — RAVEN

Well, hell, I'm always prepared for life's little surprises. But this? I did not see this one coming. Man alive, here we are, three utterly shocked people, not knowing what to do with ourselves. Awkward is the understatement of the millennia.

Clusseaud is sitting there, whiskey in hand, pale as my mom's old Halloween bedsheet ghost. Chloe is opposite him, looking defeated and worn the fuck out. And me? I'm standing in the middle of the room, not knowing where to put myself. I *want* to support Chloe; she needs my support. But then Clusseaud does too. This hit him out of nowhere, just as it did Chloe. I couldn't believe it when Chloe told me the name of her father. Ferret was just as stunned and left me to it. Asshole. For once I'm at a loss for words.

Clusseaud stands. "I'm sorry. I can't wrap my head around this. There must be a mistake. I can't accept that Terrie wouldn't have told me. This has gotta be a hoax!" He turns, walks out and slams the door so hard I worry it'll smash the frame. I've never seen him so pissed and defiant.

Chloe is pale and shaking. She needs to be my priority. I sit next to her and pull her into my lap. Finding the right words is nigh on impossible, so I keep my mouth shut and just rub her back, trying to transfer some of my strength to her. Slowly, I can feel her posture and breathing change. I know she's fighting tears; I can sense it.

117

"Hey, I'm here. It's okay, just let it out, Angel," I murmur to her, holding her tight.

There's no sobbing, her tears are silent, which to me is worse. I swear I can feel her pain and it makes me feel helpless since I struggle to comfort her.

"I'm sorry, Jamie. You shouldn't have to see me like this," she croaks.

"What the fuck! I won't pretend to know what you are feeling right now, honey, but I'm here for you when you are sad as well as when you're happy. You need my shoulder to cry on. Here it is, cry as much as you need to. It helps take the pressure off." Kissing her hair and rubbing her back and arms seems to help calm her. She leans into me.

Pushing up, with her still in my arms, I walk us through into the bedroom, with no protest from Chloe. I place her on the bed, taking my time undressing her, and pull one of my T-shirts over her head to help her put it on. She watches me with curious eyes when I follow suit and get into bed with her, pulling the covers over us.

"Come here," I whisper to her, and she scoots closer. Wrapping my arms around her, pulling her tight into my body. I can't help but want her, and my dick is standing to attention, but then it always is when she is nearby.

However, he'll have to wait. I'm not that kind of asshole. Just being together, giving her the comfort and reassurance she needs, is more important than physical desires. There's more than enough time for that later. No way am I letting her go home tonight. She'll stay with me, even if I have to duct-tape her to the bed. Not that she gives any indication of wanting to leave.

With her head on my chest and her body wrapped around me, I feel her settling and her breathing becoming deep and regular. She's finally falling asleep. It's been a hell of a day for her. I switch off the bedside light, breathe in her scent, and let the oncoming calm wash over me.

◊◊◊

My body feels like a sauna. For a second, it leaves me wondering whether I left the heat on high, until I stretch and feel a soft warm body next to mine and smile. Chloe is here, in my bed, with her back towards me, and it feels so right. She belongs here.

I carefully crawl out of bed, check my phone, which says six-thirty, and tiptoe into the bathroom so not to wake her. She deserves to sleep in after yesterday's craziness.

In the bathroom, I shuck off my boxers and turn the hot water on, stepping under the spray, and take a moment to enjoy the pelting of hot water on my skin. With my hands bracing on the wall, I lean in my head under the spray and inhale deeply. Shampooing, and conditioning my hair—yes, men do condition—I let the strain of the last few weeks wash off me. I jolt as the shower door opens, and a naked, smiling Chloe steps in.

"Thought you could use some help," she croons, winking at me. My dick jumps in appreciation of her curves.

"Did you now?" I smirk at her. She stands on tiptoes, touching her lips to mine, running her tongue along the seam of my mouth. I take over the kiss, pull her to me and let my lips do the talking. They're showing my need for her, along with my rock-hard dick, which is impatiently jumping between us against her belly.

She pulls back, panting, "You seem to be swollen there. Do you need it looked at by a medical professional?" She looks at me and wiggles her eyebrows in such a comical way it makes me chuckle.

"Yes, Nurse, please, Nurse, it seems I have a hard swollen appendage. It hurts. Maybe you could kiss it better?"

No sooner have I finished my sentence then she drops to her knees and gives my dick her attention. She tortures me with slow, teasing strokes of her tongue and sinking my cock slow-

119

motion style into her mouth, her eyes locked on me. I groan at the sight and feel of her. Without warning, she sucks hard and takes me all the way down into her throat, swallowing around me, driving me crazy, making me yell. The change from soft and slow to hard and deep blows my mind.

I lean my head back against the shower wall and give in to the sensations. Her mouth is a lethal weapon. It drives me to the edge in no time. Hastily, I pull my cock out of her mouth and draw her to her feet.

"Minx!" I growl at her, before turning her so her back is to me and she is leaning against my chest. Using my hands, I shampoo, rinse, and condition her hair, eliciting tiny whimpers of need from her. I find a soft washcloth, soap it up, and run it over the front of her body. Her moans filling the shower stall are music to my ears. Paying special attention to her pebbled nipples, I turn her towards me so I can wash her back whilst she is leaning against my front, her head resting on my chest, her breath coming in short pants, her breasts heaving. She's lost in pleasure and it's the most beautiful sight I've ever seen. I remove the showerhead and rinse her back slowly and deliberately, then turn her again with her back against me. Soaping my hands, I run them gently across her buttocks and between them, making her jump and groan as I touch her puckered hole. She must enjoy what I am doing because she pushes back on my hand. Running my hands across her hips, moving in slow circles, has her head resting against my chest.

"You are driving me insane, Jamie!" she gasps.

"Just returning the favor, Angel," I murmur in her ear. My fingers are reaching towards her center, continuing my torture, I wash between her legs, my fingers circling her clit and her hot entrance. She tries to push her thighs together to get more friction, but my hand prevents her movement's effectiveness. Her guttural growl makes me chuckle. She wants to come, but this is my show now and she will come when I decide to let her.

"Patience, Angel, patience," I encourage, as I continue my ministrations.

"You are the devil!" she moans between clenched teeth, making me chuckle harder. I know what she needs, it's same thing my dick does; to sink deep inside her and fuck her senseless, but I want her to come for me first. Grabbing the showerhead again, I rinse her front. Pointing the water spray at her hard nipples while my other hand strokes and massages her breast. "Need to make sure we get all the soap off," I offer in explanation, as her darkened, fiery eyes find mine.

Teasing her with the spray down the front of her body, I can feel her twitch against me, eyes still locked on mine. I push my knee between her legs, opening them further and with the spray turned from soft to hard jet, I point it at her needy clit. It takes a few seconds and she comes screaming. With her legs buckling, I manage catch her, hoist her up against the shower wall, her legs automatically locking around me, as I sink deep into her still spasming heat. All bets are off now. I ram into her hard. My dick has a mind of its own.

"Oh God, Jamie! I'm gonna come again!" she wails.

"Go on then, come for me, don't hold back. That's it, squeeze my cock." My eyes are rolling back in my head. I can feel the tingle at the bottom of my spine start and my balls pulling up. Shoving into her hard and fast, fucking her as though my life depends on it. All the while she is screaming my name and babbling incoherently. When she comes, her orgasm hits like a freight train, and her heat squeezes so tight around me it triggers my explosion. My knees turn to rubber and I have to lock them in place, so I don't drop both of us on the shower floor. I see stars and have trouble catching my breath as my balls empty themselves again and again inside her. With my head resting against hers, I plunder her mouth, enjoying the feel of her tongue stroking mine. It's so sensual, my dick has trouble softening.

Several orgasms later, we have to rinse off quickly because the water is now cold. It turns out to be the most exhausting yet satisfying shower I have ever taken.

◊◊◊

It's late morning by the time we make it to the clubhouse, where Mom made breakfast for everyone. I pile two plates with bacon, pancakes, and maple syrup and take them over to the table Chloe is sitting at. Clusseaud walks in, stares at us, makes himself a plate and walks straight back out. He clearly needs time to wrap his head around all of this.

Chloe sighs.

"I don't know how to act towards him now, Jamie. It was so easy before. He was the Road Captain, your brother, and that was it. Now it all seems so complicated. Not knowing what I want from this isn't helping either. I don't need a daddy figure anymore. I am too old for that now. But ask me what I want, and I wouldn't be able to tell you because I have no clue."

Vegas and Ashley walk up hand in hand, smiling. Vegas shoots me a serious look. "A word please, Prez?"

"Sorry, Chloe, excuse me, please. Don't wait, have your breakfast while it's hot," I tell her while rising to join Vegas, walking until we're out of earshot, we both watch Ashley sitting down on my chair, helping herself to my pancakes, chatting with Chloe.

"Ellie turned up late last night," Vegas starts. "We have her in the guest room. The girls had a bit of a reunion last night and their friendship picked right back up where it left off. But Raven, Ellie looks like shit. Her face is bruised to hell, and she has bruises on her arms, too. Do you think Chloe would have a look at her? She's limping a bit and I'm worried there is even more damage than what we can see. She refuses to tell us what happened."

Anger boils in me. I've known Ellie my entire life. She is a sweet girl, well, a woman now. The more I think about it, the more I become convinced that Rusty was the reason she left home as soon as she turned eighteen.

"We'll come over after breakfast if that's okay? I want to see Ellie and speak to her. Chloe can look at her then," I confirm, battling to contain my anger.

"Suits us fine, Prez. We'll join you for breakfast and then head over." Vegas nods at me.

We return to the table, pull up more chairs, and Vegas makes himself and me a fresh plate as Ashley finishes mine. Watching Chloe interact with Ashley warms my cold, jaded heart. To see both of them laughing as though they'd known each other forever affects me.

It reminds me of the young man I used to be. One that loved hard and deep, with an intensity that left me bare and vulnerable. Stone taught me the lesson early on that vulnerability was not a trait he wanted or supported in his son. Because of his life lessons, I soon dialed my feelings back and hid them under a thick coat of indifference. I didn't realize how long I felt dead inside.

Slowly, Chloe is chipping away at my protective coating, and at least when I am with her, I'm starting to feel human again. The softer side of me comes to light. I admit to myself that I miss the softer things in life. A soft, warm woman, in body and mind.

It hits me like a lightning strike to realize how much I need someone to even out my hard edges. It feels good, and I know what a lucky bastard I am that Chloe doesn't seem to mind my rough edges.

123

"Hey, Chloe, would you mind looking at a friend of mine?" Ashley is getting the ball rolling. "Seems she had a run in with a door or two… likely of the male variety." Ashley's voice vibrates with anger.

"Sure, no problem." Chloe looks at me. "You don't mind, do you?"

"Of course not," I reply with a smile. That's my girl, always trying to help others. Vegas elbows Ashley, who looks from Chloe to me and then back to Chloe, both smirking knowingly. I sigh, aware that these two will give me a lot of shit. Someone once said, "*Paybacks are a bitch.*"

15 — CHLOE

Today is Poker Run day, and I'm settled in the bone marrow donation booth. The ride started early this morning, leaving me jealous to not be able to ride myself. We—Sarah, Ashley and I—are getting ready for the first bikes to arrive back.

The club hopes to raise a stack of money in Carl's memory, to support the hospital oncology unit and raise awareness about bone marrow transplants.

It's a worthy cause, and I'm stunned by how many locals are getting involved, even before all the riders return. There are donation buckets everywhere, and most are paying cash for their food and drinks and then putting their change in the buckets provided.

Mom's running a kids' section with games and a sponge board, which will feature most club members to have sponges thrown at them.

Ally and the Wild Pixies are on the run now, but when they are back, they'll take charge of the charity auction this afternoon. Apparently, it's a promise auction. Never been to one, so this could be educational.

Casting my mind back to a couple of days ago, I never thought I'd come across such a unique man as Raven. He is full of contradictions. On one hand, he's the strict, powerful, alpha male President, leader of men. I know without a doubt, he will be dangerous when crossed. Yet, on the other hand, where I am concerned, he becomes a gigantic pile of mush. He's considerate,

125

sweet, kind, soft, and the only way his alpha traits appear between us is by the intense way he makes love to me.

I expected fucking, but not this profound physical and emotional connection. He has me wrapped around his finger as much as I have him wrapped around mine. Just one look at him, this tall, dark-haired, tattooed biker with the broad shoulders, huge biceps, and V-shaped body, sporting a six-pack you could bounce quarters off, has me all in a twist and my pussy eternally wet.

Not to mention his sick bedroom skills that are making me pant just thinking about them. Who knew the type of orgasms he gives me even existed? Multiple orgasms every night. I mean, I'm not a prude, but man alive. They are the stuff dreams are made of. Raven's large thick dick reaches places inside me that even B.O.B. never discovered! We just seem to fit, as though we are made for each other. Body and soul. I know it's way too early to even think about, but I've fallen hard and fast, and am happy with it too. Nothing else matters when we're together.

I cast my thoughts back to yesterday when we paid Vegas and Ashley a visit. Oh my God, their house is amazing! The interior is stunning, and it's set on an enormous plot. Ashley told me about their plans to extend. It's quite a sight to see those two in their own space. Their happiness is obvious.

My mood drops thinking about Ellie. I took the club's extensive first aid box, maintained by Mom, who was a former nurse, and headed to Vegas and Ashley's. After gushing over their home, Ashely took me to a spare room where she introduced me to Ellie.

She stayed with Ellie throughout the whole examination. When I looked up from Ellie's bruised ribs, I watched Ashley swallowing hard, tears in her eyes. Whoever did this to Ellie needs to be caught and beaten to shit, just like she was. Her face was a black and blue mess, some bruises older and yellowing. One of her ribs is cracked, though I don't think it's broken. Even if it was, she refused to go to the hospital for x-rays. On her back, abdomen, and thighs I found clear visible boot marks. I couldn't see any bruising indicating sexual assault or rape, but that was about the only part of her body clear of injuries.

How she drove all the way here is beyond me. Kudos to her, she's a strong woman. Though if you'd seen her yesterday, you wouldn't have thought so. She was a shaking, anxiety riddled wreck with her eyes firmly trained on the door. She'll be staying at Vegas and Ashley's resting up. I've no clue who did this to her, but Raven is worried because he assigned a man to always be watching and protecting her, no matter where she is. To see a woman in that condition shook me to my core. The way Raven reacted also reminded me of the crowd I'm hanging with.

Gone was my thoughtful lover, drowned out by a hard, cold, callous man I hardly recognized. If I wasn't a hundred percent sure that Raven is a good man, he'd have scared the living shit out of me.

I tried to figure out who the perpetrator was, but Ashley advised against asking questions. She explained what club business meant in detail. Not sure I like what I heard, but for the moment, I'll play ball.

Greg brought his friend along today, who's just passed his motorcycle test. A young man called Caleb. Another stunning example of a young man. Caleb is eager, helping with anything we need. He seems a great guy, proud of his first Harley, and you can tell he's interested in the MC lifestyle. My only concern is he's mixed-race, and I know a lot of clubs will accept nothing but white prospects. It's unclear to me whether this is the case with Stormy Souls, since I'm new to the MC scene. Here's hoping he's done his research and won't be disappointed.

Caleb and Greg carry a tray over to us with coffee and doughnuts, making them extra popular with Ashley and Sarah. Ashley looks tired and has been feeling under the weather. Coffee may perk her up.

We can hear the first bikes rumble in now. The sight of the riders filing in is breath-taking. The riders, tired and thirsty, make their way straight to the food and drink stalls. Riders continue to trickle in; a lot of non-club riders are taking part, to show solidarity and do their bit for charity.

Within no time, our stall is surrounded, we've sold out of raffle tickets, and are having to get more. Sarah's dealing with people signing up to register, Ashley is overseeing raffle tickets, and I'm explaining my heart out about bone marrow transplants and donations, to supplement the little presentation Ferret set up for us on the portable projector. Greg and Caleb, bless them, are making sure we are staying supplied with raffle tickets and drinks until the guys are back.

With the first few groups of arrivals dealt with, I notice Ashley and Sarah going stiff and their faces souring. I glance around to see what's grabbed their attention and watch a red-haired, flabby guy on crutches, with an uncanny resemblance to the comic strip character, Hagar the Horrible, except he's wearing a prospect cut. Damn, he looks too old to be a prospect. Based on his appearance, he must be in his late fifties.

Ashley leans towards me and whispers, "Watch him, and never be alone with him. He's a creepy asshole!"

Ah, that would explain why he's not patched in. Never mind. I think I saw him at the rally too but can't be sure. There were so many people there.

He limps towards our stall, throws another raffle ticket book at Ashley, and sneers, "Isn't this a pretty picture? All the old ladies together!" Not sure what his problem is, but he leaves me feeling uncomfortable.

"You must be Clusseaud's daughter." I can only describe his grin as predatory.

"How do you know? No one knows except Raven and Clusseaud," I spit at him. Ashley and Sarah stare at me, and by the way their mouths are hanging open, that revelation surprised the crap out of them.

"Tell me, how is Terrie these days? You look like her. Probably just as slutty, like mother like daughter, whores alike!" His disdain hits me like a steam train.

What the fuck just happened?

While I am still trying to collect myself, Sarah steps forward. "Rusty, I would suggest you turn on your gimpy leg and crawl back under the rock you came from. Your sparkling personality makes me want to shoot you!" Her voice is ice cold. I had no idea that the woman had it in her. Ashley takes my arm and leads me out of the stall.

"See why we tried to warn you?" she says to me while she grips my arm. I nod and still can't quite fathom what the hell just happened. Sarah stays manning the stall, while Ashley takes me to the bar near the stage and gets me a whiskey and coke. As we are walking over to a table, she explains who Rusty is and what happened before and after the rally. Bile rises in the back of my throat. How did he know about Clusseaud? Now that the cat is out of the bag, I clue Ashley in. No point in trying to keep it a secret anymore. My mind still believes it's impossible that Clusseaud could be my father. After all, when I look at him, I don't see a single resemblance.

Ashley, however, breaks me from my questioning thoughts.

"You have his eyes and nose. Not to mention, your love for all things motorcycles and the ability to ride."

True, there's that.

The last few days since that fateful revelation, Clusseaud and I have stayed out of each other's way. I'm way too pissed to deal with him and his denial. I know, pot meet kettle, but he could at least entertain the idea. Can't say I'm happy about it either. If he never realized just how stubborn and proud my momma could be, he clearly didn't know her at all.

I told Mom that I found him and, of course, she wants nothing to do with him. She forbade me to pass on her number or address. And Clusseaud? He looks at me as though this is all my fault. I didn't ask to be born. Frankly, if he'd taken care of and protected my mother, this would have been a non-issue. Feeling like I need to beat the shit out of Clusseaud is plaguing me, and I am not a violent person. At all.

If I want to keep my cool, I'll need another drink, as sure as week old socks stick to a wall. I raise my glass at Ashley.

"Ready for a refill?"

"Yup, but just orange juice for me, please. I 'can't handle my liquor' as Vegas would say," she says with a wink. I walk to the bar, place our order, pay, and as I turn around, see Rusty standing behind a very pale, very stiff Ashley. He has his hands on her shoulders, sneering and talking into her ear. I rush back to the table, but as he sees me coming, he disappears into the crowd. Ashley looks as though she's gonna vomit, pass out, or both. What the fuck was that all about?

"Ash, what the hell? Are you alright?"

"No, not really, let's just go." Her voice sounds as though she's swallowed a bag of nails, and she's shaking.

Damn it, the guys aren't back yet, so no backup there.

What do I do?

Blindly, I grab Ashley's arm and lead her back to the stall. Sarah comes running.

"What's the matter, Ash?" Sarah asks, because it is blatantly obvious something's wrong. Ash just shakes her head and sits in a chair at the back of the stall, almost as though she is hiding herself away.

Sarah, hands on hips, looks at me expectantly, like she is ready to take me down.

"I have no clue, honest," I tell her. "We needed a refill on our drinks, so I walked over to the bar. One minute she was fine, and the next she looked like that." I motion toward Ashley, before continuing, "I saw Rusty sneering at her, though, when I was heading back to our table. I brought her straight here."

Fury distorts Sarah's face when I mention Rusty. "That fucking rat bastard!" She looks around but can't see Rusty. I had the same experience earlier. It's like he vanishes into thin air. You wouldn't think it possible, since he looks like the Pillsbury Doughboy, is short, and walks with a severe limp, using crutches. Yet somehow, he disappeared. His trike is in the parking lot, so he hasn't left the venue.

Just then, more bikes pull in. Vegas and Ratchet are with them. They manned the first checkpoint, so the last of the riders should come through now.

Sarah is crouching in front of Ashley, who is still shaking. So, I run over to Vegas, grab his arm as he gets off his bike.

"Ashley needs you," is all I have to say. He breaks into a run. "Donor stall!" I shout after him, letting him know where she is. When I catch up, Vegas is sitting on the floor with Ashley in his lap, rocking her gently, letting her cry. His calm and quiet voice murmuring to her as he wraps himself around her. I've never seen so much protectiveness in such a bear of a man. He has his chin on her head and looks at me, eyes hard, flashing with anger. I wouldn't like to cross that man right now.

"What happened?" He looks me straight in the eye as he asks in a tone that would even make grown men cry.

"I'm not sure," I answer. "One minute she was fine, the next she wasn't. I went to the bar to get our drinks, and when I turned, Rusty was talking to her. That's all I know, Vegas."

A growl rips from his throat, and he tries to get up. Ashley, however, just clings to him, like a monkey.

"I'll kill the fat fuck this time!" It does not sound like a threat, more like a promise coming from him.

Ratchet, who followed Vegas to the stall, is on his phone. Within seconds, Greg is running up. Ratchet gives him strict orders not to leave the stall under any circumstance.

Greg nods.

"Is it okay for Caleb to stay around and help me? He's a close friend and might be interested in prospecting, so I brought him along to meet the members," Greg asks, looking pained, realizing that this isn't the most appropriate time for a potential prospect to meet the members.

Vegas looks up.

"No, prospect, not happening!" He thunders at poor Greg.

"Keep your hair on, man," Ratchet tries to calm Vegas.

"Call him over so I can meet him, Greg. I'll keep an eye on him and find him something to do if he wants to help," Ratchet tells Greg, who walks off to find Caleb.

They return within minutes.

"Ratchet, this is Caleb; Caleb, Ratchet," Greg makes introductions. Ratchet has a quick chat with Caleb then leads him away. Evidently, Caleb is happy to help Ratchet with the bike parking directions for the other riders. Problem solved.

Greg, feeling chastised, knowing he messed up, is not leaving our side for the rest of the afternoon. Within the hour, Raven, Slender and Pennywise are with us. Raven is all business. His exterior is harsh and his voice is glacial. Proving why he's the President. He oozes power and authority. He gets an update from Vegas. Seeing his sister on the floor being held by Vegas has rage running off him in waves. Without saying a word, he turns on his heel and walks off, taking Slender and Pennywise with him. Within no time, Sparks appears to help guard us. After making sure Ash is gonna be okay, Vegas makes his way to the clubhouse, where I am sure Raven and Slender are waiting for him.

"Sorry," Ashley whispers to me.

"Oh my God, no, don't you dare apologize, hon!" I turn and wrap Ashley into a hug. "I wish I'd known earlier; I wouldn't have left you sitting there. Would have kicked his balls into his throat if he'd spewed all that crap at me. If anyone is sorry, it's me!"

◊◊◊

The mood inside the stall is subdued. We keep busy, and the box with completed donor forms is filling up fast. So are the donation buckets. The community is getting behind the cause.

133

All of our raffle tickets have sold out. Later, Greg accompanies Ash to the clubhouse, where Vegas takes her to his room to rest and calm down. No one has spotted Rusty so far.

"Hey, beautiful, we have to stop meeting like this." I turn around to stare into a laughing Ghoul's face and can't help the smirk forming on my face. I like Ghoul, he's got a cool sense of humor and we spent some time talking at the rally.

"Hey, Ghoul, lost any bets or games recently?" I tease, sticking my tongue out at him. He puts his hands on his hips, throws his head back, and roars with laughter.

"Nope, missy, not had any worthy adversaries so far! You got some serious bike skills, though. Surprised all of us! And did our bike proud! I owe you a drink. Care to grab one?"

I turn to look at Sarah, who is still manning the stall. Dougal's with her now. She nods at me, smirking, so I head off with Ghoul towards the bar by the open stage.

Not a proper stage… more like two curtain side truck box trailers next to one another, end to end with electric hooked up and lights. Looks pretty damn good for a makeshift stage. Ghoul hands me a beer.

"How've you been? I heard you and Raven have a thing going?"

I blush beet red. "Yes, I guess we do."

"Has he claimed you yet?" Ghoul asks. "Because if he hasn't, I may throw my hat in the ring."

"Claimed?" I ask, confused. Yes, I've been around the scene, but claiming and all that I'm not familiar with.

My confusion must show on my face, because Ghoul explains, "When we meet the woman we want, we claim them as ours, which by default makes her the club's as well. Meaning she'll have protection and support from the brothers and is treated with respect and care. Bit like getting married."

I stand there, looking at him with eyes popping out of my skull, mouth hanging open, like a teenager in her first sex ed class. I had no idea. Clueless. Ghoul obviously finds my reaction amusing, because he chuckles.

I like Raven, even am falling hard and fast for him, but we've not known each other long enough for things to turn in that direction.

"No, definitely not claimed!" I stutter out.

Behind me a throat clears and when I turn to find out who sneaked up behind us, to my annoyance, it's Clusseaud.

"Ghoul, what a pleasure to see you!" He smiles, but it doesn't reach his eyes.

"What do you want?" I ask, my voice as cold as Elsa's ass. Clusseaud pointedly ignores that I even spoke, winding me up even more.

"I'd strongly suggest you keep your hands off my daughter!" he hisses at Ghoul, whose eyebrows rise in surprise.

"Come again?"

"Keep your paws off my daughter!" Clusseaud repeats.

What in the hell? How dare he! After the last few days of ignoring me, refusing to talk to me, and now this? Is he out of his mind? Oh, no! This is not happening!

"I'd strongly suggest, *dear Father*," my voice dripping with acid, "that you kindly move your ass along and bother someone who cares, which I have to tell you, is absolutely not me! Do both of us a favor and fuck off!"

"Don't speak to me like that!" Clusseaud has the cheek to growl at me.

135

"I'll speak to you however the fuck I want to. Sure, you may be my sperm donor, but that's about it!" I'm standing right in front of him, nose to nose, toe to toe.

"You're a complete dick and have zero say over my life, or who I hang out with, and if I want to throw myself at Ghoul, I'll damn well do what I please. You've no right to interfere in my life. A few days ago, you called me a hoax! Now you wanna make daddy claims! Nope, not until hell freezes over!" My voice has risen several octaves and by now has reached levels I am sure only dogs can hear; it's *that* shrill.

Ghoul has stepped up to my side, putting his hand on my arm, trying to calm me, but it has the exact opposite effect. I shove his hand away.

"Don't fucking touch me!" I snarl at him. I'm not finished with Clusseaud yet. Suddenly I find myself hanging upside down, being carried towards the clubhouse, still throwing curses at Clusseaud, whose mouth is now hanging wide open. What the fuck is going on here?

Screeching, "Fucker! Put me down, asshole, put me down right now!" I'm being carried through the clubhouse and people are laughing as we walk past. I can tell by his smell that it's Raven over whose shoulder I'm dangling, which does nothing to soothe my anger.

16 — RAVEN

Fuck my life! Can I not have a moment of peace this crazy ass weekend? I'm furious! First all this shit with Rusty, now Chloe makes a major scene with the Restless Slayers in attendance. I don't need this crap! She's hissing and spitting like a wildcat as I carry her through the clubhouse. I can't help myself and soundly smack her ass.

"Ouch!" followed by silence.

Finally! I storm into my office, kick the door shut behind us, put her on the desk and spank her ass.

"Raven! What the fuck do you think you are doing?" Her voice is only a modicum below my pain threshold, and trust me, that's quite high. She is kicking and thrashing, earning her a harder slap.

"Raven, stop, right this second!" she screams at me.

Right now, I don't care. Though I realize I can't keep spanking her. So, I take a deep breath, step back, turn, walk around the desk, and kick my chair hard enough to send it careening to the other side of the room.

"What the fuck, Chloe!" I bellow at her.

"If you want to throw a bitch fit at Clusseaud, fair enough, he had it coming, but not in front of everyone else! This is a charity event, designed to connect the club closer to the community and

137

give a good impression. And what do you do? Draw the attention of half the world to your private fucking little bitch fest!" I am breathing hard now.

"As if I haven't got enough on my plate already. Rusty threatened Ashley, she's in pieces, a VP hellbent on killing him, a sulking Road Captain, and the VP from the Dominant club wanting a piece of my woman!" Walking to the window, I try to calm myself.

"For starters," Chloe hisses at me, "Ghoul does not want a piece of me, and I am not your woman. We fucked a few times, and that is it!" If that isn't like a slap to my face, I don't know what is.

"Is that right?" I grate back. "We fucked a few times, huh?" She has the decency to flush. I know she wants to hurt me, the world, and anyone in it. I know she's hurting, but this has to stop. Right here, right now. Whether she means it or not, she needs to tread lightly. I'm not in a very forgiving mood right now.

"Second, Clusseaud deserved what he got. I am a hoax, remember? Yet he feels the need to let *daddy dearest* out? No, uh! No way! You weren't there to hear him, so reserve your judgment. Third, Rusty being an asshole is hardly my fault. Had one of you told me some of the history there, I wouldn't have let Ashley out of my sight, and he wouldn't have had the chance to get to her. And what do you mean, he threatened her?" She's stood there, hand on hips, face red with anger and all I want to do is dig my hands into her curly blonde locks, push her against the wall and rage fuck her, then stamp her forehead with *Property of Raven*. Yet I can't do either. A frustrated, angry sigh leaves my chest. She is right, of course; Rusty is not her fault at all. I can't put that on her. The scene with Clusseaud, though, I can, and will, put a stop to that.

"Chloe, regardless, you cannot make a scene like that. Club business, even if it involves you, is club business and gets sorted out within the club, not involving other clubs, and sure as shit, not the Restless Slayers," I tell her firm, but calmer.

"And if you think Ghoul does not want a piece of you, you're a fool. You're a beautiful, sexy, amazing woman. Everyone wants a piece of you. Me included. Only I don't just want a piece of you, Chloe, I want all of you."

"Why, Raven? Why do you want me?" Her question throws me for a loop. How does she not know?

Stepping toward her, I put my hand on her chest, over her heart. "Do you not feel this thing between us? Whenever we touch, it's like electricity running through me. The first time I saw you in your nurses' uniform, giving Carl shit, I fell in love with you. You're the best thing that came out of that tragedy. You're strong, independent, loving, kind, have empathy in spades, are selfless, and just the most amazing person I've met in a long time. Tell me you feel this thing between us too."

She's looking at me, eyes full of wonder.

"Is that how you see me, Raven?"

Staring into her eyes, I just nod.

"Raven, of course I feel it too. I fell hard and fast at the Slayers' Rally. The dirty karaoke did me in. But this is all so fast, so soon. If you are nearby, I can't think clearly, and just want to wrap myself up in you. I look at you and melt. You're such an incredible, principled, handsome man. I see you similarly to the way you see me. You are strong, independent, a born leader. You are hot as hell and should come with a warning sign. Had to buy asbestos thongs, dear god. It's a wonder that ladies don't throw their panties at you. You are caring, loving, kind, and empathy is

139

one of your greatest qualities. Just look at how you treat your brothers and your sister. So tough on the outside, yet so soft in the middle. And you really want me? You could do so much better than me."

"That's where you are mistaken. You are the best there is for me. My one, the other half of my soul. The soft to my hard, the gentle to my tough, the fire to my ice. You make me want to be a better man, Chloe; you round off my edges without trying to manage or steer me. I want to claim you officially at the table tomorrow. But please, Chloe, let me claim you in front of the others now. Not only am I in love with you, but the general knowledge that you're mine will keep you safer out there," I practically beg.

"Nothing to do with Ghoul then?" she teases me with a smile. I groan, pull her to me and smash my lips against hers, eating her alive. When I step back, we are both panting.

"Okay, Jamie, listen to me. I'm absolutely in love with you. Yes, claim me, your name is already tattooed on my soul anyhow. There is no one else for me. I promise I'll behave regarding Clusseaud. Tonight at least."

A relieved sigh escapes me.

"But," she continues. Here it comes. "I'm pissed with you not warning me about Rusty, so don't expect lovey dovey tonight. A rage fuck is all you're gonna get."

With that, she winks, turns on her heel and walks out of the office, stunning me for several moments before I hurry to follow her out. That woman!

We walk outside to the stage area, where everyone congregates. Out of the corner of my eye, I watch Spen and Debs in a heated argument.

Please, no more drama. I've had my quota for today and then some. Debs storms off, gets in her car, and drives out of the gates. Spen walks up to us. "I've collected all the donation

140

buckets, Prez. Gonna count it in a bit. Chloe, are you happy to be presented with a check for the Oncology unit? One of those big presentation ones?" Chloe nods at him, and I clap him on his shoulder. Dawg and Caroline amble up next to us.

"Hey, Raven, how's it hanging? Slender caught me up to speed. Just thought I'd let you know there was an incident while you were inside." Dawg looks uncomfortable. I groan. What now?

"Go on, spit it out." We take a few steps to the side. Caroline and Chloe are chatting and laughing.

"Masher came to me and Slender while we were doing our security rounds. Rusty felt up one of their member's old ladies, and the guy is out for blood. Touched her ass, not just once, but several times. Pennywise dragged Rusty off and punched him, but he escaped, got on his trike and fucking hauled ass out of here. Ferret is trying to trace him, but the fucker found and crushed the tracker."

"Fuck my life," I groan, grinding my teeth so hard they hurt.

That fucking bastard! Is he trying to take us down or something? This has gone too far. I'll put a price on his head this time. Enough is enough. I'll send him to the Devil myself. The fact he told Ashley earlier to keep looking over her shoulder because he'll find her and finish what he started years ago, makes me think he was behind the house fire and he's losing his mind. He also told Ashley he knows Ellie is here, and she's next on his list. Both are enough for me to want to kill him a hundred times over.

"Thanks, Dawg. If we find him, he's dead this time," I growl.

Dawg's eyes speak louder than words. He's on board with making him suffer first and sure as shit with sending him to the Devil.

141

I make my rounds with Chloe, my arm over her shoulder, pulling her in tight. Her arm snaked around my waist is all that keeps me from losing my shit. I make my way to Fury, Ghoul, Masher, and the Slayers' delegation.

"I'm sorry for the upset Rusty caused. Please accept my sincerest apologies on behalf of the club, and I guarantee nothing like this will happen again." I look Fury straight in the eye. He can read between the lines and knows what I have left unsaid. "I've told the vendors that all drinks and food are free for the Restless Slayers MC delegation." I continue, "I know it doesn't make up for his behavior but hope it will serve as a gesture of goodwill."

One of their men steps forward.

"If I catch that dick, I'll put a bullet in his head. He touched my old lady." He's seething.

"Be my guest," I reply.

Chloe steps up to the guy.

"Hey, sorry, I don't know your name. I can only apologize that this happened. Could I speak to your old lady?" she asks the mountain of a man. No fear, just a picture of humility.

A blonde beauty steps up next to Snake, his name on the patch on her property cut. "That would be me!" she states. "Angie." She holds her hand out to Chloe.

"Hi, Angie, pleased to meet you. I'm Chloe. I'd like to apologize to you on behalf of the old ladies for the way you were treated. It's not something that's ever happened before. Since you are the only old lady here, I was wondering whether you would like to come over and meet our old ladies and some of the Wild Pixies?" she says as she accepts Angie's hand.

Wow! And there I thought nothing could surprise me anymore. Instinctively, she did just the right thing, found the right tone, and showed her sincerity in just the right way.

"Apology accepted." Angie smiles at Chloe, turns and kisses her old man.

"You need to calm down, Snake, honey. If I can accept the apology, then so can you."
She turns back to Chloe.

"You're a nurse, aren't you? I heard about you and went by your stall earlier. Any chance you have hand sanitizer so I can wipe my ass down?" She winks at Chloe, who grins and looks at Angie's tight leather trousers.

"Yes, ma'am, follow me. We'll get you sanitized in a jiffy!" Chloe turns to me, kisses me full on, grabs Angie's hand and leads her towards the donor stall, where the old ladies and Pixies are all standing.

"You better claim her, asshole, or I'll make a move." Ghoul smirks at me.

"Raven, I have a lot of time and patience for the Stormy Souls, but something like this better never happen again. Next time, I'll hold you personally responsible," Fury threatens me, with Masher and Ghoul nodding, while Snake is seething to the side.

"I promise you, there'll be no repeat. Ever. Rusty will be severely punished," I try to reassure Fury, who nods and walks away.

◊◊◊

Despite being furious with Rusty, I'm very proud of Chloe. Her instinct guided her in doing the right thing, defusing the situation, at least partially. If I was in any doubt of her being old lady material, I am one hundred percent certain now. She stepped up without having to be asked and took control of an escalating situation.

God, I love that woman! A little shocked by that realization, but hell, at least I can admit it to myself. Making some calls, I stride back to the clubhouse and wait for Slender, Pennywise, and Ferret to arrive.

Pennywise is vibrating with rage, as is Slender.

"That bastard. I can't believe he did that. Has he lost his mind completely?" Slender rants.

"Never mind that. How did the fat fuck get away from me? I had him pinned. Next thing I know, he's charging off for his trike. Can't figure it out," Pennywise says, extremely pissed. He never backs down from a confrontation, nor does he ever lose his mark. That is the number one reason he's the club's enforcer.

Ferret's face is grim.

"He trashed the tracker, but hell, I'll find him, no matter what," he states bluntly. After all this new bullshit with Rusty, we are all on the same page. Out bad is simply not enough anymore.

The crowds part, with Ellie running through the middle. She's as white as a ghost and shaking. We all stare at her as she bursts into tears. Slender clenches his fists by his side, with a murderous look on his face as he takes in her battered face.

"He knows, Raven, he knows I'm here!" Ellie sobs. "Rusty called my cell. He's going to find me and kill me!"

Slender's reaction is instant. He grabs Ellie and puts his arms around her.

"No one is going to touch you, sweet thing, I guarantee it. I'll put a bullet in his head first," Slender says with menace.

Ellie is petrified. "I don't want to stay at Vegas and Ash's anymore. I'd never forgive myself if they'd get hurt because of me!" she wails.

"It's the safest place for you, Ellie," Slender tells her. "He doesn't know where Vegas's place is, and they have the best in top-rated security. He wouldn't be able to get closer than half a mile without all the security systems alerting. I'll speak to Vegas and see if it's okay for one of us to stay there as well, just to make sure there is backup and you're never alone."

He looks at me with a questioning look. It's a good idea. If he somehow finds the house, he'll have a welcome party he'd never suspect. I call Chloe, who appears within seconds and takes Ellie into the clubhouse, upstairs to a room to lie down.

Despite the madness, Spen comes up and announces, "I counted the money. We raised thirty-five thousand just through donations and poker run fees! Deducting the cost of the event leaves us with twenty-five thousand dollars."

My mouth falls open. Never had I expected to raise this much cash! And it doesn't include the raffle, the promise auction the girls are doing, or the fees from the open mic, which has been drawing bands from all over. We made an easy two thousand just from that.

He continues, "I'd suggest we make a check out for fifteen thousand for the hospital, leave five thousand for a memorial for Carl, and put the rest towards the minibus for Ashley's children's home. We could get a decent secondhand one, make sure it's in tip-top condition. That would save a lot and they'd have it quicker." I nod at Spen. We'll have to vote on it later, but in the meantime, it's a solid plan.

With most of the officers here in one place, other than Vegas, who's looking after my sister, I make the announcement.

"I'm gonna claim Chloe!" No one seems surprised.

"Bout time" and "predictable" are thrown my way instead.

Chloe walks back to me. "Ellie's asleep, absolutely exhausted. Poor girl. I put her into one of the spare rooms upstairs. She has the key inside with her, and I have the spare since she asked me to lock the door as I left." Chloe places the key in my hand. I pull her towards me and kiss her like a starving man. She has that uncanny ability to calm me even through the raging chaos.

"Are you ready to get the check presentation over with?" I murmur in her ear. I feel awful because Chloe looks tired, and I contributed to that. She goes back to work tomorrow and unfortunately, has the early shift. A sweet smile graces her beautiful face as she nods at me. Spen grabs the presentation check and writes it out.

We all move towards the stage where the bands are playing. They are loving the large audience. It's giving them a chance to show what they've got. Some are fantastic, and I make a mental note to invite them to play at our own rally next year. It'd be nice to showcase some local talent. I watch Pennywise sidling up to Vegas and Ash, whispering to Vegas, updating him on what's been going on. I can see by the look on his face that Vegas is not happy. None of us are.

During the next set break, I make my way onto the stage.

"Thank you all for coming and taking part in our Memorial Poker Run!" I smile at the applause I get when my voice sounds over the speaker system. "Flakey would have been proud and touched that so many of you came out to celebrate his life with us."

Whistles come from everywhere.

"He'd have wanted us to do something worthwhile in his name, so we're raising money for the hospital's oncology unit, for new equipment. Like infusion pumps for chemotherapy and a small refreshment unit where chemotherapy patients and their loved ones can make a coffee or have some ice water from a dispenser."

Applause rings through the considerable crowd.

"We also heard that Rainbow House, which is a home for children with severe mental and physical disabilities, needs a new minibus. So, we will contribute part of our fundraising effort to Rainbow House, specifically for the minibus purchase!" The noise from the crowd is deafening.

"All proceeds of the promise auction, raffle, and part of the general fundraising will go towards this, so please give generously."

"Now, I have the honor of asking one of the lead nurses of the oncology unit, and coincidentally my old lady…" Hooting and hollering breaks out and I can just make out someone shouting, "You finally found one, you ugly bastard!" which causes a lot of laughter from the crowd, making me chuckle.

"Chloe, please come up here," I call her up, watching as she makes her way onto the stage under thundering applause. It's so cute that she blushes bright red with all the attention focused on her. Spen walks up with the massive check and hands it to me.

"I hope you will do us the honor and accept this check for fifteen thousand dollars, to fund the purchase of new equipment and the refreshments station for the oncology unit." I hand the check to her. We hold a side each, while the press takes photos, and smile for the camera.

Chloe grabs the microphone off me.

"Thank you so much to the Stormy Souls MC on behalf of the District Hospital Oncology Unit." Her voice wobbles and she has tears in her eyes.

"It's amazing to see how many lives Flakey touched and even more so, how everyone has come together to remember him in this way. He was a great man, with a wicked sense of humor, and was my favorite patient." She takes the check, shakes it in the air and finishes with, "Look Carl, this is for you! Ride free, may the sun always be on your back." Tears roll down her cheeks.

The crowd roars and repeats her sentiment in a chorus. Glasses and bottles are being raised everywhere and, "To Flakey," chanted all around.

17 — CHLOE

Today was very emotional. First, the incident with Ashley, the argument with Clusseaud, Raven putting his foot down and then claiming me. Now, this huge check! It's too much and rivers of my tears are rolling down my cheeks, as I wave the check in the air to Carl. I'm sure he's watching and smiling.

The amount raised is unbelievable. I'm glad we split the fundraising between two organizations. The children deserve as much of a leg up as cancer patients do.

The promise auction is about to start as we leave the stage, handing the microphone over to Ally, who steps up with a grin. That should have been our warning.

"Right, folks, the promise auction. If you have never been to one before, let me tell you how this works. Club members of both clubs, friends of both clubs, and members of the public have donated promises, which we will now auction off. Please bid and give generously."

"First item in our long list is: leaf raking, promised by twelve-year-old Jonah. He will come to your yard and rake your leaves for you."

"Ten dollars!" someone in the crowd shouts out, swiftly followed by "twenty"; the bidding goes on and the prize eventually goes to a woman for thirty-five dollars.

"Item two," Ally's voice rings out. "I promise to deliver cakes and pies to the value of a hundred dollars to the highest bidder!" That one goes for two hundred dollars. "Item three, a car wash by club member Moggy. Topless!" Ally screeches into the microphone. Moggy's face is priceless. I don't think he knew about the topless bit. All the women go crazy trying to outbid each other. Moggy's promise sells for one hundred and fifty dollars! Not bad.

"Item four, a bike service by Ratchet and Sparks from Stormy Souls Customs!"

"Two hundred dollars to do it topless!" Caroline shouts from the side of the stage. Sparks and Ratchet both look scared, shaking their heads vigorously, but Ally's evil grin means she will not let them off the hook.

"Two fifty, topless!" Greta, one of the Pixies, shouts.

"Three hundred if you promise to take pictures and hang them in the clubhouse!" Ashley shouts. Vegas is falling over laughing.

"SOLD!" yells Ally. "Three hundred dollars to the lady over there and pictures for the clubhouse!"

The auction carries on. Local businesses pledged a lot of items. Children also got into the spirit, like Jonah. The Scout Troop promised to pick up litter, the Forestry Commission pledged logs for firepits and chimneys. So many things. At the end, Ally, laughing and a little out of breath, watches as Spen walks up to her with a note revealing the total.

"Okay, folks, here is the total of the auction: With your generosity, we raised eight thousand three hundred seventy-six dollars for Rainbow House!" The applause is deafening.

Spen steps up to the microphone. "Could I ask Ashley and Sarah to come up here, please?" As they both make their way up to the stage, Dawg appears with another presentation check.

"On behalf of the Stormy Souls MC, Flakey, friends of the club, and the community, I am proud to present you with this check for fifteen thousand dollars towards the purchase of a

150

minibus for Rainbow House." The crowd roars, and Sarah and Ashley are bouncing around the stage like lunatics. Laughing, crying, and hugging each other.

◊◊◊

I search for Raven so I can snuggle up to him and enjoy being close for a little while before making my way home. Having to go back to work at six in the morning sucks, especially after two weeks off, and what a hectic two weeks it has been.

In my wildest dreams I'd never have expected to end up with Raven, to fall hook, line, and sinker for this tough man, much less to discover that he has such a soft core. The fact that he's gorgeous helps, of course.

Feeling his arms tighten around me possessively is the greatest feeling in the world. Standing on tiptoe, I lean closer.

"Sorry, Jamie, I have to go in a minute. Work in the morning and I am exhausted." He looks down at me, as though I hung the moon, making me feel all squishy.

"That's okay, darlin'. Thank you for all your help today. With the Slayers old lady, manning the stall, and just being by my side. You've no idea how much I appreciate it." He plants a sweet, gentle kiss on my lips.

"It was my absolute pleasure, honey," I reply between kisses.

"Let me walk you to your car," Jamie tells me, his voice making it perfectly clear that he'd rather drag me to his bedroom and have his wicked way with me.

◊◊◊

I'd be lying if I said I felt as fresh as a daisy when I got up, ready, and dragged myself into work this morning. During my first coffee break, I went to the administrators and handed over the check from last night. The lukewarm thank you was a little underwhelming, to say the

151

least. I struggled to concentrate on my work, having to deal with several rude relatives and patients. I could happily live without the verbal abuse. "Bitch, hurry up!" does nothing to motivate my already exhausted mind to work faster.

On a day like today, I not only dislike my job, but hate it. If I never have to come back, it'd be too soon. At lunch break, my cell rings.

"Hello, sexy beast, what can I do for you?" I answer when I see it's Raven. This is the first time I had reason to smile today.

"Chloe, I'm downstairs in the emergency department. There's been an accident. Caroline is in the Emergency Room. You got time to pop down?" he asks me, his voice broken and strained.

It feels as though an ice-cold hand has gripped my heart and is squeezing. I don't even answer but hang up and run to the elevators. As I reach the ground floor, I race to the reception area, which is filled with pacing bikers. I find Raven and throw myself at him.

"What happened? I came as quick as I could."

Dawg is sitting at the other end of the room, head in his hands.

"There was a fire, Chloe, at Dawg and Caroline's. The fire department is still there. Caroline was unconscious when they got her out, so they brought her here. Could you find out what's going on? She's been in there forever, and no one is coming out." I see the fear in the room. Seeing that Dawg is traumatized, I know I have to try.

"Wait here," I tell Jamie and squeeze him, before sneaking into the Emergency Room, completely unprepared for the sight greeting me. They've stripped Caroline bare, and she is on the table, the defibrillator whirring. The medical team is around her working simultaneously to intubate her as well as giving CPR, waiting for the charge to complete so they can shock her. I

152

have to lean against the wall to keep upright. Marsha, one of the ER nurses, comes over to me. "Do you know her?"

"Yes, I do. She's a good friend and family to my boyfriend. What's going on?"

Marsha looks at me.

"They brought in her with smoke inhalation and unconscious. She went into respiratory arrest and coded. We are doing our best to get her back." She walks back to the team.

I flinch as they shock her for the first time. They are working frantically on her, and she is on a portable ventilator now. It takes another two shocks before they get a fragile heart rhythm. Only when the doctor orders the Intensive Care Unit team to take over, do I leave the room, with the ER doctor following behind me.

Raven spots me, his steps faltering when he sees my serious and shocked face.

The doctor clears his throat.

"Mr. Cooker?"

Dawg jumps up. "How is she, Doc? Can I see her? Is she gonna be okay?"

The doctor leads him to the relatives' room. The others crowd around me. My voice is toneless as I let them know what's been going on.

"I am so sorry, she coded, and they had to resuscitate her. They now have a heartbeat, she is on a ventilator, and will go to Intensive Care. I'm sorry I really don't know how critical she still is. They say the first forty-eight hours will show whether she will pull through."

My hands and voice are trembling as I watch the shock settle on their faces. Caroline is a popular old lady. She's one of a kind.

"How did this happen?" I ask, looking around.

"We don't know yet, darlin, the fire chief, and a couple of engines were still there when the ambulance left. We all came straight here," Raven says as he wraps his arms around me, rocking us back and forth slowly.

"Raven, I've got to go back, but please, please send someone up to get me if there is any change, okay?"

He looks at me, kissing my cheek. "Sure, darlin', as soon as I know something, I'll come and find you myself," he promises.

Back upstairs, I can't concentrate. During medication rounds, I nearly give medication to the wrong patient. Luckily, I double checked, because I know my mind is on Caroline and not necessarily on the job. It's almost five p.m. by the time Raven finds me at the nurses' station. Fatigue marring his beautiful face. My heart goes out to him.

"Hey, darlin', just wanted to let you know Caroline is doing better. Still in Intensive Care, still ventilated, but from what we were told, she is stabilizing. Her blood gasses, whatever the hell that is, are improving. The others are going home now."

I look at him from behind the desk.

"Thank you, honey, for coming to tell me. I finish in an hour. I'll look in on Caroline and Dawg. Do you want to wait for me? Come over to my house, I'll cook, and we'll chill with a movie? Or are you needed back at the clubhouse?"

"That sounds awesome, darlin'. But you are not cooking. We'll grab something on the way back. I'll make a few calls while you finish and meet you outside the ICU. How does that sound?" his tired voice replies. God, I just want to wrap him up in cotton wool and take care of him.

"Sure, that works." I smile at him. "I'll see you in an hour."

An hour later, I'm outside the ICU, waiting for Raven to finish his phone call.

"That was the fire chief. The fire is out, but they're going to wait and do their investigations tomorrow. He thinks it may have been electrical," Raven explains.

"It's Ashley's house. She rented it to Dawg and Caroline, which is why I'm so involved. Vegas asked me to deal with it. Ashley's been sick all day, so she can't manage this herself, and Vegas is busy with club business," he continues.

I just grab his hand and open the door to the unit using my badge. We step towards the desk and are shown to Caroline's bay. Dawg is sitting by her side.

I walk up to Dawg and wrap my arms around him from behind.

"Hey, Dawg, how are you holding up?" Stupid question really, and I regret asking it as soon as it leaves my mouth. He turns towards me, and tear tracks are marking his cheeks.

"Dawg, she's strong. She'll get through this. From what I heard she is stabilizing. That's a good sign." I impress on Dawg. He just nods and turns back towards Caroline.

While I speak to the nurse looking after her, Raven claps Dawg's shoulder and just stands there with him.

"Is there anything you need, brother? Anything we can do for you now?"

Dawg's detached voice drifts over when he answers, "No, nothing anyone can do for me. I'll just stay here with her. She's my life, you know?"

Walking over to Caroline, I take her hand.

"Hello, lovely lady. What are you doing, scaring the shit out of me? Just hurry the hell up and get well. You owe me a drink and a girls' night in. Taking a nap is okay, my friend, but tomorrow, I want to see you with your eyes open. Or I'll have to administer some of your own medicine to you. Wire brush, disinfectant, and a resounding smack," I quietly tell her, leaning

155

over close to her ear, then gently and carefully I kiss her cheek, even with all the tubes in the way. "See you tomorrow, my friend."

Neither Raven nor I speak as we drive home in my car. His bike stays at the hospital, in the staff car parking lot, where it'll be safe. It's a clear sign he's planning on spending the night with me, and I'm not arguing.

The atmosphere is subdued as we get to my place. Since we forgot to get dinner, I open the freezer and get all the fixings for fried chicken. Attempting to distract Raven, I ask him to make a salad. After finishing our dinner of fried chicken, gravy, biscuits, and a salad, we grab a beer out of the fridge and try to watch a movie. *American Sniper* is playing, but we're not paying attention.

"What do you think might have happened?" I ask him, looking at my hands.

"No idea, Chloe. I wish I knew, but I feel like a damn failure. This is the second time a fire has destroyed Ashley's house. Last time, she got out and wasn't hurt. This time, Caroline hasn't been so lucky. It feels as though I failed to keep everyone safe."

My empathy for him goes deep. I heard the story of Ashley and Nathan barely making it out of a burning house years ago, in retaliation from a rival one percenter MC. But this? Now? Despite knowing it's not Raven's fault, I appreciate that a man like him would take this personally.

"Raven, honey, this isn't your fault. You're not responsible. For all we know, it may have been electrical or something equally unanticipated." I try to comfort him as best as I can. He looks at me, eyes full of sadness and agitation. His knee bouncing with nervous energy.

"I know, Chloe, but why do I feel I missed something?"

"I don't know, honey, I really don't. Let's not overreact; we need to wait for the results of the investigation." I stroke my hand across his stubbled cheek. Guilt is radiating off him in thick waves. So, I switch off the TV and straddle him, sitting on his lap. I place my chin on top of his head and wrap my arms around him, trying to infuse him with peace.

"Come on, let's go to bed," I whisper in his ear, before getting up, grabbing his hand, and pulling him along with me.

Undressing him in the bedroom is one of my favorite activities. I love the feel of his taut muscles and soft skin, the smattering of hair on his chest, and the sensations it arouses when I run my fingers through it when caressing him. Yes, I'm a chest hair fan. I find it incredibly sexy, especially on someone as cut as Raven. He is so handsome, so far out of my league, that I still pinch myself every time we're together, struggling to believe he's with me and wants me. Once we are both naked, he lets me take the initiative.

I push him onto the bed and gesture for him to turn around onto his front. God, just looking at his tight ass cheeks has me salivating, making me want to bite them. Instead, I straddle them and start rubbing, stroking and massaging his neck and shoulders, which are so tight and tense they feel like rocks.

Bit by bit, he relaxes under my ministrations. Small groans come from him as I move further down his back, continuing to massage and stroke. It's not a sexual thing, but his little groans and sighs are making me wet. When he tenses his glutes, they rub my clit in the best of ways and I cannot hold back the small moan escaping me. Lightning fast, he moves, and I find myself under him with my arms stretched out above my head.

"You little devil!" His voice is husky, his eyes on fire.

"Are you complaining about your treatment?" I tease him, smiling.

157

"Such a tease," he murmurs as his mouth closes over mine and I lose all sense of reality. And reality does not resurface for several hours, when we both curl around each other and fall into an exhausted sleep.

Raven's phone wakes us around six a.m.

"Yes?" he answers. I can hear Dawg's voice, but not what he is saying. "Oh, thank God!" Raven replies. "Give her our love and we'll come and see her later, before Chloe has to start work. Does she need anything?... Okay, I'll ask her... Sure, no problem, brother, see you soon!"

"Caroline's awake and breathing on her own. They are taking her off the ventilator as we speak. Honey, Dawg asked if you could get her some clothes and personal stuff? Soap, deodorant, toothpaste, that kinda thing?"

"Sure, no problem, we're roughly the same size, so I'll grab her some of my leggings and T-shirts. I can buy undies on the way, plus soap, toothpaste, and everything else she needs. Luckily, I am on a late shift today so I don't start until one p.m., gives us plenty of time to get all this."

We stay in bed to cuddle a little longer, which ends up turning into a couple of orgasms. We take a prolonged shower, leaving my knees deliciously sore.

It's about midday once we make it to the hospital, Raven carries Caroline's bag. We make it up to the Intensive Care Unit, where we find out they've moved her to a medical floor as a step down since she is doing better.

Caroline smiles as we walk in. Dawg's sitting on the side of her bed, holding her hand.

"Hey, girlfriend, how dare you give me a fright like that!" I tease her.

"Sorry," she half croaks, half whispers, throat still aggravated from the smoke and the recently removed breathing tube.

158

"Wasn't the plan, Chloe, I can assure you!" she coughs. I just step up and give her the biggest hug possible, while Dawg and Raven hug and clasp each other's shoulders.

18 — RAVEN

Relief crashes through me like a tidal wave seeing Caroline sitting up, awake and smiling. Unable to help it, I imagine it was Ashley or Chloe in that hospital bed. I know I'd be broken if I lost either of them. For the first time in my life, I talked to the man upstairs. It's not that I don't believe, it's just that I don't talk to Him. I learned a long time ago to rely on myself more than on others, including Him. It seems He heard me this time and I send up my sincere thanks.

Whilst the women are hugging, I pull Dawg to the side.

"Any news from the fire chief?"

"Yup, it was arson. They found accelerant by the front door," Dawg hisses between clenched teeth. "Some bastards set the place on fire with us in it." He's raging.

Chloe and Caroline's heads shoot up.

"What did you say?" Caroline croaks in shock.

"Sorry, sweetheart, I didn't want to tell you like this. You were asleep when the fire chief called. They declared it arson." Dawg steps to Caroline, takes her in his arms and holds her while she cries.

"That's heinous," Chloe whispers with disbelief. "Who'd do such a thing?"

That's the million-dollar question.

"Did you have any beef with anyone before you came here?" I question Dawg.

"No, nothing, nothing at all, and even if I had, how would they know where to find me? No one apart from the club knows where I live," Dawg blusters. I get his fury with this nasty attack, which could have cost Caroline her life and the club another family member.

"What are you gonna do now?" Chloe asks.

"Find a hotel room!" Dawg snarls.

"Watch your tone, man!" I admonish him.

"No, honey, that's okay. I understand. I'd be the same if it happened to us," Chloe says in his defense.

"Listen, you two, you can stay at my apartment until you have something else. I spend most of my time with Raven anyway, so it doesn't matter. You'd be in town and close to the hospital. Bit longer commute for you, Dawg, but gotta be better than a hotel room."

My mouth flaps open in surprise like an old saloon door. That's so typical Chloe. I'm so damn proud of my old lady right now. Without even trying to act like the president's old lady, yet again, here she is, caring for my family. Our family. Caroline cries harder, if that's even possible.

"Thank you so much, my lovely!" she sobs.

Dawg straightens and gives Chloe a bear hug.

"Thank you, love you, girl. Are you sure we won't impose?"

Chloe's laughter rings out, lightening the mood. "Impose? I get to spend every night with my sexy-as-sin man, and you're asking about imposing? No, thank you for giving me the excuse." She winks at Dawg, whose eyes are getting glassy. My woman is truly one of a kind.

"I'm off at ten tonight. Raven, could you go back to my apartment, get some of my stuff and take it over to your house? Caroline, I'll leave you some T-shirts and leggings to wear until you can replace your own. We're about the same size. Bought new underwear for you on the way in. Raven, spare key is in the kitchen. Top right-hand cabinet. Can you drop it off with Dawg and Caroline here later?" she asks, but her instructions sound more like a sweetened-up drill sergeant's order.

So, I click my heals, salute, and reply, "Yes, ma'am!" Shooting a look at Dawg, who snickers, I threaten, "You tell anyone about me taking orders, I'll have you on shit duty for a year." Winking at him.

"We have Church tonight, Dawg. You're excused. You stay with your old lady, make sure she's okay and not getting up to any mischief," I declare. "I'll fill you in when I pick Chloe up." Chloe opens her mouth, but I railroad right over her.

"No, don't even try to argue this one. Someone tried to kill members of our family. Until further notice, we will accompany old ladies at all times, including Ellie. At the very least, to and from home, and the home will be checked before anyone leaves. I'm not taking any chances with anyone's safety, especially not yours. So don't start!" I growl at her. This is not an argument I'll tolerate, and she needs to know that right now.

"Okay," she quietly answers. I count that as a win.

◊◊◊

Everyone is in church, apart from Dawg. The agitation in the room is palpable. A ton of shit landed on our plate, yet again. I clear my throat and call the room to order.

"First, most of you will have already heard, Caroline is improving, so that's fantastic news. Second, I am claiming Chloe."

162

Clusseaud jumps up, nostrils flaring. "The fuck you will!"

Now *that* I hadn't counted on, what is he playing at?

"Keep your hands off my daughter!" Ah, so that's what's bugging him.

"Clusseaud, as much as I value you as a brother, choose your words carefully here," I grate at him.

"One, a few days ago, you called your daughter a hoax and wouldn't even acknowledge her existence. You've really given up the right to play daddy now. And may I remind you also that if I don't claim her, Ghoul has made his intentions known. Two, you're well aware, along with everyone else, that keeping my hands off Chloe isn't an option. Not now, not ever." I glare at him, my fury rising. The glare turns more into a death stare.

"Sit your ass down and shut up. I don't need nor want your blessing."

"Does anyone apart from Clusseaud have an opinion?" I grate into the room.

"Chloe's a special one, Prez. You hold on to that one," Dougal throws in. The vote goes as expected and Spen is tasked with ordering the *'Property of Raven'* cut for my new old lady.

"Unfortunately, the reason I called you to church is not all good news. Rusty is in the wind. He has threatened Ashley, yet again, beaten and threatened Ellie, and Ashley's house burned to the ground with Dawg and Caroline inside. The fire chief informed us it was arson. They have nowhere to stay, so Chloe is letting them use her apartment until they find something else."

Spen raises his hand.

"Go ahead." I nod at him.

"I am not gonna bore you with details tonight, but we have enough money to facilitate a loan for Dawg, so they can buy their own place as soon as possible. Is that something we should consider?" He looks around the table. Nods greeting him from every direction.

Zippy pipes up, "How much could we afford to loan him? Just out of curiosity."

Spen nods at his question.

"We can afford to loan him about hundred and seventy thousand without leaving us real short, but it'll have to be repaid. I've done some clever investing over the years for the club, so financially, we're very stable; I can make the funds available within two weeks."

Surprised whispers and murmurs go through the room. I'm just as surprised as everyone else. I knew we had investments, of course, but never bothered following the returns.

"Okay, let's vote then," I say, starting the vote. As expected, the ayes have it.

"Now to our other problem." I exhale, trying to keep myself calm.

"With Rusty being in the wind and an arsonist targeting club members, I'm putting a brother with all the old ladies and associates. They'll be escorted to and from work and someone will watch them wherever they are. Ferret, can you track Rusty's phone?" I look straight at him.

"I've tried, boss, but the bastard isn't stupid. Must have it turned off. Only switches it on when he phones Ellie, and although I can ping the cell tower he calls from, it's too quick to get an accurate location. By the time we'd get there, he'd be long gone. Uses different locations each time. Sometimes from town, sometimes from the greater Duluth region. So, the area is too wide to cover. The question is, how are we gonna find him?" Ferret explains, rubbing his hands over his tired eyes.

"Slender, Pennywise, Ferret, Vegas, take Halfpint and Eli, call in favors, ask contacts and leave no stone unturned. He has to be found. And this time he will not get away with it. Out bad is the least of his problems!" I growl. When Moggy opens his mouth, I railroad straight over him.

"Once we have him, it will go to another vote. Whether I'd like to see him dead or not doesn't matter. It'll be a club decision. Make sure he gets into the dugout alive."

"While we're here, I'd like to raise something else!" Ratchet stands, which is unusual because he is normally one of the quieter brothers, and not a man of many words in meetings.

"Have at it," I encourage him. Usually if he has something to say, it's well-grounded, so I'm more than happy to listen.

"At the Poker Run, I had a shadow. Prospect has a friend who really would like to get to know the members. He stuck with me the whole time, did everything I asked, has smarts and a good head on his shoulders. He's great prospect material. Only problem is, he is mixed race, so strictly speaking the bylaws forbid him to become one. I'd like to ask that at the next meeting we put the bylaws on the agenda and until then think about whether skin color makes a difference to us. I, for one, would be happy to sponsor him."

Well, I'll be damned! That thought never occurred to me, but then we never had a situation like this. The bylaws state members must be white and male.

"Okay, it's too much to discuss now, but I agree. We can put it up for the next church meeting and all of you think about it until then."

The sound of rumbling bikes hits us at the same time as shots ring out.

"What the fuck?" We jump out of our chairs, weapons drawn and run out the clubhouse within a couple of seconds. The scene greeting us makes me want to vomit. Greg, the prospect, is on the floor bleeding from both his legs, with Fury standing over him, holding a gun to his head. Fury's face is an ice-cold mask of, well, fury. No pun intended.

"Fuck with me this time, Raven, and I'll put a bullet in his head! You'll be next!"

What The Fuck?

A gasp comes from behind me. In the chaos, no one had noticed Ellie stepping out, hiding behind Slender. Her face frozen in shock. She must have come running downstairs from Slender's room, where she stayed while we were in church. She's having either Slender or another patched member with her everywhere she goes, since Rusty is still on the loose.

Stepping forward, I need to find out what the fuck is going on.

"Fury, what the hell is going on? What are you doing here? More to the point: why the hell did you shoot my prospect and why are you threatening me?" My tone is as glacial as I feel.

It's not just Fury and his officers in my yard, but a sizeable delegation, including a van, which I bet holds his reinforcements. There's no beef that I know of with the Slayers. They're our dominant club and we have a peaceful relationship with them. Poker run aside.

As I look around, my men all look as shocked as I am.

"Where is Rusty? Bring him out to me!" Fury bellows at us. I inwardly groan. What has the fuckwad done now? Nothing could have prepared me for what Fury does next.

He drops the prospect to the floor, storms over to me and holds his gun to my head, despite all of my men having their guns drawn on him. I see murder and hatred in Fury's eyes, making me realize just how serious this is, having only known Fury as a jovial and approachable man.

"I wish I could, man. He's in the wind. We have everyone searching for him. Hell, all our contacts are searching for the fucking weasel. You know I wanted him out Fury; you know that

166

whatever it is he did to piss you off, I'd hand him over to you, no questions asked." I try to calm Fury, at least a little. Otherwise, I may not see the end of the day.

"Why don't you and your club join us in church and fill us in on what's happened, since we are clueless as to what the fuck is going on?" I ask, trying to diffuse the tension in the air.

Masher steps up to Fury.

"Let's take this inside, Prez. You can't shoot him out here, too many witnesses. It'd start a war and I don't want to lose any of our men to these animals."

My eyebrows hit my hairline. Animals? Really? What the fuck is going on here? I feel Masher grabbing my arms, twisting them behind my back, while Fury's gun pushes into my temple. They march me and the rest of my guys into church. Ellie hides behind Slender and Pennywise, who tells her to stay at the bar. As we walk into church, my men sit down, with a Restless Slayer standing behind each chair. I stand at the head of the table, with Ghoul sitting in my chair, Masher now having his gun trained on me, and Fury pacing like a captured wild animal.

"Who's the girl?" Masher snaps.

"Ellie is under my protection," Slender grates out. Masher looks thoughtful, tapping his finger to his lips.

"Ellie? As in Eliza, Ellie Greenwood?" I'd rather he hadn't figured it out, but it was bound to happen.

"Yes, as in Rusty's sister. He beat her to within an inch of her life and threatened to kill her, as well as my own sister," I rasp out, barely able to contain my anger.

Masher nods at one of his men, who leaves the room then seconds later comes back in, dragging a kicking and screaming Ellie behind him. Slender is out of his chair, attempting to

167

jump over the table to get to her, but is slammed down by two Slayers, subdued and held in a choke hold.

"Calm down, man," Masher bellows at him. "We only want to ask her a few questions." He stops struggling for now and gives Ellie an encouraging smile.

"What the hell is this all about?" I snarl at Fury.

"You come into my house, shoot a prospect, hold me at gunpoint with no explanation, and now you drag a girl in here who isn't even an old lady and pull her into club business? At least I presume that is what you are doing? Conducting club business in front of civilians? What's next? All the old ladies being subjected to this?" By now I am so mad, I'm ready to lose my shit. It's all bullshit, anyway. We've been coexisting for many years and never had an issue.

Fury spins, foaming at the mouth, cocks his arm and before I can react, his fist flies straight towards me and the world goes black.

19 — CHLOE

My phone is ringing with Dawg's name on the screen, so I pick up.

"Hey, sweetheart, could you give us a lift when you're finished? Caroline is being discharged. I tried to ring the prospect, but there's no answer. Same with Raven. They're in church as far as I know. Would you mind?" Dawg asks me.

I frown. Raven always answers his phone. "Sure, Dawg. I finish in just under an hour. You can meet me in the waiting area by the front entrance. I'll grab you both and get you settled at my apartment. Then make my way to the clubhouse," I reassure Dawg. He thanks me and hangs up. Hmm, it's unlike Raven not to answer his phone for one of his brothers. Another call bell rings, and I pull myself together so I can finish the rest of my shift.

"Hey, you two!" I smile at Dawg and Caroline just over an hour later. "Let's get you home and settled. The fridge is full, and the place is all yours for now." I grin at them, grabbing Caroline's bag as Dawg helps her to my car.

"Have you tried Raven again?" I ask, but Dawg shakes his head. "They'll still be in church."

After dropping them off at my place, I hand Dawg the keys, show them around, and make sure I settle Caroline in bed. I say my goodbyes and head back to the car. As I drive up to the gates of the clubhouse, I realize something is very, very wrong. Greg is on the ground, leaning

169

against the gate, bleeding. He doesn't look good. I screech to a halt and jump out without bothering to turn off the engine.

"Greg, oh my God, are you alright?"

"Chloe, you need to leave. Go now! Slayers are here. They shot me in the legs," he rasps out, pain distorting his face.

"Fuck that!" I yell, run to the clubhouse, into the kitchen, grab the large first aid kit, and sprint back out to Greg. I clean his wounds as best as possible. Luckily, the bullets went straight through and didn't appear to hit anything major. Grabbing the scissors, I turn Greg's jeans into short cutoffs, in order for me to inspect the wounds. After bandaging them with pressure bandages from the gun-shot kit, I pass him a bottle of water.

"Sorry, Greg, I'll have to leave you here. There is no way I can carry you inside." I hand him pain killers to go with his water. "Take those, drink the water, and try to relax. Your wounds need stitches, but I can't do that out here. I'll get someone to help you. Just hang in there, bud."

Greg grabs my hand, trying to stop me as I walk away. I can hear him swearing.

"Chloe, don't go in there! Stay away from the clubhouse! Raven will kill me if anything happens to you!" followed by a screamed, "Fuck!"

I take a moment, for the first time since I arrived, to look around, noting the number of strange bikes in the yard. They appear to be abandoned rather than parked, and a dark van with Slayers' insignia is in the parking lot. This can't be good. Taking a deep, calming breath, I try to shake off the anxiety and nerves. I call Ashley. I'll need her as backup. No way am I going in there alone.

"Hey, girlfriend, what's up?" she titters at me.

"Ash, get your ass to the clubhouse right the fuck now. Bring Ally and anyone else you can find. The Slayers are here. They shot Greg and left him by the gate."

All joking aside now, Ashley barks out, "Be there in five, don't do anything stupid!" I disconnect, thinking who else could come and help. I make a call to Dawg.

"Dawg, I need you. Slayers are here. Greg has been shot, and I have no fucking clue what's going on. Get here as fast as you can!"

I hear a muttered "Fuck!" before the line goes dead.

Within minutes I hear Ally's bike roar up, Ashley on the back, and followed closely by Dawg. They ignore Greg, he just waves them towards me.

"Whatever the fuck is going on, must be serious shit if they shot the prospect," Dawg states.

"I'll stay with Greg, keep him company. Anything you want me to do?" Ally asks. "Just keep an eye on his dressings and make sure they don't bleed through. Give him some more water to drink. Watch his blood pressure," I advise her, before turning, exchanging looks with Ashley and Dawg.

Ally nods at me and hands me the gun from her waistband. "Take this as an insurance policy. I'd rather you didn't use it, but if you have to, go for it." I look at the Ruger LPC, make sure it's loaded, and the safety is on, nod in thanks to Ally, and wait for Dawg, who also has his Baretta in hand. Ashley pulls a rather large Glock out of her bag.

"Don't judge me, it's Vegas's. I've been training with it since Rusty went underground!" She shrugs her shoulders and marches forward.

As we approach the entrance, we hear a roar and a loud crashing noise. We run to the door and storm through it, guns in hand and trained into the room, where half an army of Slayers is standing around the table, keeping their eyes trained on the Souls' members, Slender is subdued in a choke hold and Raven is on the floor unconscious with Fury standing over him. We have the element of surprise for now, but it won't last.

"Step away from my old man, Fury!" I scream at Fury, who stares at me puzzled, with my gun trained on his head.

Ashley pulls Ellie behind her. "What the ever-loving fuck is going on here?" She demands. The whole situation screams utter chaos. Guns all around, everyone pointing at everyone, a situation which will only take the slightest trigger to escalate into a bloodbath.

Dawg makes the first move by slowly holstering his gun, holding his hand out, trying to placate the Slayers, followed by Ashley. Vegas nods at the rest of the Souls, who all holster their guns as a show of goodwill. Masher puts his gun away next and everyone else follows suit, apart from Fury.

"Fury, don't make me shoot you! I like you and the guys, but I'll not tolerate being threatened by you after just having patched up the first victim of your trigger-happy soul," I growl at him. Yes, I can growl with the best of them. I may be a nurse, but hell, I can stand my ground if I have to.

The agitation radiating off Fury is phenomenal. His eyes are darting between me and Raven, who's still out cold. In the end he holsters his weapon, as do I. Ghoul gets up, winks at me on his way out and shuts the door. The damn nerve of that man. Seconds later he is back with a bucket of cold water, tips it over Raven, who regains consciousness instantly. Groaning and coughing, he tries to sit up, reaching for Ghoul's outstretched hand.

"Your old lady just saved your ass, man! Best say thank you later!" he tells him. Raven's eyes meet mine and I can see his fear and temper sparking in them. He watches me standing with Dawg, Ashley, and Ellie right behind us. They release Slender and shove him into his chair.

"Where's Rusty?" grates Fury.

"That's the million-dollar question," Ash throws in before anyone else can open their mouth. "If we, fuck… if *I* knew that, I'd put a bullet in him myself." Sounding ice cold and a tad bored.

It gains her raised eyebrows from the Slayers.

"That fucking bastard raped my Meghan! At the rally!" A gasp goes round the room as Fury explodes with his outburst, his eyes wild. Behind us, Ellie wails as she sinks to the floor.

"Oh my God, I am so sorry, so, so, sorry!" she sobs.

Megan is Fury's eighteen-year-old daughter. The Slayers rally was the first one she was part of. Watching Raven, Vegas, and the rest of the Souls go from shock to disbelief, anger, disgust to shame, is an awful sight to see.

Tears are flooding down my and Ashley's cheeks, as I step forward, followed by Ash, and walk up to the gigantic beast of a man, who's struggling to keep himself together, ripped apart by pain, guilt, grief, and unimaginable anger.

We walk straight to him, take him between the two of us and wrap our arms around him, not afraid to show our tears and the pain we feel for Meghan, Fury, and his club.

"Oh, Fury," Ashley groans. "I am so, so sorry. How is Meghan? Is she okay? Is there anything we can do? I've been at the receiving end of his threats and violence for years. I just recently told Vegas and Raven. I hid it for years because I was ashamed and scared. Anything, Fury, anything at all, you name it, and we'll do it," she cries.

173

Whereas I just look him in the eyes through all my tears, my lips pressed into a firm line, and nod my agreement. If I speak, I'll lose it and cry my heart out.

Fury seems to calm a little, whispering, "Thank you," in a broken voice.

Ghoul raises his voice. "Everyone out, into the bar, have a drink and calm the fuck down."

Dawg nods and asks, "Can someone give a hand with bringing the prospect inside?"

Church empties until only Masher, Fury, Slender, Vegas, Ghoul, Raven, Ellie, Ashley, and I remain in the room. Ashley seeks comfort in Vegas's arms. Ellie is sitting in a chair now but she's so far gone into her head, she can't quit crying. Slender is sitting next to her, murmuring, attempting to calm her.

And me? I am still next to Fury, with my arm on his, looking at Raven, who's sitting in a chair, staring at me with pride, fear for me, and barely contained anger at my arrival on the scene.

Raven moves his jaw, groaning. "Fury, I cannot tell you how sorry I am that this happened to Meghan. Shouldn't happen to any woman. If I had Rusty here, I'd gladly hand him over and watch you rip him limb from limb, but he's not here, I swear. We're out looking for him ourselves. I promise we'll find him and deal with him." His voice is steady and sincere.

"You bet your ass you are!" Fury laughs without humor. "My daughter was raped and abused in more ways than one! She's broken and may never recover from this. Scarred for life by that fucking animal," he rants. Ellie shakes off Slender and walks to Fury.

"I am so sorry for my brother's actions. Rusty's changed in the last year or so, beyond recognition. He deserves to be put down for what he did to your daughter and the women from this club. He's crazy and has gone off the deep end. Rusty beat me and threatened to kill me.

174

This club took me in and protected me ever since. Please don't take your hatred out on them. It's not their fault. They would never condone this kind of treatment towards any woman and they definitely would never protect him for doing this." Fury looks her up and down. She still has some bruises that aren't fully healed.

"He did that to you?" he questions.

"Yes, he did." Ashley steps up to Fury, phone in hand, showing him pictures she took of Ellie when she first came to the club for shelter. Fury's eyebrows rise as he scrolls through Ashley's phone.

"I know he is your brother, but he raped my little girl. He'll die for this," he hisses. Ellie looks him straight in the eye and nods.

"I won't try to stop you. I understand, but don't take it out on the entire club for one man's actions. They didn't know and if they did, they would have taken him out," she tells him.

Fury turns to Raven.

"You have some gutsy old ladies here. Count yourself lucky! I warned you last time to keep him under control. Usually, it would be your club's responsibility to deal with him, but this has gone too far," he glowers.

Raven nods.

"I know. I can't undo what he did, but please tell me if there is anything, anything at all we can do to help your daughter, Fury." His sincerity seems to calm Fury.

"I'll get Ferret on to the hunt; he'll do anything possible to hunt him down electronically. Rusty will need money and a place to stay. He can't stay hidden forever. The man will leave a trail," Raven states.

175

Pennywise stands. "I'll take a few men and visit his favorite hangouts, ask questions, and tighten the noose. Would you like some of your brothers to come with me?" He looks at Fury, waiting for his reaction.

"Scar!" he shouts into the bar and a bear of a man with scars all over his face walks in. "You're with Pennywise, looking for that bastard!" Scar grunts and follows Pennywise and Dougal out to the bikes. Raven calls in Moggy, Ratchet, and Sparks. They're taking all the motels in town and a fifty-mile surrounding radius, followed by two Slayers.

I strut over to Raven, sit on his knee, and whisper to him, "Sorry, Raven, I couldn't just sit back and do nothing,"

"We'll talk about this later and I guarantee you won't like it," he hisses in my ear. He's pissed. Really pissed. I look between Raven and Fury.

"Can I stitch up Greg now without you two killing one another?" I flippantly throw at them with a wink. Humor often is the best way to deal with strained situations.

"Sassy, you need a firm hand," gruffs Fury.

Followed by, "Tell me about it!" from Raven.

I wave and walk out to the bar area, spotting the prospect laying on the pool table, where he is being shamelessly teased about his extremely short cutoff jeans. Shooing the taunters away, I get to work, cleaning and sewing up the entry and exit wounds for Greg, while someone tops his pain relief with whiskey.

He's an exhausted, high, and drunk prospect by the time I finish. A few guys grab him and lead him upstairs to bed, where I set up an IV for fluids, to replace the blood he lost. Happy with my work, I move back downstairs.

Raven stayed in Church with the other officers. It's getting late and everyone needs a break. Ashley called Sarah, and together they're making food in the kitchen for the unexpected guests. I task the club bunnies with making spare rooms ready and taking care of the guys who need a little extra special attention.

"Fury, we have made rooms ready for your men. You can stay with me and Raven, as long as you don't mind the pull-out sofa," I tell him. He nods in agreement.

"Masher and Ghoul can stay with us. We have enough room," states Vegas.

"Slender, you and Ellie too, of course!" Ashley adds. Within twenty minutes, we serve a meal in the kitchen. Nothing special, just pasta Bolognese, but it gives sustenance after the four-hour ride the Slayers had to get here and a somewhat hostage situation. Plus, it shows hospitality even after all that went down. Ferret calls but has no new information. After a couple of hours, Pennywise returns with his group; he equally had no luck. Ratchet, Moggy, and Sparks's group are not back yet and not expected for the time being.

"Since there's nothing more we can do tonight, I suggest we all make our way to our beds and meet back here at eight a.m. sharp." Raven lurches to his feet, exhausted by today's developments. Ashley and Sarah show folks to their rooms, while Ally and Ebony wash up. Vegas gets his party ready to go, waiting for Ash to return so they can leave.

I link my arm through Raven's and whisper, "I'll just check on Greg again. Be right back." Without waiting for a reply, I dart up the stairs, look in on Greg and leave more pain killers on his bedside table. Before I join Raven back downstairs, I make sure Greg is comfortable and tell him I will be back to check on him tomorrow.

Vegas and Ashley are on their way out the door with their overnight *guests,* followed by Raven, Fury and me. Since Raven lives so close, we walk to our home for the night. Raven opens

177

the door, switches on the lights, and I disappear straight into the bedroom to get bedding for Fury.

The men are talking, so I take my time, giving them a little space to settle and talk things through. Making as much noise as I can, I return to the front room, making sure they're aware I'm on my way.

I pull out the sofa bed and get it ready for Fury before I turn around and face him.

"Fury, I truly am sorry for the way I acted when I walked into the clubhouse. Drawing a gun on you is not the nicest thing to do. I hope you understand I needed to stop you from doing my family any further harm. I love my old man and felt the need to protect him, since he was out cold on the floor. You'd have done the same, and I'm sure your old lady would have too." Finishing with a hug for Fury, I make sure my apology sounds sincere.

Fury sits down on the opposite sofa, whiskey in hand, but silent. Raven sits on the table to the side of him, when Fury puts his head in his hands and his shoulders shake.

"My baby, he hurt my baby girl! The best piece of me and he hurt her!" We can hear him sob, his voice full of torture. "I couldn't keep her safe. I failed her! I'm going to kill that bastard!"

The level of distress radiating from him is unreal and painful to watch, making me want to kill Rusty myself. Kneeling in front of Fury, I wrap him in a hug while Raven has his hand on his shoulder, trying to convey compassion and understanding. We sit there until Fury composes himself.

"Fury, you have my word. We'll find him and deal with him. I guarantee it," Raven declares with conviction. Fully aware that he just sentenced Rusty to death.

20 — RAVEN

My eyes open at the sound of loud banging on the door. I groan. My face throbs with my pounding headache, brought on by Fury's fists and the stress of yesterday. Chloe's already gone to work and didn't even wake me when she got up. The banging is relentless. Hearing Fury moving in the front room, I drag myself out of bed and join him just as he is opening up the front door.

"I've had some ATM activity from his card!" Ferret announces as he steps inside.

"Where is he?" Fury growls.

Ferret looks from me to Fury and on my nod, he states, "Canada."

Fuck my life! Canada is over six hours away. Figures that he'd go where he feels he's out of reach of club justice. Bitter hatred runs through my veins at the mere thought. Fury has his phone out and is informing the Slayers. I nod to Ferret.

"Thanks, man, see what else you can pick up. Church in an hour!" I send out a group text, calling church, walk into the kitchenette, where Chloe has left a full pot of coffee for us. God, I love that woman.

Her thoughtful gesture means a lot. Despite being angry, I wanted to throttle her for her interference yesterday. I appreciate her reasoning, and though I hate to admit it, she did the right thing. I just can't deal with the fact I wasn't able to protect her and instead she protected me. She handled the situation like a champ. Not only de-escalating the situation inside the clubhouse but also by patching up the prospect and taking the reins there. She could have withered and cried, but she didn't. She took stock of the situation and handled it like a queen. The fight we had over it last night was not pretty and, admittedly, it ended in a standoff. Chloe ripped me a new asshole, grabbed her pillows, and threatened to sleep on the floor. The makeup sex was stellar, though. Nothing like a bit of angry fucking to settle the temper. The second round was more me apologizing for being a complete ass to her.

"Hey, fucker, are you listening?" Fury's agitated bellow rips me out of my rather pleasant thought. The situation remains tense and fragile between our clubs and the atmosphere is rampant with explosive aggression, just waiting to detonate.

I pass Fury a coffee while fixing my own.

"Sorry, man, got caught up in my thoughts. What were you saying?" I try to radiate calm. Even though that is not what I'm feeling, not by any means.

"We need to send men out to go get him," Fury states.

"Fury, let's wait for church, give Ferret a chance to narrow his location down and then put a team together. We'll do this together, both clubs working together, making sure we cover all angles." I try to calm him.

"No, this is your club, your mess. If it wasn't for your club, this would've never happened. My daughter would still be whole. You not dealing with that fucktard when you had the chance caused this fucking mess." Fury's anger billows around him like a hurricane, waiting to let loose. It will only take the tiniest of actions to push his button now. Realizing just how precarious and dangerous the situation is, for both clubs, but mostly for mine, I try to figure out how to manage the volatility surrounding all of us.

Fury's cell rings, thankfully distracting him.,

"Hey, girl, what's up?... Is she okay?... She did what? Oh my god! How bad is she?...

Tanya, please keep a real close eye on her, I'll be back this afternoon... Yes, call me anytime and thank you for looking after Meghan, for being there for her. Yes, please contact the therapist, you know. The Souls will pay for her private treatment."

The hateful look Fury shoots me, freezes me on the spot. I nod in agreement. Of course, we'll carry the cost. It's the least we can do. Fury hangs up, opens the door, walks out, slamming the door on his way out, nearly breaking it off its hinges.

"Shit!" I scream into the now empty house, clenching my fist, punching the wall so hard it goes through the plaster, leaving a large hole behind. The pain serves to divert me from my frustration and anxiety. This could bring serious retribution to the club.

◊◊◊

As I enter the clubhouse, a wave of nausea hits me, caused by the wall of Slayers, staring at me with unbridled loathing and malice. Everyone files into church, Fury sitting at the front of the table next to me, his knee constantly moving, bouncing as he fidgets in his chair. Pennywise and his group have returned, tired and gritty eyed. "Ferret, you're up!"

"I traced some card use at a cash machine in Winnipeg, Canada. Hacking into their CCTV system was easy. You can watch him arriving with his trike, taking out money, and leaving. I'm waiting for him to make another transaction to pinpoint his location. He's not using his cell; I can't ping his location. So we'll have to wait for him to make another mistake," Ferret finishes, frustration gleaming through his eyes.

"Not good enough!" Fury jumps up and snarls.

181

"That fucker sodomized my daughter. She tried to take her own life yesterday, and you're telling me you can't find that asshole?" An explosion of yells and mumbles breaks out in the room. Almost everyone is on their feet.

"You find him, Raven; you and your club. Dig deep, because I need to get back to my daughter. I'll make an exchange. We're taking his fucking sister and your Sergeant At Arms. We ride back today. You have two weeks; you don't find him, I'll shoot them," Fury threatens. The room goes silent enough to hear a pin drop.

Slender stands. "I trust my brothers and am happy to go with you in exchange for time to find him, but taking Ellie goes too far!" he speaks up calmly. "Ellie stays here."

Fury roars with laughter.

"I think you misunderstand who's in charge here. You have half an hour to get her here and we leave." There's no talking to Fury, no opportunity for discussion. Masher shoves Slender over to Ghoul, who restrains him. Not that Slender is fighting. He knows that the slightest provocation will not end well this time.

"I'll go speak to Ellie and explain what's going on. I need your guarantee that she will not be harmed." Vegas looks Fury dead in the eye.

"I'll shoot Slender first, so she's safe," Fury says dismissively.

I nod at Vegas, who gets up and leaves, followed by Masher and a couple of Slayers. I'm bulldozed by the one-percenter dominant President and his officers. There's nothing I can do to stop the train wreck from happening. Instead, I promise a long, drawn out, painful death to Rusty, and anyone who supported him.

◊◊◊

As long as I'll live, I won't forget Ellie's panic-stricken look as Slayers lead her and Slender to the waiting van, her flinching when the driver's door slams with a bang. Slender, with his arm around Ellie, talking to her quietly, trying to calm her and keep her rational. She must be scared out of her mind. Ashley came with Vegas, who's pacing, shouting and cussing. Yet we're all helpless to prevent them from being taken from us, even if it's just temporary.

Ashley is wrapping herself around Vegas, trying to calm him and herself. Me? I'm desperate with the need to beat on something to release the anxiety. Concern about my family being driven away from us, my hatred of Rusty, my rage, it's all building toward an explosion of epic proportion, but the feeling of helplessness is the worst of all. Pennywise and Ratchet are toe to toe, fists are flying. I don't stop the fight. They are just trying to relieve stress. Dougal and Dawg pull them apart after a couple of bloody rounds.

Ashley sneaks over to me and wraps her arms around my waist, burying her face in my chest. I can feel her shaking, part shock, part straining to hold back the tears that want to escape.

"Jamie, promise me you'll kill him this time. No more chances! He can't live!" whispers Ashley, tear-stained eyes on me.

My pacifist sister, who's suffered so much already, begging me to put an end to this. How terrible that must feel for her. I don't even want to consider how conflicted she must be. She hates the violence, always has. It's rare for us nowadays. So for her to beg me like this, shows just how affected she is by all of this.

"Don't worry, princess, we'll send him to the Devil this time. I swear on my life."

Ashley's pained eyes are killing me. She takes a deep breath, goes on tiptoe, and kisses my cheek.

"I trust you, Jamie. Always." She turns and walks back to Vegas.

"Church! Now!" I bellow at the men, encouraging everyone to hurry back inside.

The mood is somber. The utter silence is unnerving. No one whispers or comments, everyone still shell-shocked by what happened in the last hour. I look to my right where Vegas is sitting, and the chair to my left, which is left empty, making Slender's absence even more visible and poignant.

"Ferret, is there any way you can call in favors to speed things up?" I watch as Ferret opens his cell and leaves the room, nodding at me.

"We need to find him, and fast. We need to get Slender and Ellie back here, asap. It's unthinkable to put them at a higher risk than they already are. Suggestions, guys! We need to pull some tricks and an ace or two out of our sleeves if we want to keep them alive and safe." I look every man in the eye, not that they need reminding just how precarious and serious this situation is.

"We ought to split into groups, mount a search, feet on the ground, so to speak," Dawg suggests.

"I know Canada is a long way away, but if we want results, we need to act, and act now." Pennywise nods. He's our enforcer, and I trust him implicitly. "I agree. We need to get on the road, pound pavements, follow up on Ferret's leads. He can pass info over to us directly. We stand a better chance of catching his ass if we are on location at the time he uses an ATM or makes a different mistake."

"Volunteers?" I ask. Hands raise around the table. Dawg, Dougal, Pennywise, Vegas, Ratchet, and Sparks. They'll make a skilled team.

"Dawg, are you sure, man? Your old lady has only just gotten out of the hospital. You can sit this one out man, look after her first," I tell him.

184

Dawg laughs. "And you don't think Caroline would feed me my balls one by one if I didn't take that dickweed out of circulation?" he asks me, eyebrows raised to his almost nonexistent hairline. I've known him for many years. The fact that he is braiding his beard shows he is ready for action, and nothing would stop him.

"I'll get Caroline. She can stay with Ashley while we're away. Would help Ash if she had company," Vegas throws in.

Clusseaud who's been silent so far, I'd almost forgotten he was there, clears his throat. "I'm with them. Have a score to settle myself. I know Winnipeg. Rusty and I used to run around there back in the old days. Not sure how much it's changed, but I may know a few places he might frequent, if they're still there, that is." I nod in agreement.

"Right," Vegas states, "go home, pack, we'll meet here in two hours and get going. Clusseaud, can you sort out the fastest route? Don't want to spend more time on the bike than needed." Clusseaud nods.

"Ratchet and I will take the cage, so we can get the fat fuck back here without giving him the chance to ditch us once we have him," Dougal states. I nod in agreement.

"I want him alive," I reiterate to the search party.

"You may teach him a lesson in etiquette, but he has to be alive and conscious. Well, alive anyway." My voice vibrates with anger.

"Aww, and I was looking forward to playing with him a little." Pennywise's voice drips with sarcasm and mock disappointment.

Ferret returns. "I called in all the favors owed to us," he starts. "An old army buddy of mine runs a PI and security business, with connections to the law. I can only imagine the systems he has access to. He'll help. The man is on the trail now."

185

"Thanks, man, means a lot." I let him know.

"A search party is going to Canada, trying to find the cunt. Any information you get, relay straight to Pennywise and Vegas. They'll be on their way in two hours." Ferret just nods, gets up and leaves for his IT cave.

I know how hard this is on him. He's a vet, has been on several tours, and Iraq fucked him up big time. PTSD is his bitch. Hence, calling in favors is a huge thing for him.

As I look around, I notice everyone has left, and bikes are starting up in the yard. When I enter the bar, Vegas is sitting with Ashley in his lap, whispering to her. I can see her nodding, so I take it Caroline staying with her won't be an issue.

"How long will you be?" I overhear her asking Vegas.

"I don't know, babe. Depends on what leads we get. I am hoping we'll be back within the week." He looks at me, pain in his eyes. He is just as aware as I am that Slender will be in real danger in a week's time.

"But I can't be sure. I'll call you though and check in with you every day, darlin'. Don't worry, it'll be fine," he tries to reassure her.

They both get up and leave to make their way home. Spen is behind the bar; he grabs a bottle and pours me an obscene amount of Makers Mark, which I take with shaking hands and down it in one, holding my glass up for a refill.

"How's Greg doing?" I ask, since Chloe tasked him with looking after the prospect, until she's back from work to check on him.

"He's doing okay. High as a kite on pain meds, and cranky, but doing better than yesterday."

"Good," I reply. Grabbing my refill, I trudge back into my office, fall into my chair, and put my head on my desk. My split lip and swollen eye hurt from laying on them, so sit up and lean back in my chair and close my eyes.

Self-deprecation is my middle name, so I analyze and analyze. What did I miss? Could I have stopped the situation getting so out of hand? How did I not see what a filthy bottom dwelling cunt Rusty really is? My questions remain unanswered, frustrating me even more. I hate feeling helpless, and that is exactly what I am right now.

21 — CHLOE

If I could erase the last twenty-four hours forever, I would.

After checking on Greg, who seems better, I returned home to a totally obliterated Raven. He was so drunk he staggered around, mumbling about everything being his fault, berating himself. I had no clue what to do with him. He wouldn't answer my question when I asked him what happened, leaving me with no choice but to call Ash. Ashley told me about the Slayers taking Slender and Ellie as "*collateral*"—meaning hostages—until we find Rusty. She mentions that a search party left earlier today to hunt him, as well as Fury threatening to shoot Slender after a week.

It took me ages to get Raven into bed. Every time he was in, he came back out into the front room, resulting in me going to bed with him. I snuggled up to him, stroking his hair until he settled. I've never seen him nor could've imagined him being so full of remorse and self-hatred. It isn't his fault that the son of a bitch pulled the wool over everyone's eyes. There's nothing I can do to help him… or is there? I crawl out of bed and tiptoe into the living room, so not to wake him. Picking up my phone, I dial Ferret.

"Ferret!" Wow, he sounds groggy as he answers his cell. Groggy and grouchy.

"Hey, Ferret, it's Chloe. Have you got a minute?"

"What can I do for you?" His voice is slightly more friendly now, though I wouldn't call it warm by any means.

"Ferret, I was thinking. Rusty is in constant pain. He'll need pain prescriptions and those have to be filled at a drugstore. To get a doctor to give him prescriptions, he'd have to be seen or have his current doctor send his prescriptions to a new pharmacy. Any chance you can access health records?"

"Damn it, Chloe, you're a fucking genius! Not sure how I missed that. I can't, but I know someone who can. I'll take care of it. You know, you're not supposed to know anything about club business," he reprimands.

"You know what, Ferret? Fuck you and your club business. Raven is a mess, and two of our family are being held against their will until we find this piece of shit. I'll protect my family any way I can. Club business be damned," I grate at him, causing him to burst out laughing.

"Good girl, you're a capable old lady. Now get off the phone, look after your man, and let me work my magic."

I stare at a blank screen. *The little shit hung up on me!* The thought makes me grin. I love my new family. Blood isn't always family. Loyalty, respect, and love are, though. That's what makes us all family. A bit of a crazy and dysfunctional one, but I realize just how proud I am to be part of it.

◊◊◊

I wish I could just call in sick from work. Groaning, I swing my legs out of bed and rub my gritty eyes. Next to me, Jamie's dead to the world, his snores rattling the windows, which makes me grin. I wouldn't like to be him when his alarm goes off. He'll be suffering like hell after his drunken escapade yesterday. A pang of hurt finds its way into my chest. My heart goes

189

out to him. Jamie is dealing with an impossible situation. Vegas and his crew left late last night, leaving Moggy, Zippy, Greg, who is recovering from his gunshot wounds, Halfpint, Eli, Ferret, Spen, and the old ladies. Ashley is looking after Caroline and no one has heard from Debs since the poker run. Then there's Ally and myself. Oh, and of course Mom, who has taken over Greg's care this morning.

I grab a quick shower, get ready, make a pot of coffee because Raven will definitely need it. Grabbing a quick slice of toast before I fill a pint glass with water, leaving it on his bedside table with ibuprofen. I stroke his hair, turn on my heal and hustle to work. As I pull into the parking lot, my cell rings.

"Hi, Caroline, how can I help you? Are you okay, hon?" Caller display is a wonderful thing. I smirk to myself.

"Hi, lovely lady, yes, I am fine. Ashley, not so much. She's been throwing up and about two minutes ago, almost passed out. She keeps telling me she's fine, but I don't think so."

Hmm, I screw up my brows, thinking. "How often has she been sick?" I ask.

"Twice," answers Caroline.

"That's not so bad, Caroline. Just remind her to drink water, little sips, and keep eating. I know she's stressed and worried about the guys being on a run. Just keep her as calm as you can. She'll be fine. But call me if you get worried, and if she passes out, call an ambulance to get her checked out. Sorry, honey, I am at work now. I'll call you during my lunch break to see how she's doing," I try to reassure Caroline.

Ashley being sick is not ideal. Caroline still needs to be taken care of, so checking on Ashley later will be my number one priority. Guess I will drive over after my shift to make sure they are okay.

"Okay, hon, we'll keep an eye on each other. Catch you later," Caroline's voice is bright as she replies. Hence, I'm not overly concerned.

It turns out to be a darn busy day in the oncology unit. It's chemo day for a lot of our patients, so not the most pleasant of days. Between wiping brows, handing out vomit bowls, sitting with patients, drying their tears, speaking to relatives and loved ones, end-of-life decisions, the pros and cons of hospice care, and making a referral to the local hospice, the day flies by.

Before I know it, it's six p.m. and I feel horrible because I clear forgot to call the girls. Not taking my lunch break is a regular thing. The staff are stretched thin and overworked. Not bothering to check my phone, I know it'll show missed calls from Caroline. I jump in my car, drive to Pizza Hut, and order two large pizzas with everything, plus garlic knots. One for the girls, one for Raven and me to have at home. We already have a salad in the fridge.

I'd like to say getting to Ashley's was easy, but it wasn't. She must be pissed because the gates didn't open automatically when I drove up to them. Their house is as secure as Fort Knox.

I have to get out, walk to the security phone, and ring the house. After the third try, I roll my eyes. I know Ashley is watching, so I get back to the car, grab the pizza box, and hold it up to the camera. Funny, the gates suddenly judder open. Jumping back into the car, I drive up to the house.

"I'm so sorry, ladies, I meant to call, but didn't get a break today, so thought I'd come and see you with pizza instead." I smile and use my best contrite voice.

Ashley stands in front of me, hands on her hips.

"Pepperoni?" She squints at me.

"And meatballs, bacon, ham, and pineapple!" I grin back at her.

"Okay, you are forgiven, just this once, though!" She almost rips the pizza box out of my hand as she storms off to the living room, where Caroline is sitting on one of the oversized, overstuffed couches. She slams the pizza box onto the table, opens it, grabs a slice, shoves it in her mouth and groans likes she is having an orgasm. Caroline and I just stare in bewilderment at our weird friend.

"What? I'm starving!" She looks at us as though we're the weirdos instead.

"Obviously," Caroline grumbles. "Not sure how you can be, since you've eaten almost everything in the cupboards."

She looks at me, shudders and tells me, "Chocolate Nutella with smoked sausage and a pinch of salt! It was disgusting! No wonder she threw up."

"What's going on, Ashley? Are you sick?" I question her. But looking at her, she doesn't look ill, well, weird food taste aside.

"Nope, I'm fine, just felt queasy this morning. Must be the stress of Vegas being away. Had some trouble sleeping last night and my anxiety was riding high. He phoned about lunch time, letting me know they got to Canada and are looking for a place to stay. So, I'm not so worried anymore," she states as she takes another big bite of pizza.

"Err, I can tell!" I tease, pointing at her third slice of pizza on its way to disappear into her mouth.

Caroline mutters something under her breath.

"What was that?" I ask.

"I said, I think she has a bun in the oven! No wonder either. When I got here, we crashed their goodbye sex fest," she says, wagging her finger in mock disgust at Ashley, making gagging noises.

"Nope, no way, no how! I am on the pill and am super strict with when and how I take them. I had a cold, but I made Vegas suit up. There is no way. I get like this with anxiety sometimes. Especially when Vegas is away." Chloe looks from Caroline to me, and back again, completely serious. Okay then, that was that.

After sticking around for a cup of java, I make my excuses and head home.

Finally, a quick shower and getting changed later, I throw the pizza and garlic knots into the oven to heat through, fix the salad and load two plates. Pizza will only take another ten minutes, so I call Jamie.

"Hey, sweetheart!" he answers. "Are you back now?"

"Sure am, and have pizza with garlic knots and salad ready, if you're hungry.",

"Baby, you are amazing. I'm so sorry, I can't get away from the office yet. Would you mind bringing the pizza to me? I know, honey, not ideal, and I promise to make it up to you!" Raven mock grovels, knowing full well I'll take him his dinner.

"See you in a moment!" I reply, before covering our plates, and making my way to the clubhouse. Knocking on the office door, I find Raven and Ferret with Spen in deep discussion. Ferret paces with the phone to his ear. You could cut the atmosphere with a knife.

The discussion stops as I enter. Raven looks tired, Spen deflated, and Ferret agitated. I sigh, place both plates on the table, and uncover them. Raven's eyes light up as he draws me to him and kisses me so thoroughly, I have to lock my knees as they turn to jelly to stop me from falling over.

Giggling, breathless and flushed, I smack his shoulder, pull back and make my way into the kitchen to get two extra sets of cutlery. *I didn't want pizza anyway.* I quietly mock myself as I return to the office with the forks. Ferret has now stopped pacing and is no longer on the phone.

"There you go, gentlemen, have at it. Pizza, garlic knots, and salad. You look as though you need it. Want me to get you a beer with that?"

Ferret groans. "You are an angel! Boss, you have the best old lady ever! Has she got an older, single sister?" He winks at me as he turns towards Raven, who bursts out laughing,

"Keep your mitts to yourself, man, or I'll have to break them," He warns Ferret with laughter creasing the corner of his eyes, as I walk to the bar and grab three longnecks for the guys, which I hand out as I return to the office.

"I'm sorry, baby, I'll be a while yet." Raven looks at me with regret.

"That's okay. I'll find Mom and check on Greg. See you later at home." I smile at him. Home sounds so right. Pressing my lips to his, I devour his mouth with mine, letting him know just how much I missed him today.

"Love you, Raven!" I whisper against his lips.

"Love you too, Chloe," he replies and slaps my backside as I turn to walk out.

As I open the kitchen door, I see Mom at the counter, making sandwiches, salad, and dividing it onto two plates, finishing it off with a handful of fries and chips. My mouth is watering at the mere sight and my stomach grumbles loud enough for her to turn around laughing. "Sorry, I didn't have my lunch break, and my pizza is in the office!" I murmur apologetically.

"I know, Chloe, I saw you walk in there and then come out of the kitchen with extra forks. So, I made us some sandwiches. Thought we could have a chat? Get to know each other a bit? We haven't had time to do that yet." She smiles at me, walks over with the two plates, and we take a seat at the long table.

We dig into our food, and Mom brings out a bottle of wine.

"Now, that's exactly what I need today," I giggle at her.

"Thanks, Mom, this is delicious!" I groan in appreciation.

"There are more fries and I've got a pint of Ben and Jerry's in the freezer." She winks at me.

"Let me tell you a bit about the club and myself. Always good to know a bit of history." She smiles at me. "I knew your mother. She was becoming a fast friend before things went haywire with her and Clusseaud."

That has me sitting up straight.

She continues, "Your mom and I were in high school together. That's where we met Derek and Bobby. I fell madly in love with Derek. He was already a prospect for the Stormy Souls when they were still under the leadership of Stone. Clusseaud was a hang around then. He often came out with Derek, Terrie and me. That's how he met your mom. Clusseaud and Derek were friends with Rusty, who was a full patch by then, and Stone's right hand.

"Raven and Ashley were just kids, and Nathan not even born. I never liked Rusty but put up with him as he was their VP even then.

"Derek patched in, and Bobby got his prospect patch. They were so proud to finally get their patches. Your father was so in love with Terrie, he'd have cut his own arm off for her. He truly loved her.

"Anyway, the night of the patch in, Rusty sent a club bunny to Bobby. He knew your mother was coming over to the party. She'd told Rusty but wanted to surprise Bobby. He'd invited her but wasn't sure whether she'd show."

She looks at me, sadness in her eyes.

"I'm pretty sure he arranged for your mother to find Bobby and the club girl. Bobby later told us that nothing had happened, and he kicked the bunny out of the room, or was in the process of doing so, when your mother came in. He was so shocked to see her that he opened his big mouth and made matters worse.

"I saw Terrie run out of the clubhouse, but never managed to catch up with her. When I went to her house the next morning, her mother told me she'd left during the night, cursing the MC and your mother for getting involved with them.

"It destroyed Clusseaud. It took him years to get over her. He turned into a loner, used club bunnies now and then, but never got into another relationship. He was bitter and hard for some years. Rusty encouraged him to put the club first and foremost in his life. He was a terrible influence for both Bobby and Derek from the beginning. There was a shootout about twelve years ago. Before the club went legit. Clusseaud was shot, and Derek died whilst throwing himself over Rusty to protect him.

"Rusty got shot in his hip but survived as most of the bullets hit Derek. It was the most horrendous day of my life. I lost my old man, and Pennywise lost his father, as well as Raven, Ashley, and Nathan lost their father to prison. Not long after that, Ashley's mother died."

Mom's eyes are glassy with tears. My head is swimming with information overload. I want to ask questions, but I don't want to interrupt. It feels as though she is purging her own demons by talking about the past.

"It was a chaotic time for the club. Raven had to take over the reins at a really young age. I tried to help look after Ash and Nathan, and it helped me deal with my grief. Ever since I've been looking after this lot. It comes naturally." She smiles at me.

196

"I know you are angry with Clusseaud. I'm not saying he was right in everything he did, because he wasn't. All I am asking you is to cut him some slack. Rusty manipulated him and put him into a situation he could not get out of. Terrie left without a word, and, at first, he was too hurt to go looking for her. Later, when he did, it was as though the earth had swallowed her, gone without a trace." She sighs as she finishes her story.

Huh, that puts a different spin on Clusseaud, and my mother, too. I'm not sure what to think right now. This conversation has left me confused and I'll need some time to sort through my thoughts. Standing, I smile at Mom.

"Thank you for telling me all this. I had no clue."

She also stands, walks around the table, wraps me in a hug and says, "Hi, I'm Helen, mother of Pennywise, and everyone else in the club. Welcome to the family!"

22 — RAVEN

Running my hand through my wild hair isn't helping to reduce the pressure inside of my head. A video just hit my cell and I feel sick at what it shows. A beaten Slender, whose face looks rearranged, but he's still smirking, so I know he is holding up. What seriously disturbs me is seeing Ellie in the background, held by her arms by two Slayers, very pale and obviously shaking. "Just thought I'd give you an incentive, Raven." Fury's voice comes through the speaker, causing Ferret to pace harder, shouting down at his phone.

"For fuck's sake, how long does this shit take? This is life or death, man, try to hurry it up!"

I get his desperation. His PTSD tortures him full force. I know he has flashbacks; sees himself in the middle of war, trying to help his brothers in arms, losing them all over again, not sleeping, and when he does, he suffers from extreme nightmares. We all witnessed that earlier, when he dozed off in his chair for no longer than five minutes but woke screaming and drenched in sweat. It took him a few minutes to get his bearings.

I've never served, but I have the utmost respect for anyone who has. There are a few vets in the club. Most came after leaving the armed forces, searching for a new family, brothers who mean something to them. They found their home here.

198

The tension in the room is unreal. I walk out to the bar, grabbing beers. As I stand there, I can hear voices from the kitchen. Mom must be in there. I smile when I hear Chloe's voice. She's the one thing keeping me sane. It should piss me off she involved herself with club business by calling Ferret, but her idea was spot on, turning out to be a valid lead. How can I be pissed under those circumstances? That'd be insane.

Just thinking about her hot body next to mine has me sporting a half chub. But it also has me wondering how she's coping. Managing the current violence within the club, her relationship, or rather non-relationship to Clusseaud, her demanding job, and me not being there for her the way I should. Is she gonna run away screaming? It'd destroy me. Fear races like ice water through my veins. I've never loved anyone with this kind of intensity. Losing her would break me.

"Yes!" I hear Ferret shout and break into a run back into the office.

He looks at me and smiles with an evil look in his eyes. If I didn't know him so well, it'd strike the fear of God into me.

"We've got the fucker," he rasps.

He grabs pen and paper. "Hang on, Tuff, let me take notes. Can you send the details to my cell? Email me what you've got. Yup, got it, thanks, Tuff, I owe you one. You'll let me know when he makes his next appearance? Thanks, buddy."

I stare at him as he turns towards me, closing his phone.

"He's in Ashern, Manitoba. Registered with a clinic there to get his pain prescriptions filled. Just waiting for him to pick it up and take it to the pharmacy. Then we'll know for sure. The address he gave is the Ashern Motor Hotel. The guys are in Winnipeg, which is a few miles from there. It'll take them at least two hours to get there. I'll send them a message after we discuss how to approach."

I plonk my ass into my chair, open my beer, and hand the others out to the guys.

"Thank fuck," I mutter on a relieved exhale.

"So, Prez, how are we gonna play this?" Spen asks and Ferret nods.

"How many motels are there in Ashern?" I ask.

Ferret pulls out his phone and checks the map.

"Three, as far as I can see. The Ashern Motel, Sharptail Motel, and the Interlake," he replies.

"Book rooms in any of the other two for the guys. They are to stay there until they hear from us. We need to know for sure that he is there, which means waiting for him to fill his script."

Ferret nods. "Tuff will call as soon as he drops the script off to be filled."

"Cool! We can grab him when he picks it up," I jeer. Spen is rubbing his hands.

"Can't wait to punch that bastard's lights out."

We listen to Ferret on the phone, letting Vegas know the plan. Next, Ferret books the reservation at Sharptail Motel under Robert Smith and calls Vegas back with the details.

I can hear Vegas laughing his ass off over the name. Once Ferret finishes his call, he nods, turns, and walks out of the office. He and Spen look dead on their feet.

"Go back to your old lady," I tell Spen. His head shoots in my direction.

"Er, Prez...sorry, you haven't heard? We split up. Debs upped and left me. I was an idiot. She caught me getting cozy with a bunny at the poker run and just walked. By the time I caught up with her, she was gone," he tells me, looking ashamed.

200

Shaking my head at what he's just told me, I look him in the eye. "You are a first-class dick. You didn't deserve that woman to start with. What the fuck, Spen? Tell me, though, was it worth it?" I ask him, feeling disappointed.

Spen looks at me, regret in his eyes.

"No, boss, it sure as shit wasn't. I've been trying to find her, but her parents won't tell me anything. Not sure how to put this mess right, or if I'll even be able to." He trudges towards the door.

"Night, Prez." And walks out.

Picking up my phone, I unlock it and make my call.

"What?!" Fury snarls at me.

"Was that necessary?" I ask him. "You've only been gone twenty-four hours. I get you're pissed and want to kill all of us right now, but to drag women into this. Really? I didn't think you'd sink that low. If you need to beat Slender, at least leave Ellie out of it," I growl at Fury. "And before you come out with any more shit, I'm calling to let you know that we have a solid lead. We have his location; the boys are hot on his trail and we should have him back here in a day or two. I'll call you when they're on the way back." Not waiting for his reply, I hang up the phone.

I can't trust myself to speak to him right now. I am too frustrated and wound up to remain rational. Leaving the office, I shut the door on today and stride to the kitchen, hoping that Chloe is still there. As I get to the door, I can hear Helen talking about Derek—her late husband— as well as Clusseaud, and Terrie. I didn't know that Helen knew Terrie. Not wanting to chance being caught eavesdropping, I knock, open the door and watch as Helen walks around the table, hugs Chloe, and welcomes her to the family. Smiling from ear to ear, I nod at Helen, who spots me. She lets go of Chloe and my girl turns and walks straight to me, wrapping her arms around me, going on her tiptoes and kissing the hell out of me.

A kiss with meaning and emotion. It's as though she tells me I love you through that kiss. I wrap her in my arms and pull her close. So close that my now throbbing hard dick digs into her, causing a small whimper to leave her.

"On that note, I'm out of here. Raven, not in my kitchen," Helen admonishes me, setting Chloe off giggling.

◊◊◊

I keep Chloe close to me as we walk home, unable to tolerate even an inch between us. We walk in and as soon as the door closes, Chloe jumps me. I literally have to catch her. She is clinging to me like a spider monkey, kissing the living shit out of me, making me hard as steel.

"Please, Jamie, I need you, now. Right now!" she groans between kisses, pulling on my T-shirt, trying to get it over my head. Pushing her hard her the door, helping her to get rid of my shirt and hers, I grab her ass and carry her to the bedroom. I would like nothing more than to fuck her hard against the wall, but I want to feel all of her skin, and ripping clothes off each other is much easier and quicker on the bed. She bounces as I drop her on the mattress. I follow her, covering her body with mine.

We wrangle our clothes off, not caring where they land. A deep groan leaves me as I feel her hot, smooth skin against mine. Her soft body against my hard one drives me crazy. My cock is pulsating and so damn hard. I want nothing more than to bury myself deep inside my woman, but I know I won't last for shit, so I need to make sure she comes first, at least once.

I break our frantic kiss and hold her arms above her head.

"Don't move, or I'll stop." I smirk at her.

She mewls, "Jamie, I need you now, honey!"

"You've got me, Chloe, and I've got you." I wink at her, kissing the side of her long neck, watching her shiver as I lick from there to her shoulder blade and blow a cooling breath over the area.

"Jamie," she whines. Her nipples are pebbled to hard points and begging for my mouth.

"Yes!" she hisses as my mouth closes around one while my fingers torture the other one, rolling and squeezing, pinching, then laving them with my tongue. Taking turns on each side has her writhing on the bed, her hands clenching the sheet above her head. Slowly, I work my way down her abdomen, watching it pull in every time I kiss lower. Her little moans and whimpers are driving me nuts, and I am struggling not to shove my dick straight into her.

As I work my way lower, her clean-shaven mound has me almost combusting. I groan. Hearing her giggle makes me smile.

"You like?" she teases.

"I definitely like," I rasp out while my tongue makes contact with her mound. Spreading her legs, I move lower. I love the smell of her arousal. Unable to wait anymore, I start eating at her like I'm ravenous.

Flicking my tongue over the hard nub of her clit, has her moaning and writhing. Licking slowly and deliberately from her clit to her entrance, parting her folds, cleaning her arousal, tasting it on my tongue, drives me as crazy as it does her. I can't stop myself from entering two fingers into her. A low growl leaves her as I do.

"You taste scrumptious." I smile, teasing her with my tongue, and leisurely fucking her with my fingers. I can feel her flutter around them. She's close.

"More," she begs. "Harder, Jamie!"

I love to hear my name on her lips and am happy to oblige. Entering a third finger, I fuck her deeper, hitting that sensitive spot inside her. I wrap my lips around her clit and suck hard. My girl comes with a scream, her pussy squeezing my hand again and again.

I flip her over onto her stomach and pull her up on her hands and knees, without giving her time to recover. I slide in with one forceful push and bury myself to the hilt. Her pussy is still squeezing, strangling my dick. Grinding my teeth, I count to ten, imagining my grandmother in her underwear and flannel nightgown, to stop me from shooting my load. When my eyes have uncrossed, I move. Slow at first, letting her catch her breath, but not for long. Soon I hammer into her with all the force I can muster.

"Yes, Jamie, oh God, yes," she moans. "Feels so good when you fuck me deep."

I change my angle, allowing myself to go even deeper. I can feel myself bottoming out on every hard stroke. Her pussy, hot and tight around me, crushing my dick.

"You are so hot and tight. My dick loves your pussy," I groan. I can feel my body heating and the unmistakable desperation to explode building. A tingle starts at the base of my spine, traveling upwards, building massive pressure, causing my balls to draw up.

"You're gonna make me come again!" she wails, and I can feel her walls flutter around me.

"Come for me, sweetheart!" I growl at her. Seconds later, she tightens around my dick, making it impossible to hold back anymore. I can feel myself losing control. My vision dims as an intense orgasm rips through me, preventing me from moving, other than to rut deep inside her; I hold on for dear life as it crashes over me.

Rolling to my side, taking her with me, both of us breathless and sated, it takes a while for us to catch our breaths and calm down. We just lay there, our hands roaming each other's bodies. For the first time in days I feel at peace with myself and the world, far removed from reality. We don't speak, just look at each other, while we continue to caress one another.

After a little while, I pull her up and into the shower with me. Grabbing her shower gel, I soap her body, taking time to shampoo and condition her hair, which she lets me do with a pleasurable groan, before I rinse her off. She then reciprocates, washing my body, making me hard again. The water is running cold by the time I fuck her silly again.

"You'll kill me one of these days. Is death by orgasm a real thing? I can think of worse ways to go." She winks at me, which has me throwing back my head and laughing.

"Are you complaining?" I inquire, not expecting an answer.

She throws her towel at me and giggles while sprinting into the bedroom. She digs through the drawers and throws on one of my T-shirts and sleep pants. I don't know why, but it makes me feel ten feet tall. I want to beat my chest like Donkey Kong and shout at the world, "Mine, she's mine!"

We walk into the front room and snuggle up on the sofa together.

"Thank you, Chloe," I tell her. My tone serious.

"Whatever for?" she asks, looking up at me.

"For caring for me, caring for my brothers, and not running away screaming, which I honestly couldn't blame you for," I admit.

"Also, for the ibuprofen and water this morning, and leaving me a pot of coffee." I smirk at her. "I really appreciated that more than you can imagine."

She throws her head back, laughing. I love that sound. Full and uninhibited.

"Did it work?" she asks, teasing me.

"Yes, it did, thank you." I smile and lean over to kiss her nose.

"And thank you, Chloe, for calling Ferret. It is not usual for the old ladies to get involved in club business, and normally I wouldn't condone it, but this time, I'll let it slide and just say thank you." She looks at me, her eyes serious.

"Raven, I'm not the girl you leave in the dark. I can cope with most things, as long as I know about them. The one thing that'd drive me away would be lies and secrets. I realize you can't share all club business with me, and I honestly wouldn't want you to. But whatever you do, don't leave me in the dark, or lie to me because you feel you need to protect me. I am a grown woman and have been around the bike scene for years. I can take it. And I need the truth to deal."

I nod. That is fair enough. I can be honest with her, even if I can't share everything with her.

She stands, grabs my hand, pulls me up and leads me into the bedroom, pushes me to the mattress and crawls up my body. I can see fire in her eyes, which has me harden in an instant. She grabs me by the root and lowers her mouth to my cock. I groan as I watch it disappear. The heat of her mouth scorches me. She takes me deep, all of me. Relaxes her throat and swallows around me, which has me hissing.

"You're killing me, babe," I grate out. She hums and sends vibrations all the way through my cock, straight to my balls. It's me who's fisting the sheets now, trying to not act on the need to fuck her mouth.

I move my hands into her hair, grabbing onto it, pulling on it, which has her humming and swallowing around me again, making me shout out. She increases the suction and pressure, making me see stars. When her hand goes to my balls, rolling them and squeezing them in her palm, I can't help but push my hips up into her. Humming again, she drives me crazy. She's not holding me back when I start fucking her mouth, swallowing around me when I hit the back of her throat. When she pulls tight on my balls and rolls them in her hand again, I can only shout and warn her.

"You need to stop, or I'll shoot down your throat." In reply, she ramps up the suction and swallows around me once more. My entire body tenses. I explode on her tongue and she swallows every drop of me. Only letting go when I start to soften. She crawls up and kisses me, our tongues dueling for domination. I don't mind that I can taste myself on her.

23 — CHLOE

Thank God, it's the weekend and I'm off work. The longer I stick at my job, the more frustrated I become. While I love working with cancer patients, it's had me in tears more than once. Flakey's just one recent example. It eats me up inside and I feel burnout approaching at lightning speed. Yet, every time I think about what else to do, I come up empty. I understand now why many medical staff seek solace in alcohol or drugs. Not that I do drugs at all or drink a lot, but I've bought a bottle of wine after a stressful shift.

I turn onto my side and watch Raven sleep. He looks so relaxed and chill. For the first time in over a week, he's sleeping soundly.

"Stop staring at me. It's weird," he mumbles at me before even opening his eyes.

"How did you know?" I ask him.

"It's Chloe-dar! I can sense when your attention is on me, and so can he." He grins, pointing at the tent under the sheets.

"Oh, is that right? Nice tent you're sporting, babe, are you going camping? Or would you like a hand taking it down?" I smirk at him. He stops laughing pretty fast after my hand wraps around him tight and gives him a few hard strokes.

A languid make-out session, and a few orgasms later, he turns towards me.

"What's bothering you?" he asks. I take a deep breath.

"Really? It's everything, and nothing. The job is tough and has me struggling emotionally. Don't get me wrong, I love it, but there are only so many times you can talk to someone about death, give them sad news, '*sorry there is nothing else we can do for you,*' even the elation of somebody successfully beating their cancer is draining. Because every time someone survives, I think about the ones that don't. It just doesn't feel like I am making a difference anymore." I shrug my shoulders, feeling lighter for just having voiced my thoughts and feelings.

"Can't even imagine what that must be like, babe, and am so proud of you, for doing what you do, being as professional as you are. But I do get not being happy. I can't tell or even advise you what to do, sweetheart. Only you know yourself well enough to know what's best for you. Know I've got a big shoulder for you to lean on, though. Am here for you and will support you with whatever you decide," he says, engulfing me in a hug.

This man! Now I'm choked up, struggling to hold back tears. Instead, I squeeze the living daylights out of him. I'm such a lucky bitch to have found him. The tough biker, who growls, snarls, and spits fire to protect his crazy family of weirdos. Only I see the soft man under the hard shell, making me feel awed and privileged, not to mention proud to be his, as he is mine.

◊◊◊

After a lazy morning, I finally get my ass into gear and head into town. We desperately need groceries and I want to check on my place. Open windows etc. and water the plants, making sure it's ready for Caroline and Dawg, once he's back. I tick off my to-do list until there's only Ally, Ashley, and Greg left on it. Since I'm in town already, paying a visit to Ally's is no hardship. As I walk in, Mom and Greg are sitting at one of the tables.

"What the hell are you doing here, Greg? Are you crazy? Your wounds haven't healed yet, and if you tear my stitches, I'll make sure you'll have a cross stitch pattern in your scars next time." Furious isn't the word I am looking for, I'm that pissed at the little shit. Mom throws her head back and laughs.

"Not funny," I tell her.

"Freaking women," Greg mutters under his breath, which has my hand going to my hip, cocking it at him, and glaring at him with the evil eye.

"Would you like to expand on that? Share with the class?"

"Couldn't stand being cooped up any longer with Spen and Mom hovering. For fuck's sake, I am a grown man. I make my own choices!" He growls. Actually, growls at me.

"I can see that, and such sensible ones, too." My voice drips with sarcasm while I point at the fresh blood stain in his jeans.

"Shit, God damn!" he swears, heading to the bathroom.

"I warned him, but he would've gone out on his own, on the damn bike, if I hadn't taken him." Mom rolls her eyes. "Men! Sometimes I wonder if they ever grow out of the defiant teenager stage."

"Fat chance in hell," Ally replies as she walks up to our table, four coffees in hand and a plate full of cupcakes.

"Had a call from Sparks this morning. Don't think they'll be much longer. All I could hear in the background was Vegas laughing and Dawg cussing, so I guess they're having fun." She smiles at Mom and me.

"You got a first aid kit, Ally?"

"Sure have, darlin. Why?" She looks at me.

210

"Can I grab it and help Greg out before he messes up my handiwork completely?" I reply, rolling my eyes.

"Sure, help yourself. It's hanging on the wall over there." She points at the hall behind the counter.

I get up, grab it, and make my way to the men's room. I open the door to find Greg with his jeans round his ankles, trying to dab at his opened stitches with a hand towel.

"You can't be in here!" he screeches like a girl, panic in his eyes.

"I can and I am! Now put that towel away, douche canoe, and let me change the dressing. See how much damage you've done? Idiot!" I yell right back.

His mouth flaps open and shut, like a fish, but he complies. As I remove the soaked-through bandage from his leg, I can see only one stitch torn, so I grab a wound closure strip, apply it, then rebandage the leg.

"You can pull your big girl panties up now, buddy," I tell him with a wink, as I gather the rest of the first aid kit, turn and walk out, feeling his glare on me. Now that was fun.

Spending another hour laughing, yes, at Greg, but also just having fun with Mom and Ally, we decide to leave Greg, after asking one of the staff to watch the naughty little boy—much to our entertainment and his embarrassment—to get our hair done while in town. We're lucky enough that the salon can accommodate us.

"Hi, Sharon," Ally greets the owner.

"What is it going to be this time?" Sharon grins at Ally.

"Well, let's see. How about half and half? I'd like the right side electric blue and the other side fire engine red please." She smiles at Sharon, who just laughs at her, propels her to a chair and gets started.

I decide on a trim and a manicure. The constant handwashing at work ruins my hands, so I'm gonna treat myself. Mom decides on a trim of her long black wavy hair, since she always wears it in a ponytail. Easy conversation and laughter keep us amused for the next couple of hours. When we leave, I feel like a normal person again. It's amazing what a manicure, haircut, and laughing with friends can do for your soul.

After releasing Ally's staff from babysitting duties, Mom takes a disgruntled Greg back, and I drive over to Ashley's. This time the gate opens as I drive up to the house. Caroline is on the step waiting for me.

"Thank God you're here!"

Not the greeting I was expecting.

"Ashley has been throwing up all day on and off. She's not looking too pretty!"

I sigh as I walk in to find Ashley in deep conversation with the toilet bowl, talking to the big man.

"Oh God, I'm dying. Make it stop already."

Stroking Ashley's hair, I sit with her as she continues to retch. When she finally feels she's done, I help her to the couch and get her a glass of water.

"No, no, no, I can't drink that. Even the mere thought makes me want to hurl again. And don't tell me I'm pregnant. It is two in the afternoon, so it's not morning sickness," she huffs.

"Okay, Ash, you are not pregnant," I try to reassure her with a smirk.

She glowers at Caroline. "See? I don't need a damn test!"

"Yeah… yeah, whatever," Caroline replies.

With a devious chuckle, I shoot a text to Ally.

"I think you could both do with a pinch of Ally, so I invited her over!" I smile at my sullen friends. Friends? Yes, it feels as though they are, despite not having known them for long.

Half an hour later, Ally arrives with a large paper bag.

"Coffee for you, Caroline, Mocha for you, Chloe, Coffee for me, orange juice for Ash… carrot cake, fresh out the bakery for all of us, oh, and this is for you, Ashley!" She smirks as she waves a fancy pregnancy test at her.

Ashley looks at me and Ally.

"You're such bitches," she whines, tears in her eyes.

Yup, hormonal!

"We love you, though. Now, if you are sure you are not pregnant, what have you got to lose?" I tease her.

"I'm scared," Ash whispers.

Ally gets up and grabs her by the hand. "Come on, girlfriend, I'll come with you."

"I can pee on a stick myself, thank you very much," Ash huffs.

"Yes, you can, but I need to make sure you don't dip it under the faucet instead. Denial, and all that!" Ally winks at her.

"You are no longer my best friend. You are the Devil!" Ashley stomps ahead of Ally into the bathroom. Two minutes later they reappear, a sulky Ashley, followed by an eye-rolling Ally, placing the stick on the kitchen island. Now the waiting begins.

Caroline and I are chatting, eating carrot cake, while Ashley bickers with Ally. Ash picks up a piece of carrot cake, her eyes go wide as she bites into it, and she groans as though she's having an out-of-body experience.

"Bitches, this is mine! I don't share," she declares, making us all grin.

213

Whilst she scarfs down almost a whole carrot cake, well apart from the piece that Caroline and I had, the timer dings. We all look expectantly at Ashley, who ignores all of us and the timer. Ally finally gets up, picks up the test, and walks over to us.

"Don't make me look," Ashley pleads with her.

"Stop being such an idiot and look!" Ally tells her in her no-nonsense voice.

Ash takes the test from a grinning Ally. She first turns as white as a ghost, then pink-cheeked, and a huge smile graces her face.

She jumps up and screams with tears running down her face.

"I'm pregnant!" Dancing around like a lunatic. We all join in, hugging her, dancing with her, laughing and crying with her. The stick tells her four weeks, which coincides with the rally.

"Oh my God, what is Vegas going to say? This is way, way too soon!" Ashley's voice quivers and her breathing has sped up.

"Calm down, Ash!" Ally says calmly. "Concentrate on your breathing. Slowly, in… and out." Ashley follows Ally's instructions and averts the looming panic attack.

"Vegas will love it! He told you he wants to see you growing with his baby, before and after he proposed. He'll be a super dad and you an awesome mom!" Caroline reassures her.

"Yes, but it's so soon! I'm not ready!"

"Ashley, no mother in the world is ever ready. Same as there is never an ideal time. You'll rock this pregnancy and mom shit! Plus, you have lots of crazy aunties to babysit for you!" I hug Ashley tight.

"I can just see Vegas being an alpha daddy," Ally jokes.

"God help her if it is a girl, she won't be dating until she is fifty, and each time a boy comes to pick her up, Vegas will sit there, cleaning his shotgun!"

Ashley's eyes go wide at Ally's statement, while we all struggle not to pee ourselves laughing.

"Girls, please keep this to yourselves for now," Ashley begs us. "With everything going on and their run, they have enough on their plates, and I need to tell Vegas first."

"Okay," we all agree.

"But do it soon, Ashley. He ought to know," I tell her gently.

"I know, and I will. Pinky promise," she replies. After another hour, I make my excuses and drive home.

The sight that greets me as I drive onto clubhouse property is not one I'll forget in a hurry. The parking lot is full of bikes, a van, and people are bustling around with grim faces. Most of the patches read Restless Slayers MC, with only the few Stormy Souls left behind mixed in. It scares the living shit out of me. In the center stands Raven, surrounded by the Slayers' officers, tension so thick, you could cut it with a blunt knife.

"Hello there, gentlemen, nice to see you so soon again," I trill as I get out of my car, trying not to let the growly men's atmosphere intimidate me.

"Are you staying overnight?" I ask, and a very serious Ghoul nods at me.

"Okay, I'll get the girls to make the guest rooms ready for you and then help Mom in the kitchen to fix you a meal. You must be hungry and thirsty from the ride." I smile, trying to disarm them. And it partially works. Ghoul has a smile for me, which sets Raven's teeth on edge, and Fury nods at me.

A girl steps out from behind Masher, the Slayers SAA.

"Hi, I'm Tanya, Masher's daughter. I think we met before at the rally. You were the girl who won the slow riding contest against our club?" She smiles at me.

215

"Hi, Tanya, yes indeed, I am. Thanks to your club for lending me a bike." I grin, winking at her.

"Wanna come inside and help me?" I ask her.

"Sure, let's go. Way too much testosterone out here!" she teases, hugging her dad, who smiles softly at her. While walking up the stairs and into the main room, I have to ask myself, *What is she doing here? She can't be older than twenty. Why would Masher bring her along?*

After getting the guest rooms ready, I join Tanya with Mom in the kitchen where I left them, preparing a humongous pot of chili with a mountain of grated cheese, tortilla chips, and floured tortillas. I show Tanya where the plates are, and we set the large dining table with bowls for chili and cheese. We grab a ton of beers from the bar, place one next to each plate and hope for the best.

Mom walks out, calling in the guys, and within no time hungry, grumpy, stressed-out bikers fill the kitchen. The meal goes on in silence, with just me, Tanya, and Mom making conversation.

"Nice nails," Tanya comments on my new nails in rainbow colors with tiny, sparkling butterfly applications.

"Don't let the growly bears intimidate you," she whispers. "I've grown up with these men. They are angry, and on a mission. So am I, but normally their bark is worse than their bite. It'll all sort itself out in the end." She tries to reassure me. However, I remain doubtful.

24 — RAVEN

"ETA about one hour." Vegas's tired voice comes through the cell I have on speaker so Fury, Ghoul, and Masher can listen in.

"Don't worry, I haven't broken him, just played with him a little on the way," Dawg throws in. "What can I say? I got bored!" His laughter sounds slightly maniacal.

Vegas groans and I can hear Pennywise chuckle.

"Don't worry, Raven, he's conscious and alive, just as you asked. Got to say, though, I learned a thing or two about Dawg. That man is a lunatic." We can hear Rusty groaning in the background.

"He's mine!" Fury grates. "No further damage to the dickweed. I don't care what Raven said." On that note, I hang up on the guys.

"Where are ya gonna keep him?" Ghoul asks. So, I take them all up to the bunker, or what we call the dugout. It's the place we conduct our more... nefarious business.

An old World War II bunker, which we converted into holding cells, and a main room that sports a large drain just off the center. We have shackles on the wall, ceiling, and floor that can be raised or lowered with a remote. There's a bench with a variety of tools and instruments belonging to Pennywise, as well as electricity, a water supply, and plenty of seats.

Masher whistles. "Nice set-up. Fury, we could do with one of these."

217

As glad as I am that he's impressed, the thought of having Rusty in here soon makes me feel itchy. Itchy to get on with it and let him have his just desserts.

Chloe went home over an hour ago and I decide to end the guided tour here. Exhaustion makes my limbs feel like lead, and for the first time, I feel my age. I look at Fury. His drawn face speaks volumes. I don't blame him for the way he's been acting. I'd be the same if someone raped my daughter. The thought makes me shudder and I'm more certain than ever that kids are nowhere in my future. I'm getting too up there in years and who knows what could happen with the life I lead. You could be there one minute, gone the next. It wouldn't be fair to Chloe. Which reminds me, we'll have to revisit this topic and have a discussion. I am not opposed to a vasectomy. At least I won't ruin any kid's life like my parents did mine.

◊◊◊

Over an hour later, the rumble of bikes announces the arrival of our *honored* guest. As the van and bikes roll into the property, a large welcome wagon is waiting for them. Vegas, Dawg and Pennywise get out of the van, while Clusseaud and the others park their bikes. "Wow, what a welcome home party," Dawg jokes. "Your local parcel delivery service has arrived, faster than UPS and with satisfaction guaranteed." He winks.

For the first time in days, I can hear snickers of withheld laughter from the men.

Pennywise steps up to Masher and Fury.

"Would you like to give me a hand, showing our guest to his new quarters?" He smirks. Within less than a second, Fury is at the van, door open, dragging a hog-tied, gagged Rusty out of the loading bay, smashing his fist straight into his face.

"Ohhh," Dougal hisses. "That's gotta hurt!" He turns and walks into the clubhouse, straight to the bar. Fury, Masher and Pennywise transport Rusty to the dugout, and everyone else follows Dougal.

As beers are being passed around, Vegas nods his head towards the office. When we get inside and close the door, he sits in front of my desk and puts his feet up. Normally I'd kick his ass, but this once, I'll let it slide.

"We caught him as he was coming out of the pharmacy. He didn't see it coming but made no fuss to start with. He knew he didn't have a chance in hell of getting away," Vegas reports.

"There were five of us and only one of him. Dawg went a tad crazy, and I didn't have the heart to stop him."

His evil smirk tells me he quite enjoyed Dawg's antics.

"I want to know where he learned all that stuff? Need to go to Dawg school."

My eyebrows hit my hairline as I wait for him to continue.

"He made us stop at a hardware store, bought sandpaper and denatured alcohol. I bought the shit and asked him if he was gonna paint and decorate when we got back. The crazy ass just grinned at me, took Rusty's boots off, and threw them out of the window. He had Pennywise pin him down, then proceeded to sandpaper Rusty's toes. I mean, he took the skin of the tips straight off. Man, did his cheesy feet stink up the van. Gonna have to air that shit out." Vegas takes a sip of his beer.

"Then he told Rusty his feet needed cleaning. It was only when I heard Rusty's muffled screams that I turned round and watched Dawg, not only tipping alcohol all over Rusty's raw toes, but rubbing it in as well. Rusty passed out and Dawg called him a sissy."

I can't help but chuckle at the animated retelling of their journey back.

219

"How's the prospect?" Vegas asks.

"He's doing okay. Pissed Chloe off today and apparently screeched like a girl. I can see a road name coming on. Mom could hardly breathe. She was laughing so hard when she told me the story. Chloe threatened to turn his scars into cross stitch." I laugh at Vegas.

"Oh, let me see… Screecher? Needlework? Cross stitch? The possibilities are endless." Vegas's evil grin makes me glad he's my brother and not my enemy.

"Thanks, man, for taking charge of this. Appreciate it, brother," I tell him, slapping his back.

"No sweat, Prez, anytime. Are you okay with me taking off now? I got a woman at home who is due to scream my name tonight."

I slap him round the back of the head.

"That's my sister, you dirty fucker! TMI!" His laughter follows him out to the bar. Next, the door opens, and Fury, and Pennywise, enter.

"You got Rusty. Now hand over Slender and Ellie," I grate at Fury between clenched teeth. Fury nods, walks to the door, and whistles.

Less than a minute later, both Ellie and Slender were escorted into the office. Ellie looks at her feet, shaking, and Slender, poor Slender. His face is hard to recognize and the fingers on his right hand look broken.

"You bastard!" I hiss at Fury. Right now, I'd like to put a bullet in his head more than anything else.

"You knew we were on the case; you knew. I kept you up to date on everything that happened," I seethe at him, trying not to reach over and strangle him.

"Calm your tits," Fury states. "Chill. We haven't done much damage. His pretty face will heal. You needed an incentive."

I stand and walk towards Fury, ready to lay him out, as Pennywise steps in front of me. "Don't do it, man, keep your head," he hisses at me. I straighten my shoulders and give him a curt nod.

"Pennywise, can you take Ellie and Slender up to his room? I'll ask Chloe to come and see to them." Pennywise nods and leads Slender and Ellie out of the room. I make a call to Chloe.

"Hey, sweetheart, could you come over and have a look at Slender and Ellie please? Slender is a bit… worse for wear," I sigh.

"Sure, babe, I'll be right over. Let me just grab my kit," she answers, voice heavy, knowing I wouldn't have asked had I not been worried.

Looking at Fury's scraped knuckles, I scoff.

"Well, looks like you got an early start on Rusty. Hope you don't mind if we reconvene tomorrow morning. I'm beat." Fury looks as if he'd like nothing better than to shoot me but walks to the bar. I turn, switch the office lights off, and lock the door. Never had to do that before.

I make my way up to Slender's room to check on him and Ellie. Ellie is sitting on the bed crying, stroking Slender's hair, who's laid on top of the covers, caked in crusty dried blood.

"I'm so sorry, man."

"No need, Prez. He'd have taken it out on one of us. Rather me than her," he grinds out, hissing in pain, looking at Ellie.

"Watching what they did was difficult, believe me." Her voice trembles as she speaks.

221

She looks at me, and I struggle to contain my anger.

"They made you watch?" I growl. She nods her head in confirmation.

"They wanted me to see what they'd do to Rusty and to me if you didn't find Rusty in time. They would have shot him." She nods to Slender, still shaking.

The door opens and Chloe walks in with a bottle of whiskey, her medical kit, and a few glasses. Taking one look at Ellie, she pours a double and encourages her to drink it. She repeats the same with Slender and me, then gets to work. I take Ellie outside as she straightens his nose. That's gonna hurt like a bitch and she's seen him suffer enough. There's no need for her to witness this as well.

By the time Chloe calls us in, she has cleaned Slender's face, washed the blood out of his hair, and bandaged him up as much as possible. He doesn't look as gruesome now as he did when they led him in.

"We'll leave you be now," Chloe tells them and grabs my hand. "Ellie, my number is on the dresser. If you are at all concerned about him, call me. He might have a concussion, so try not to let him get up until the morning, see how he feels. I left some pain relievers on the dresser. Give him two every four hours. He should sleep with them and feel better in the morning. But as I said, call me if you think you need me. I'll come over, no matter what time of day or night." Ellie nods while Chloe gives her a one-armed hug and drags me out of the room.

She stays silent as we make our way through the clubhouse, but I don't miss the filthy look she shoots Ghoul, who has the decency to look down at his hands, knowing full well what pissed her off. If Ghoul ever thought that Chloe might have liked him at all, that feeling is now dead and gone.

Outside, she lets go of my hand and walks towards Clusseaud, who's still sitting on his bike, smoking a cigarette. I watch from a distance as she speaks to him. He gets off the bike, hugs her tight, and they stand there talking for a few minutes. Then Chloe kisses him on the cheek and makes her way back to me. We make the brief journey to the house in silence.

The silence is deafening, and I don't know what to say to her. This is the point where she's realized that although we are legit, we are no choir boys for sure, and this is only going to pan out one way. Bloody and deadly. I don't know how to reassure her and can feel the distance gaping between us like a chasm.

The knock on the door rips me out of my musings. I open it and there's Clusseaud. Wringing his hands and running them through his hair, like a mad professor.

Stepping aside, I let him in. He sits on the sofa opposite me and Chloe.

He clears his throat. "I went to the dugout just now and spoke to that rat bastard."

He looks at Chloe. "I am so sorry, sweetheart, that I ever doubted you. I shouldn't have. You were right. He told me everything. Even that he knew Terrie was pregnant."

A gasp comes from Chloe and her hands go to her mouth.

"What?" she whispers, utterly shocked.

"He had a PI on her for a year after she left. That's how he found out she was pregnant. He set the whole thing up. Starting with the club bunny in my room that night. He also told Terrie afterwards that I had been fucking the bunnies forever. Which is a goddamn lie."

Chloe repeats, "He knew?"

"Yes, he did, and he made sure we were kept apart by feeding your mother and me lies about each other. I loved your mother more than anything. It killed me when she left, and for a time, I turned into a real asshole. A womanizing asshole. It took years for me to get over Terrie, to not think about her every day, to not wonder what she was doing, how she was, where she was. But in the end, I had to rebuild myself and get on with life. Chloe, I promise, had I known of your existence, I'd have fought. For you and for Terrie. I can't turn back time. All I can ask is for you to forgive me and maybe let us build our relationship now. The one they cheated us out of from the very beginning." He stands, so does Chloe, tears running down her face. She walks to Clusseaud and throws herself at him. He catches her, holding her tight in his arms, both faces soaked in tears.

"It's okay, Dad, we found each other now. Some positive has come out of Flakey's tragedy," she sobs into his chest. He just nods and strokes her back.

"I wish it didn't happen this way, but yet, it has. I'm sure he's up there looking down, smiling at us," Clusseaud replies.

Clusseaud and Chloe stay in the front room, talking. They have a lot of years to catch up on. I lean down and kiss Chloe's cheek.

"I'm beat, babe, and gonna head to bed. You do your thing. Clusseaud, you're welcome to stay on the couch if you like. It'll give you two some time and space to catch up."

"Thanks, brother." Clusseaud smiles at me. A genuine smile I haven't seen in God knows how long. It soothes my wired thoughts, and as I hit the mattress I am dead to the world within a second flat.

My alarm wakes me, I turn to find Chloe already out of bed. Jumping in the shower, I scrub the sleep out of my eyes, get dressed, and make my way to the front room, where Chloe and Clusseaud stand, joking, drinking coffee. Good, seems they worked things out last night. She turns to me and hands me coffee, visibly more relaxed now.

I take the cup, pull her to me, and wrap her close. She puts her head on my chest and lets out a deep sigh. I know she's found the calm she was looking for by the way her shoulders relax. Clusseaud looks at me and nods. He sees it too. It's only seven a.m., and I already know it's going to be a helluva long day. One that will stay burned into my memory forever.

"Hey, sweetheart, why don't you call Ally, Sarah, and Caroline? You could have a girls' day?" I want her as far away from here as possible.

"Sensible idea, honey. I might ask Tanya if she wants to come along, too."

"Sounds like a great idea, Chloe," Clusseaud joins the conversation. I know he's with me on this one, one hundred percent.

After breakfast, she calls the girls. They arrange to meet at nine at Ally's. We walk over to the clubhouse, where she disappears upstairs. I can only assume to check on Slender and Ellie, and to speak to Tanya.

They come down the stairs, and to my amazement, Ellie's with them. Tanya walks up to Fury and Masher, gives her dad a kiss and whispers something in Fury's ear, to which he only nods.

The three girls wave and walk out to Chloe's car. We watch them from the window as they get in and drive off.

"You have breakfast?" I ask Fury.

"Yup, had breakfast an hour ago."

I shrug my shoulders and turn to the men who are all in the bar. "Let's go!"

Every single one follows Fury and me out of the door and up to the dugout. Rusty's payday has finally come.

25 — CHLOE

The door chimes at Ally's as Tanya, Ellie, and I walk in. Ally, Sarah, Ashley, and Caroline are already in a booth.

"How are you feeling, Caroline?"

"Much better, Chloe, thank you. Dawg picked me up last night and waited on me hand and foot. Thanks again for letting us stay at your apartment." She smiles at me, her voice almost croak free now.

"That's fantastic," Ellie adds, clapping her hands.

"I don't know about you, girls, but I have to say, with Dougal, absence makes the heart grow fonder, was definitely true." Sarah wiggles her eyebrows.

"Oh, come on!" laughs Ashley. "They've only been away a couple of days!"

"And? I bet you got it good from Vegas last night!" Ally pipes up. Ellie is snorting, trying to suppress her laughter.

"Don't make the single girl jealous," she teases. I keep a close eye on her; neither I, nor Ashley, nor Sarah have missed her constant hand wringing. But this is not the time or place to have that conversation.

"Well, I sure couldn't complain last night," Caroline interjects, causing Ally to howl like a dog.

Tanya roars with laughter. "You all are too funny! I'm gonna choke to death on my coffee."

At that precise moment, Ashley changes color, gets up, and sprints to the ladies' room. Ally, Caroline, and I look at each other, smirking.

"What? What have I missed?" Sarah looks from one to the other, with Ellie and Tanya following with interest. I shrug my shoulders.

"Not our story to tell, Sarah." Knowing that she'll now be like a bloodhound on a trail. Ashley has zero chance of getting out of this one now.

A very pale Ashley returns to the table. "You alright?" Ally asks.

"Hmm-hmm." Ash nods.

"Spill it, sister. What's going on?" Unable to keep from grinning, I watch the drama unfold as Sarah gets her hooks into Ashley, who pleadingly looks from Ally to me and back to Ally, a big "HELP" sign flashing above her head.

"What's happening?" Tanya whispers to me, I just shake my head.

"Just watch," I snicker.

Ashley is shifting uncomfortably in her chair as we all watch the drama unfold.

"Ashley Saunders! You tell me right this moment what's going on or I won't let you have Leo next weekend!" Sarah's full-on glare hits a helpless Ashley.

We can see the moment she caves. "I'm pregnant," she whispers.

"You what?" Sarah jumps up and looks at her best friend as though she's grown two heads.

"I'm pregnant," Ashley says a little louder and then, "Oh my God, I'm pregnant!" she screeches, smiling from ear to ear.

Sarah jumps up and down, smiling the biggest smile I've ever seen.

"That's great news. Congratulations! Does Vegas know? What'd he say? When are you due? I'll be a godparent, right?" Sarah is on a roll now, peppering Ashley with question after question.

"Stop!" Ashley yells at her friend. "I only found out yesterday and am so sick every day I haven't thought about anything else yet. Other than tying my hair back in the mornings so I don't get vomit in it. I haven't even confirmed it with the doctor, and no, I haven't told Vegas yet, I'll do that tonight. So please, keep that gigantic trap of yours shut. Otherwise, I'll withdraw godmother privileges." She smirks at Sarah.

"Oh, you wouldn't dare!" Sarah replies in mock outrage that has us falling over each other, laughing.

"Watch me," Ashley sasses back. "I need some fresh air. Mind if we walk through the park for a bit?" Ashley looks green around the gills.

"Sure, let's do that. Be nice to stretch the legs a little." Tanya smiles and shuffles out of the crowded booth.

The park is just around the corner, and we stroll around the large pond in its center. Ally brought some bread, so she, Caroline and I feed the ducks, while Sarah is talking Ashley's ear off. Tanya is standing further away by the benches, in deep conversation with Ellie, who looks uncomfortable. No one could blame her. Only yesterday she was a hostage of Tanya's father's club and had to watch Slender's beating.

Somehow, I have a feeling that Tanya is one tough cookie. She grew up in the club, lives and breathes it. I'm just hoping she doesn't upset Ellie further. Not her fault that her brother is worse than a sewer rat.

But to my surprise, I watch Ellie and Tanya hug, and a load of worry seems to fall from Ellie's shoulders. They return to us and feed the ducks as though nothing ever happened. On the way back, I trail behind the others with Ellie.

"Are you alright, hon?" I look at her, gentling my tone.

"Yeah, I'm okay. Tanya talked to me and apologized for what the club put me through. I cannot believe that Rusty raped that poor girl. I met Meghan, you know; she came to see me when we first got there and talked to me. She is such a sweet girl. I wish I could reverse what he did, but I can't." She sighs. "The poor girl will carry this with her for the rest of her life! I wish I had the guts to make him pay myself." She looks forlorn as she word vomits all this up.

"I know he needs to pay, and I know he'll pay with his life. He deserves it, Chloe. He's my brother, and at some point, I loved him unconditionally, but he has changed beyond all recognition. Turned into a wild animal. No one can put him on the right path anymore. He deserves what he is getting. He did it to me too, you know?" She looks at me with hazy eyes.

"Please tell me you are joking, Ellie, I thought you said he didn't touch you that way?" My heart almost stops. Watching the pain in her eyes makes it even more real.

"Well, I lied. I was too scared he'd find out and kill me. Please, Chloe, don't tell anyone about this. I have nightmares every night and almost all men scare me now. But most of all, *he* scares me. I know I need help and I promise I'll get it when this is over, but I can't deal with all of it simultaneously."

Swallowing back the bile rising in my throat and my deep-seated hatred for Rusty, I put my arm around Ellie.

"Ellie, no one can tell you how to deal with this and I am so sorry this happened to you. You know I'm here for you, right? You can talk to me any time, any place. And of course, I'll keep this private. Just promise me you'll come to me if you need me."

Ellie's eyes shine with gratitude. Gratitude I don't deserve, since I've done exactly nothing, but I take her smile when she breathes a quiet: "Thank you, I promise."

We spend another hour walking aimlessly, chatting, until we return to the diner, where Ashley wolfs down an enormous piece of carrot cake and an order of chamomile tea, which has all of us shuddering in disgust.

"Don't argue with the pregnant lady," she sasses.

◊◊◊

All the ladies are now seated in the clubhouse bar. After Tanya received a phone call, she asked to be taken back, and as one, we all left together. We are the only ones sitting around since the men are still noticeably absent. I have a vague idea of where they are, but despite my hatred for Rusty, I wish I was wrong.

When the door opens and most of the men file in, all it takes is one look at their grim faces and blood splattered clothing to know that, despite all my wishing, I was right. It's strange to think that as a nurse, someone who helps preserve life, I'm even sitting in the same room with men who are going to be murderers. At least, most of them are going to be. Even though in part, I agree with their decision, at the same time I wish it wasn't necessary and could be dealt with by the police.

Yet, as a nurse, I have seen so many rape victims; I know that a lot of cases don't make it to trial, and those that do can take years, leaving the victims of this heinous crime with little support, or resources to pick themselves up. Plenty of suicide attempts went through our hospital

ER during my time there. I believe Ellie when she tells me Rusty won't change, and I am well aware he's put others through hell. Even if Rusty went to prison, Stone has always supported him, so it's very unlikely that he would suffer the consequences other rapists do when inside.

So, while I struggle with my conscience—and I am struggling hard—I agree he has to be removed from society. He's been a menace for too long already and left his mark on too many people. My mother, Ashley's mother, Ashley herself, Sarah, Ellie, Meghan, myself. The list goes on and on. Those are just the ones we know about. It's unlikely that we are the only ones.

Vegas moves over to Ash and draws her close. He wraps her in his arms and whispers to her. She looks up at him, fear written all over her face, swallows, and nods.

Slender limps to Ellie, talks to her and she nods as well.

Raven looks at me. I make my way across the room to him and wrap my arms around his middle.

"Hey, Raven, you look beat. Anything I can do for you?" I snuggle closer to him, needing to feel his presence.

He sighs.

"No, darlin, nothing you can do for me. Nothing anyone can do." Showing his own struggle with the situation.

"Vegas and Slender want Ashley and Ellie to have a chance to look him in the face. Give them a chance to purge and say what they need to say to him. I disagree with that, but they have outvoted me." He looks down at me, dark circles under his eyes.

"I agree with them, Raven. I'll tell you why too. They've been so affected by his behavior for all of their lives. It's important for them to get closure in one form or another. Let them have their say, but don't let them witness the end. They don't need that to be the last image they see of him."

Raven looks at me, frowning.

"Hmm, never thought of it that way. Maybe you're right. Maybe they deserve to have the choice to gain some closure. Chloe, I have to ask you. Are you able to support them? Are you willing to come with us and take them outside before things get out of hand? I can't guarantee that this will not get really ugly before they are back outside."

His words make me think. *Can I? Will I be able to support them through the day? Am I strong enough to not get damaged by this myself? Is this too much to ask of me?* The questions are pelting me like hailstones. I look into Raven's eyes, they calm me a little and he just holds me, aware of my internal battle.

Taking a deep breath, I answer, "Yes, Raven, I can support them. I can handle it. I'll take them outside as soon as they had their say."

He nods and draws me closer. The metallic odor of blood, a smell I'm very familiar with, clings to his cut. I push away, walk behind the bar, and get a damp cloth. He looks at me and is about to protest, but I leave his cut alone. Instead, I wipe a few blood spatters off his face before I lean in to kiss him.

It's not a hot, steamy kiss by any stretch of the imagination, but a warming, comforting, loving one. Showing him I am here with him, for him, and will support him whatever may come at us. I'm his and he's mine forever.

Never more certain than I am right now that I want to take care of this man and my new crazy conflicted, rowdy family, for better for worse.

232

We are no spring chickens anymore, both of us over thirty, heading for forty, knowing my time for kids has come and gone. I'd hate to be an older parent, my kids being asked who the grandma is picking them up from school, but I want to be with my man and our family for the rest of my life. I know that for certain.

Sarah and Dougal are still in a heated discussion. Sarah finally loses her temper.

"I know! I don't want to see him, asshole. Have nothing to say to the scumbag, but you will not stop me from being there for Ashley. If you think that's how this will work, you can fuck right off!"

The room goes silent as Sarah stomps over to Ashley and Vegas.

Dougal rolls his eyes, throws his arms up in defeat and spits, "Damn women!" before stomping off in the opposite direction, causing Dawg and several others to chuckle under their breath.

26 — RAVEN

Making the trip to the dugout this morning was tough. This is one of our own, disgraced beyond belief, not just himself but the entire club with it, and despite everything he remains unrepentant. I take no delight in what comes next but pull my Prez britches up and get on with what needs to be done.

As we enter the room, they've already moved Rusty from the cell. He's shackled to the floor and ceiling, and stretched so only his toes remain on the floor. He's buck naked, not a pretty sight, and not just because Dawg and Fury had some fun with him. I watch him dance on his bleeding raw toes, hissing when his toes come in contact with the puddle under them. From the smell, I believe it's alcohol of some sort. That must sting like a bastard.

Fury stands next to me. Masher, Slender and Pennywise are ambling around the trussed-up Rusty, whose face is bloody and his body bruised. We nod at Masher, Penny, and Slender. Time to get this party started.

"So, dickweed, tell me," Masher starts, looking Rusty straight in the eye. "Did you stick your puny dick into one of ours? Our family? Our princess?!" His voice increases with each sentence until he is bellowing. Rusty turns his face away, not answering.

Masher rewards him by letting each Restless Slayer step forward, each beating and kicking him. Rusty, spitting out a few teeth and some blood, grins at Masher.

234

"You ain't breaking me, you little fucker!"

"Oh, really?" Masher asks calmly.

"Did you hear that, Pennywise? He still thinks he has the upper hand. What do you think?"

"Time to teach him a thing or two," Pennywise replies, his serenity belying his anger. As though he ordered a beer at the bar. He walks to his bench and weighs a short knife in his hand as if to test the weight.

Smiling at Rusty as he comes into his line of vision, he turns to Slender.

"Hey, I heard nipples are the most sensitive part of a woman's body. You think that applies to men as well?"

"Wouldn't be able to say, dude, that's a cockroach in front of you, not a man," Slender replies evenly, using a knife to clean his nails as if bored.

"Might have to test that."

Within a blink of an eye, Penny has the knife on Rusty's chest, drawing a thin line from his neck to the center of his sternum. Just a shallow cut, enough for blood to gather.

"Eli, bring the matches," he commands.

Eli complies, stands at Penny's side, box of matches in hand, waiting for instructions.

"Strike a match and heat the knife with it. You better do a solid job, else cauterizing the next cut won't work and the roach will bleed all over my floor."

Eli nods, strikes a match and holds it under the knife. He repeats it about ten times until Eli grunts, "Fuck this." Before heading back over to the bench, grabbing the gas torch and firing it up, to heat the knife.

Penny grins at him.

"I think Striker here got tired!"

Everyone roars with laughter. Quite a story to tell when Striker gets asked about his road name, and how it was given by Pennywise.

Pennywise turns back to Rusty,

"Pliers, nurse!" he orders Striker, as though they're doing an operation. Striker hands him a pair of pliers.

"Wouldn't want to burn my fingers now." And with that, clamps a nipple in the pliers and slices it clean off.

Rusty's screams are such high pitch, everyone winces.

Penny repeats this with the other nipple, holds his hand out to Striker, who hands him a bottle.

"Now then, Rusty, since you're supposed to be a brother, I don't want infection to set in. Let me clean this for you!" He pours the medicated alcohol Striker passed him over Rusty's chest, running through the shallow cut and the removed, burned skin of where his nipples used to be. Rusty screams and passes out.

"Damn it, good one, Pennywise, will have to put that trick in my toolbox." Masher slaps Pennywise on the shoulder.

"Don't worry, folks, I got more where that came from. For entertainment value. Striker, you good?" he asks. Striker looks green and swallows hard. We forget that prospects now don't deal with wet work so much. The members who have been around longer remember the time where this was part of our daily routine.

Pennywise walks over to the hose.

"Oh, please, let me!" Dougal begs, chuckles going around the room.

"Be my guest, man."

Dougal grabs the hose, turns on the water supply, steps in front of Rusty and opens the spigot.

When we say hose, we're talking about a fire hose, not a garden one. It would take too long to clean the floors with one of those, hence we invested in the higher-grade option. The water comes from our own well and is ice cold.

Dougal points it straight at Rusty's head. As Rusty comes round coughing and spluttering, unable to deal with the amount of water entering his mouth, nose and eyes.

Dougal shouts over the hose noise, "I always wanted to wash your filthy mouth out. Don't need soap for that."

After about a minute, he stops and puts the hose away as we watch Rusty dangle and cough up water.

Masher steps up to Rusty again.

"Man, I'm getting hungry. Anyone else for BBQ? The smell of smoked flesh just does that to me."

I've heard about Masher's penchant for cooking equipment, but never seen it in action. Though I am not prepared for what he has in mind.

"Ghoul, care to assist?" He grins at Ghoul, who rubs his hands with an evil smile, and walks straight to the workbench, picking up a baton, a hammer, and to my surprise some BBQ skewers. He turns to the crowd and bows.

"Ladies and gentlemen, thank you for your kind demonstrations and rapt attention so far. I shall make sure you won't get bored. Please, can I ask my glamorous assistant Fury to step forward?" Masher asks as Fury steps forward, smiling from ear to ear.

237

He grips the baton.

"Could you lower the shackles and get him into a comfortable position so he can enjoy the full effect of his little treat?" Fury asks with glee in his eyes.

Chains rattle from the ceiling and Rusty flops like a fish, weak and groaning. Someone kicks a chair into the middle.

"That'll do. Thank you very much," Fury states, smiling at the room.

Rusty starts thrashing as Penny, Slender, Masher and Ghoul throw him over the chair and hold him down.

"Lube, please. We want your fat ass to enjoy this, don't we?" Fury commands.

Ghoul throws him a can of WD40, which he sprays liberally onto the baton, making Rusty struggle harder.

"Do you know what it feels like to be helpless and raped?" Fury snarls. Without further ado, he takes the baton and rams it up Rusty's ass as far as it will go, making Rusty scream like a pig in the slaughterhouse.

"Now you do! Enjoy, fucker!" Fury screams and fucks Rusty with the baton, again and again, until the only thing coming from Rusty is whimpering. Fury removes the club, throws it to the side with disgust, and walks back to my side, huffing. The chains rattle again, pulling Rusty up to his feet.

Masher smirks.

"Fury, you opened his asshole too wide, man. I don't wanna see that shit from over here!"

"Let me help you with that then," Ghoul announces. He steps up to Rusty, who is by now only hanging in his chains, his head lolling, but his eyes opening once in a while, showing he's still conscious.

Ghoul stands to the side of Rusty, takes a metal skewer and the hammer, shoving the first skewer all the way through Rusty's left buttock into the right until just the ring sticks out. He puts the hammer on the floor.

"Huh, will you look at that! Didn't even need the hammer. There was enough fat in his ass for it to slide right through," Ghoul says like it shocked him while Rusty is moaning and hissing. Ghoul changes sides and repeats the process with the second skewer, which has Rusty screaming.

"Oh, did that hurt? Sorry, Rusty, my bad. I'll take your mind off it in just a second!" He grabs the hammer and a nine-inch rusty nail and drives it straight into Rusty's hip. I don't think I ever heard screams quite like it. After repeating the procedure on the other side, Rusty passes out again. The room smells of fear, piss, shit, and sweat, making me nauseous.

"Let's take a break and let him come to on his own," I announce.

Vegas, Dougal and Slender step up to us.

"I want Ashley to have the chance to come down here and tell him what she thinks of him." he states. Dougal and Slender nod.

"Same for Sarah and Ellie, though I'd rather Sarah didn't see this," Dougal chips in.

Fury answers for me.

"Tanya is here with me. She was the one who looked after Meghan, and she's furious. She wants her own go at him. I'm planning on letting her after we get back!"

"I am against letting the women in here. They don't need to see this," I argue.

"Okay, let's put it to the vote," says Fury.

"Anyone for the women having a chance at their revenge?" Fury asks, and eighteen hands go up in the air without hesitation.

"Anyone against?" This time four hands go up, including mine.

I don't like it but can no longer argue. Outvoted, I turn and walk up the stairs to the open air. All of us make our way to the clubhouse, where we find the ladies sitting in the bar.

◊◊◊

It takes Chloe to explain to me that the girls may need closure, to understand why having the option is important to them. I made clear, watching and seeing Rusty will impact them and may leave them more scarred than they already are. But it made me realize it ain't my decision to make, it's theirs. Chloe said she'll be there to support them, although I wonder if she's taking on too much here, struggling with work demands as it is.

After an hour, we all make our way back to the dugout. The men walk in first, dispersing through the room, and putting a few chairs out for the girls to sit on.

Only Tanya remains standing, hands shaking, and face contorted in rage and anguish, wrapped in Masher's arms, who whispers to her. I watch Vegas caring for my sister, who shakes like a leaf. Slender has his arm around Ellie, who sits on his lap with her head buried in his chest. Sarah sits next to Ashley with Dougal and Vegas bracketing them. They're pale but hanging in there. Chloe is by my side, holding my hand, squeezing tight. Outwardly, that is the only sign she's showing of the emotional rollercoaster going on inside her.

Chloe takes a closer look, standing up front with me. She gasps as she spots the burned open wounds on his chest and leans against me, head pressed into my shoulder as she notices the skewers through his buttocks, keeping them together. Rusty is a mumbling mess.

240

Fury steps into the middle of the room.

"Ladies, we wanted to give you the opportunity to tell Rusty whatever the hell you need to tell him. Or exact your own vengeance if you like. It's an opportunity. You do not have to do anything if you do not want to and we'll understand if you'd rather leave. We'll carry on our vengeance here, so if you are squeamish, I suggest you leave now. No one will think any the less of you," Fury addresses the ladies.

Ellie steps forward, holding Slender's hand, tears rolling down her face. It's plain to see her grief, her pain, disappointment, but also her resignation. She leans into Slender, as though he's her life raft, her eyes going wide when she gets closer to Rusty, crying harder.

"Oh my God, what happened to you?" she sobs. Rusty tries to pull off a condescending grin, but it looks more like a grimace.

"Why? What do you care? I obviously didn't teach you my lessons well enough," he spews back to her.

Slender steps forward, punching Rusty in the mouth. Ellie grabs his arm and pulls him back.

"Stop, Slender! Don't let him goad you," she begs. She stands up straighter and looks Rusty in the eye, her voice more even now, despite tears running down her face.

"Rusty, you are my brother. I loved you so much when we were younger. I don't know what happened to you, what made you become the evil, vile, travesty of the person you once were. You're beyond help, and without remorse. Beating me does not make you strong, just a sad shadow of a man. Goodbye, Bill," she finishes, turns, and walks away, led by Slender, whose eyes are on Rusty and promising hell to come.

Ashley is next, holding Vegas's and Sarah's hand with Dougal supporting Sarah. There's zero mercy in Ashley's eyes, only anger. Her voice is ice cold as she looks Rusty in the eye.

"Not so strong now, are we, Rusty? Got any more threats of gang rape and killing me? You're the filthiest cockroach I ever had the misfortune to meet."

She wrestles out of Vegas and Sarah's grip and steps towards Pennywise.

"Give me the hammer!" she demands. Pennywise sends a questioning look towards Vegas and when he nods, passes the hammer to Ashley.

"This is for my mother," she tells him, raises her arm and slams the hammer onto the toes of his right foot. The noise of the bones breaking, a satisfying crunch.

Rusty's face turns red with the effort not to scream.

"And this is for me and the hell you put me through!" She lets the hammer fly onto his left foot. This time, he cannot suppress the scream. Sarah steps up, ripping her hand out of Dougal's.

"You filthy bastard, rot in hell!" she bawls at him before spitting in his face. Dougal and Vegas lead the two women away. Chloe is still gripping my hand tightly, and Tanya remains wrapped in Masher's arms, hatred in her eyes.

"Go with the others, darlin'. You don't need to see this," Clusseaud begs Chloe. But Chloe just holds on tighter. "Make her leave, Raven, please, she shouldn't be here!" he snaps at me.

"I agree, Clusseaud, but it is her decision. I can't make it for her," I tell him.

"Dad, I know you both want to protect me, but I will stay until it's over." Chloe's eyes are serious when she looks at her father.

242

My emotions are mixed. I agree with Clusseaud. I know what's gonna happen will be gruesome, slow, and torturous. But equally Chloe wants to be there for those who can't, so I'm going to let her and support her after, the best I can.

After the door closes behind the women, Ghoul approaches Rusty with a nod to Masher.

"Man, I forgot the best bit earlier, as you checked out so rudely."

He grabs the blowtorch, pulls out the end of the skewers, which has Rusty groaning in agony, and starts heating the ends.

Within minutes, a sizzling sound comes from his buttocks, and Rusty screams as the hot skewers singe him from the inside out. Chloe hunches her shoulders and retches, burying her nose into my chest.

"My turn. I promised I'd show Pennywise and Masher a few of my tricks. It's amazing what a small piece of sandpaper can do!" Dawg smirks

He grabs a pair of rubber gloves.

"Don't want to go anywhere near that shriveled dick without gloving up," he states, which has Rusty's head shooting up, his eyes full of horror. He's not begging, though; I'll give him that.

Dawg grabs hold of Rusty's flaccid dick and starts stimulating him until he can't help but have a physical reaction. The erection is pathetic, but it's there, despite Rusty groaning in disgust. Dawg grins and pulls out a small square of sandpaper from his pocket. He rubs the end over Rusty's dick, at the sensitive head. Slight at first, increasing the pressure until Rusty is screaming at the top of his lungs. When he pulls the sandpaper away, it's eroded most of his dick and rough flesh is hanging in its place.

"Now, to prevent infection, my friend…" He stops his sentence halfway through as Ferret comes barging in.

"I have news!" he announces. He looks directly at Dawg. I just spoke to the inspector from the fire department. He sent me some video they recovered from Ashley's house. Rusty set the fire. Clear as day."

"Really?" Dawg appears calm, too calm.

"Well, my brother, as I was saying, to prevent infection," he nods at Pennywise, who hands him the bottle with alcohol, "I'll disinfect your dick. God knows where that has been anyway and we wouldn't want you to go to Satan dirty now, would we?" He pours the rest of the alcohol over Rusty's flayed dick and shakes his head in disappointment when Rusty passes out screaming.

"And now for my party trick!" he states. Dawg walks to the side of the room where a leisure battery sits, with two welding electrodes next to it. He nods at Pennywise, who grabs a bucket of water, tipping it over Rusty, while pulling the now cold skewers out of Rusty's backside.

Rusty is more unconscious than conscious at this point. Dawg inserts one of the welding electrodes into the mincemeat dick and shoves the other one up Rusty's ass, then connects both the rods to the leisure battery. Not enough force to kill him, but enough to shock him hard and frying his insides where the rods are inserted. The smell of singed flesh is overwhelming.

Disconnecting and removing the rods, Dawg steps back, grins at Fury, who's paled a little after that, and bows.

"He's all yours now."

We all know what that means. Rusty has come to the end of the road. Another bucket of cold water brings Rusty back to a semi level of consciousness. That'll have to be enough. Both Masher and Fury step forward with Tanya between them.

She takes a knife from her belt and stands up close to Rusty.

"You dirty fucking pig! Where you are going, you won't need this anymore," Tanya says with venom. She grabs his dick and balls and cuts them clean off.

Rusty is bleeding like a stuck pig now, and that's the end of him, or so I thought. Only to watch as Fury takes the dick out of Tanya's hand and shoves it down Rusty's throat, holding his mouth shut while Rusty gags and retches. "This is for my daughter! See you in hell!" He holds Rusty's panic-stricken eyes until the light leaves them and he goes slack in the shackles.

It's finally over.

27 — CHLOE

When Tanya stepped up to Rusty, I thought she was going to hit him, but the reality was so much worse. I had to throw my head to the side to vomit, *barely* missing Raven and some other guys behind us.

I should have left when Raven told me to. I should have left!

The mantra repeats itself in my head, over and over again. I am shaking so hard, my teeth are rattling, my brain wants to panic but is too overwhelmed, and I want to run until my feet can't carry me any further; run far away from this place and these people.

People I thought I knew.

I look at Ghoul, and I think to myself, *I thought he was such a pleasant guy.*

But to see the lengths he will go to torture someone makes my stomach churn, killing the little attraction I held for him stone dead. The same goes for Dawg. Just goes to show, I don't know shit about these men, and what I believed about MCs vastly underestimated the fierceness and the violence I've seen today.

This bone chilling experience shocks the literal shit out of me. I mean, I knew Rusty wasn't going to live, and to some extent, I condoned it. I just hadn't expected the harsh reality of MC retribution. I expected something more like an execution. Like in the movies. Cover their eyes and shoot.

I can't even look at Raven right now. He stands stiff and stoic, asking Pennywise and Slender to clean up, whatever that means, and hasn't looked at me at all. He truly is the cold, hard, president right now. Not the loving, sweet man I've gotten to know. The question is, which is the real Raven? And can I live with his 'job', plus the stresses of club life even without witnessing events like today?

There's always going to be a certain amount of violence. I'm not a fool to believe otherwise. It's the MC nature to handle their own problems and not go to the law. But can I deal with it all? Honestly, I don't know. All I know is right now, I have to be away from Raven and away from the club. I can hear people talking to me, but don't hear what they are saying. So, I just nod and plaster the fakest smile ever on my face as we file out of the dugout. I hear Raven talking to Fury, Ghoul, and Masher.

"You had your retribution; I'd appreciate it if you'd peal out of here." Leaving no doubt that the Slayers aren't welcome.

"The matter is closed!" His acrimonious tone not concealing his infuriation.

Feeling dirty, nauseous, still smelling the foul stench of urine and blood, I don't even look at him, but walk up the path to the house, open the door and go straight to the bathroom. After emptying my stomach of food and every last bit of bile, I turn on the shower, sit on the toilet, and strip. My clothes are going in the garbage can; they would only remind me of today, and I know I could never wear them again. Stepping into the shower, I turn it as hot as I can stand and start scrubbing myself with my loofa until my skin is bright red all over and stings. Then I let the shower wash the never-ending rivers of my tears away. I cry for Ellie, Ashley, Meghan, Rusty, despite everything he did, and for myself.

I've lost a piece of myself today. My belief in benevolence, mercy, and humane treatment of others annihilated.

After drying my sore skin, I drag myself into the bedroom, get dressed, and pack a bag. There's no way in hell I'm staying here tonight. I need to get my head straight and consider not only what I've seen, but whether I'm able to live with this knowledge and more specifically, with Raven.

Closing the door behind me, having left my keys on the bed, I throw my bag in my car, start it, and drive out of the now empty parking lot. Stopping at the gate, Halfpint is there, and motions for me to lower the window.

"You alright, Chloe? Where are you off to?" he asks me.

"Got called in at work, so heading to the hospital now." I smile at him.

"Poor you. Hope you won't get too busy." He smiles back and opens the gate for me. My heart clenches at the lie I told, but I tamp it down; I need distance from Raven.

With every mile I put between us, my chest feels tighter.

"Ally? Are you home?" I've dialed her, as I knew she wasn't there tonight.

"Sure, chick, what's up?"

"Ally, I need your help. I'm on the road and on my way to you. I packed my stuff and left; Raven doesn't know yet. I just need space to sort out my head. Can I come and see you?"

"Sure, honey, I'm with Ashley and Ellie at the moment, but they are okay. Slender and Vegas are here with them. I'll meet you at my house in fifteen minutes."

I sigh.

"That works for me, Ally. Please don't let anyone know you spoke to me. I need distance and a shoulder more than being chased by bikers." My voice is cracking as my composure slips.

248

"Of course, hon, I'll be there soon!" With that she ends the call.

◊◊◊

My head is thumping, and I look around, dazed and confused. Why am I on a couch? Where am I? Groaning, my head drops back onto the pillow on it's own accord. I try to make sense out of where I am and what's happened. Slowly, memories resurface. Nausea overwhelms me and I jump up, run to the bathroom, half wondering how I knew where it was, and vomit repeatedly. My toiletry bag is sitting on the floor. I grab my toothbrush, clean my teeth, and my mouth, which feels like an old rotten carpet.

Sitting on the closed toilet lid, everything comes crashing in at once. Yesterday's events, my flight from the clubhouse, my confusion and fear. Ally taking me in for the night, telling Sparks her mother came to visit and to stay at the clubhouse. Followed by the alcohol consumption. Ally got me loaded last night, well, more like overloaded.

Leaving the sanctuary of the bathroom, the smell of freshly brewed coffee leads me into the kitchen, where Ally is sitting at the table with two cups filled to the brim. Man, I could kiss her right now.

"How are you feeling?" she inquires, none of the jovial Ally this morning. This morning it's somber, caring, no-nonsense Ally.

"Better after ridding myself of last night's alcohol." I groan, wincing as the sunlight streaming through the window hits my face.

"What are you going to do?" she asks. After a minute of thinking, I try to give her an answer that makes sense.

"I'll take a few vacation days. I've got plenty left. Then I'll take myself somewhere calming and consider my options." The sadness in my voice surprises even me. I've not felt so lonely and heartbroken in a long time. It's not a feeling I relish, hence me staying single for so long. I dread switching on my phone. I switched it off after calling Ally.

"Okay, let me tell you a few things now that you've slept and are more together than last night. Raven clearly loves you. Even a blind person can see that. You leaving without so much as a note, that will kill him. I covered for you last night, but I won't cover for you anymore if you don't contact him and tell him what's going on. It's not fair. He'll be going out of his mind with worry."

All I can do is nod and wait for her to continue. I know she isn't finished with me. "What happened yesterday, with Rusty? I knew it wouldn't be pretty. Which is why I stayed away. It's the first time in the club's history that something like this has *ever* happened. I've known the guys for a long time, almost all of my life. They're not inherently violent; they're good men who love and protect their families with everything they have." She looks at me before continuing.

"They love hard and true, but also will go to any length to protect what is theirs. That goes for both clubs, although the Restless Slayers are certainly running a different ship. They are a true one-percenter outlaw club and do things differently. Don't mistake their mentality to be the same as the Souls' mentality. That would be a dire mistake," she explains with patience.

"Also, keep in mind that under that cut is just a man. With feelings, problems, concerns, fears, and yes, also physical strength and strong character traits. They've all been through some shit in their life, experiences that formed them. Just like you and I."

"Raven's job as president is a difficult one. He has to be a leader, even when he has doubts or makes a tough decision. He holds the men together, giving them their home, and supports them in every way possible. In return, he gets the respect due to him. He's a hard man, but as soft and squishy as a marshmallow, especially where you are concerned, Chloe. I've never

250

seen him act the way he does around you with anyone else. Ever." I swallow hard and continue to listen.

"They are not angels, but hell, they aren't devils either. They are as loyal as they come and would do anything for their women. Life with them isn't always easy, but it is rewarding. Not just sex-wise, which they seem to be fantastic at, and I can only talk for myself and Sparks there. From what I've heard from Ash, Caroline, and Sarah, everyone's world gets rocked regularly. Life is never boring with them. But equally they need a lot of tolerance. They need strong, independent women who can look after themselves to a certain extent, who can stand up for themselves when they get too pushy or overprotective."

My eyes water again as I take in what she has to say.

"I understand if you want out, and I understand if you want to stay. Regardless of what happens with you and Raven, I want our friendship to survive. I like you, Chloe, and I'll be there if you need me, but I won't lie for you." Instead of talking, I get up, walk around the table, and give her the biggest hug I can muster.

"Thank you, Ally. I love you and wouldn't dream of you having to lie or cover for me. I'll call Raven a bit later and explain when I've got my vacation days sorted and know where I'm going. Thank you for your honesty and for being so direct with me. I needed to hear that," I tell her with sincerity.

"I promise I'll try not to hurt him. I love Raven with all my heart, but I have to consider all angles here, since only I can live my life; I have to be happy and at peace with the decisions I make. Can you understand that?"

"Sure, I get it, Chloe. I totally do. Now then. I've got to open the diner. Are you alright here? I'll bring you up some breakfast, give you time to sort yourself out," she says as she gives me one last look.

When I nod, she turns and walks towards the door, spinning on her heel at the last second, with her colorful hair flying.

"Don't take too long. I need my friends and sisters close, and that's what you are, girl, a sister from another mister. Ugh, forget I said that. Now I've got Clusseaud's face in my head!"

Laughter bubbles up as I watch her shake her head at herself, walking out the door. It leaves just as quickly as she closes the door behind her.

Grabbing my dreaded phone, I switch it on. As it starts, ding after ding hits my ears. A long stream of messages, lots of missed calls from Raven, Vegas, and Ashley. I sigh as I dial my voicemail. Let's get this over with. Raven's voicemails, all ten of them, I save and don't listen to immediately. Ashley's and Vegas's are concerned, asking where I am and what's happened. All of those very valid questions. The last one's from Ash asking me to call Raven. She sounds angry in that one, and guilt washes over me. My actions have hurt people I care about.

There are several text messages from Raven, Ashley, Vegas, Dawg, Caroline; everyone wanting to know where I am. Raven's messages sound rather frantic, as do the voicemails when I finally muster the courage to listen to them. Tears are streaming down my face by the time I listened to, read and deleted everything.

Next, I look at a vacation lake cabin booking site, not too far away. There's a lovely little cabin in the woods, near a lake; quite remote, but not so remote you're never found. I reserve it despite not having even requested my vacation time yet. I realize I made the first decision about the rest of my life. Or at least a partial one.

"Hello?" my manager answers her phone.

"Hi, Cindy, it's Chloe." I take a deep breath.

"Cindy, I need two weeks' vacation time starting from Monday. I've been feeling off lately, and my mental health has taken a beating. If I don't take time off, I'm gonna burn out." I hold my breath, hoping she'll understand and give me leave on short notice.

"Chloe, that is impossible. There is no one to cover for you. We'd have to use an employment agency, and that is not in the budget. Sorry, but I won't authorize this. I'll see you on Monday," Cindy huffs through the telephone.

I sigh, and for once, do what is right for me.

"Sorry, Cindy, but you won't. You leave me no option but to quit, effective immediately. Please notify payroll to pay my outstanding wages plus my outstanding two-week vacation time. It was a pleasure working for you," I say with finality.

"You don't mean that. You can't do this, Chloe," she objects.

"Yes, I can, and I am doing this. My mental health has to come first. I am just sorry you don't understand. I'll be by to pick up my personal stuff in two weeks and to return my uniform and equipment. Thanks for everything, Cindy. Bye." Not waiting for her reply, I end the call, breathing a sigh of relief. A weight has lifted from my shoulders.

Next, I go through my emails, confirm my booking and make the payment, order groceries to be delivered to the cabin for when I plan to get there and then go grab a coffee.

There's a knock on the door. Ally enters with a breakfast tray full of food. Pancakes, waffles, bacon, eggs, everything you could want. It would easily feed three people. She grabs a coffee for herself, sits opposite me and starts dividing the breakfast onto our plates.

"Ok, so far I've listened to my voicemails, rented a cabin, and quit my job."

Her eyes go wide as she listens to me.

"Next, I'll call Raven. I feel awful about doing this to him, but I have to." My voice is firm. I look at Ally, who nods.

"I get it, girlfriend, I do. I'm glad you are improving your life. But can I suggest something helpful?"

I nod, wondering what the hell she is up to now.

"Chloe, I've got two bikes. The one I love and ride every day and a Sportster I don't. I would like to sell it to you. It's five years old, has only done about a thousand miles, and is in shop-floor condition," she tells me.

"Which one? Eight hundred, or twelve hundred cc?" I ask, my interest piqued.

"It's the twelve, my dear. It's been slightly modified." She winks at me.

I consider my savings, which I'll need right now until I find another job, and find myself cautiously asking: "How much?"

Ally grins. "It comes with a price!"

Her eyes twinkle with mischief. Oh, dear God, what is she up to now?

"Do tell," I answer, prepared for the worst.

"Okay, the cost of the bike… You promise you'll attend at least three rallies with the Wild Pixies and consider joining us. You owe me three girls' nights and give me five hundred dollars for the bike, which you can pay in 50-dollar installments. In return, I'll have the bike transferred via van to the cabin, so you can ride and clear your head. When you're ready to come back, give me a shout and I arrange for it to be picked up and brought to wherever you end up. Be that with Raven or elsewhere." She offers the bike like you would dangle a carrot in front of a rabbit.

I can't believe what she is offering. This is just too much.

"Ally, I can't accept that. It is too much! I'll give you a thousand dollars and pay for the transport," I counter offer.

"Four hundred dollars and I pay for transport." She grins.

"Ally!" I scream. "Stop being silly!"

"Okay, three hundred dollars and you pay for transport."

"Ally!" I screech at her, laughing.

"Listen," she tells me, all serious now. "I can afford to sell to you for five hundred dollars. The bike sits in the garage, gathering dust, and it's just costing me extra in insurance. You might as well take it off my hands. I'll know it'll be loved and treated well, so five hundred it is."

So much for negotiations. She has me pinned, and she knows it. I can tell by the twinkle in her eye. She's well and truly got her hooks in me.

"Okay, five hundred, but I pay in installments of hundred dollars, and I pay for transport there if you organize transport back," I reply swiftly.

"Done!" she agrees happily.

Just like that, I have a new bike to ride and a real chance to clear my head.

Oh hell, what have I done? I just quit my job and bought a bike! Panic should be running rampant. Instead, all I feel is calm and serene.

28 — RAVEN

It's seven a.m. and I've not slept a wink. Chloe left without a word, not even goodbye. I realized letting her stay was iffy, but had no idea she'd react like this. Her leaving wrecks me, leaving me broken and in pieces. Yet there're no regrets as to our relationship, only fear that it has ended like a lightning strike. The idea that we're over is unacceptable. I refuse to believe it and have resigned myself to fight by any means possible, be those dirty or fair.

She's not answering her phone. Ferret couldn't track it because it's turned off. Waiting for her to call is my only option right now, but it's driving me fucking nuts. I spent last night pacing back and forth and throwing myself from one side of the empty bed to the other. If I don't do something, I'll go crazy, and I must keep it together. We have church today and the aftermath of yesterday's shitstorm will have to be addressed, Chloe or no Chloe.

I grab my keys and gear, walk to the parking lot, and cock my leg over my bike. A ride is the only thing that could give me any semblance of peace right now. As I roll out of the gate, thoughts race through my mind.

I should have kept her away from all this. I should have thought more carefully about falling for her. Is she strong enough to be an old lady? If she balks at the first hurdle, maybe I should just let her go.

The rear wheel slipping, making the bike swerve, knocks me back into reality and schools my concentration. Without destination, I just open the throttle and let the bike find its own path.

◊◊◊

Five hours later, I pull up in front of Ally's. Locking up the bike, I sit on it sideways, hang my helmet over the bar and light up a smoke. Taking a deep draw, relishing the burn in my lungs, as I let the calm of the ride wash over me. Throwing the butt, I walk into the diner, and sit my ass down in the empty Souls' booth.

Ally comes over, smiling.

"Ah, I was wondering when you'd show up."

"Is she here?" I ask, not daring to hope.

"Nope, Raven, but she was. She needed to sort her head out. Your kind of justice overwhelmed her." Her calm but serious tone gives me hope.

"She loves you, you know. Give her time," Ally tells me while filling my coffee cup. I nod and place my order. Might as well eat. I won't get around to it once I get back to the clubhouse.

My phone rings, and by the ring tone, I can tell it's her. Thank God.

"Chloe, are you okay? Where are you?" Aware I am shooting questions as I answer the phone, I strain to hold myself back.

"Hi, Jamie, I'm sorry I just left. I got scared and needed to clear my head. I've booked a cabin for a week to do some serious thinking. I need to work out if I can live with what the club, therefore inherently you, brings with it. Whether I can cope with the consequences." I hear her unsteady voice.

"Chloe, I get that. I am sorry, I should've insisted you leave. Made sure you didn't witness what happened to Rusty. I'd even understand if you never want to come back. But I beg you, Chloe, I miss you like crazy. I love you more than anything. Please don't just give up on us."

"I love you too, Jamie, so much, but I have to live with my conscience. If I can't, we're doomed to fail. If that is the case, I'd rather know now, before we start to resent each other."

I let the silence wash over me for a moment as she finishes speaking.

"You're right, honey, if that is how you'd end up feeling, then it's better to stop this now. No matter what you decide though, I trust you explicitly, and there won't be any blowback from me or hassle regarding what you saw yesterday. I don't want to pile more pressure on you. Just please remember, I love you and want you by my side. Also, whatever you decide, please stay in touch. Let me know you're safe and okay, please, honey?" As I say those words, I know I don't mean the *whatever you decide* bit. My heart sits in my chest as heavy as a boulder, pain flaring in its place, which I unconsciously rub.

"Okay, Jamie. I can do that. Thank you for understanding. It's not just you and the club, either. I quit my job today, I need to work out my life from here. Give me a week. I'll stay in touch, I promise."

"Okay, I can do that," I reply to her.

"Love you, Jamie," she whispers before the call disconnects.

"Ferret?" I calmly speak into my cell. "Chloe just called me. Can you see where she is? Okay, let me know in a bit; I'll be on my way back soon, just having something to eat at Ally's. Catch you later, bro, and thanks!" As I end my call, Ally slams my food on the table.

The evil look she's giving me is scary as shit.

258

"Don't do it, Raven. Leave her alone. She deserves to have the time she needs to make her own decisions. Don't you damn well interfere now, you might lose her forever," she hisses at me like a rattlesnake, ready to strike with her hands on her hips. I decide it's in my best interest to agree with her, or I might find myself in the ER with whatever she puts in my food the next time I see her.

◊◊◊

"Quiet!" I bellow, as the murmuring and chatter seems unending. Church is church and I want to get this over with. It's four p.m. and I have an empty house waiting for me. The noise levels drop.

"Clean up finished?" I raise my eyebrows at Slender, Pennywise and Dawg, who if he wasn't secretary already, would make a great back-up enforcer. I shudder at how his mind works.

"Yup, boss," Pennywise answers.

"Made sure we cleaned the dugout thoroughly, burned the clothes, scattered the ashes into a field a few towns over, wrapped him in chicken fence with cinder block and sunk him in the lake. The bass and pike will have a feast."

Slender and Dawg grin as Halfpint interjects, "Remind me not to go fishing there. Might pull up more than I bargained for."

Chuckles rise around the table.

Sparks pipes up, "Dawg, you're an evil mofo underneath that calm exterior, a new motto for the future; Don't piss off the Dawg!"

Even more chuckles.

"Quiet, you jackasses!" Vegas hollers at them.

I nod at him in thanks. "Let's get this done so we all can go home." I add.

"Since this is the first regular meeting in a long time, we'll start with Spen."

Spen gives an update about finances and businesses. "The renovations at Stormy are going great guns. Might even be able to open early. The stage is about to go in. They set the bar up, ready to be stocked. The interior, as in tables, seats etc., is finished, as are the other rooms. We can start looking for dancers and new bar staff, although I would suggest keeping Neil on as manager. Zippy, your tattoo studio is just about finished. Can you go in on Monday and let them know where you want the sockets and equipment so the second fix can go in? Order your chairs or benches or whatever it is you use, so they can go in next. With a bit of luck, you'll be ready to accept customers in about three weeks. So, start advertising." Spen looks at Zippy as he finishes.

"I'll need someone at reception," Zippy states.

"Well, you better find someone then." Spen smirks at him. "I'm not your employment agency, man."

Zippy adds, "I've got a lot of requests through word of mouth. I reckon I could have a reasonably full book within the first four weeks."

"Excellent stuff," I say, to get the meeting back on track.

"Is there anything you need to clarify regarding the bar?" I ask Spen.

"Nope, nothing so far. Just have to advertise, then interview dancers and bar staff. We should be able to open within the next eight weeks," he replies.

"Good, I'll leave the advertising and all that in your hands, Spen. Get with me when we reach the interview stage, and Vegas, you and I will do that together."

Striker shouts, "I want to interview the dancers. They have to audition, after all."

Snickers go round the room.

"I'll let that slide as it's only your second proper official church today," I tease him. "Next time, it'll be the dirtiest job I can find."

Striker pales.

"Not necessary," he groans.

"At the last meeting, we discussed looking at the charter bylaws and possibly changing them. According to the current bylaws, we cannot accept prospects or members that are not white. Ratchet would like to sponsor Caleb, who I've met and have to say he's a decent kid. He's mixed race. Now, I'm all for him prospecting. He's ready to show us what he's got. But we have to discuss and see if everyone's good with removing the clause and amending it to allow only male members. I don't want to discriminate against race, orientation, age, or anything else, especially since we have disabled members, anyway." I look around the table, seeing lots of nods.

Vegas states, "I really don't care whether future brothers are orange, blue, or green with purple spots. As long as they become brothers and fit into our family. I say let's get with the times and change this."

"Agreed," calls Moggy, "But I draw the line at women. Ally can deal with hormonal road rage. I ain't."

Clusseaud pops his two cents worth in. "As long as they can ride, comply with the charter, do what needs to be done and fit in, nothing else should matter."

"Let's vote." I point at Dawg, who has his book out, ready to record the vote. It's a one hundred percent vote to amend the bylaws, which Dawg will update. After he amends the bylaws, the officers just have to sign it and it'll be official.

"Ratchet, get Greg in here a moment?" I request. Ratchet nods, leaves, returning with Greg in tow, who looks a little worried. Prospects only get into church for extraordinary reasons.

"Greg, call your friend. He needs to come by the clubhouse. We have a decision!" I bark at him, amused at the way he nods vigorously but does not speak.

"That's it, Prospect, back to work," I growl. He leaves swiftly, making sure to close the door behind him, and chuckles rise from everyone. Greg's an excellent guy. Six more months and it will be his turn to patch in. Our little family is growing. That thought sends a stab into my chest. I may have spoken too soon. My thoughts wander to Chloe, so much so that I don't hear Vegas clearing his throat.

Until Slender kicks my ankle, as Vegas is standing and staring at me with drawn together eyebrows.

"I've got an announcement to make," he starts. What the hell now?

"Ya'll know I proposed to Ashley and we want to get married within the next few months." I groan. Being stuffed in a monkey suit is all I need.

"Why the sudden rush?" Dawg asks before I can.

"Well, we'd like the next generation of prospects to grow up legitimately. We're pregnant!" he shouts, a big grin splitting his face. Chaos breaks loose as everyone comes up to congratulate him and slap his back. You can tell he is very proud of his announcement.

"Err…" I clear my throat and raise my voice to be heard over the background noise. The room quietens, all eyes on me.

"What if it's a girl, Vegas? You gonna hand her over to Ally to prospect?" I work hard to suppress my laughter seeing Vegas's color change rapidly.

"No way, it has to be a boy!" he almost screeches like a girl. He looks at me as I open my mouth.

"Don't say it, Raven, I beg you, don't say it."

Oh. Vegas knows me so well.

"I can't wait to see my seventeen-year-old niece to be, bringing home her first 'boyfriend' or being picked up for prom. In fact, I'm gonna sell tickets for that show!"

I roar with laughter, as does the rest of the club. Vegas looks panic stricken and seems lost for words, his mouth flapping like a fish out of water. God, I love winding him up.

Church turns into a celebration. A sorely needed one after the last few weeks.

At least Vegas and Ash are happy.

I'm happy for them too, I just wish the situation with Chloe would resolve itself, and I could share this with her. Being an uncle could be awesome. Since I don't want kids of my own, which is something I have to discuss with Chloe, if there *is* an 'us' left to even have a discussion about kids. A little niece or nephew would be the next best thing. One thing is for sure. That little baby will be the most fiercely protected human being in the world and will grow up with lots of crazy uncles and aunts.

Our family is growing, after all.

29 — CHLOE

Three days, countless rides, and lots of *me* time proves to be the balm my battered soul needs. Work doesn't bother me anymore. After much soul searching, I realize that I'd actually rather work anywhere else but continue to work as a nurse.

Jamie, well, we message every day, just to say *hi* and *how are you?* Some messages are more than that. Deep conversations about God, the world, and everything, making me feel closer to him than ever.

The time and physical distance eventually sets off the realization that I love him with my whole heart and soul. With all his faults, strength, and everything that goes with the territory. I'm not ready to give up on us. On what could be. Sitting here, in this gorgeous little cabin, I feel more alone than ever. Missing Jamie is such an overwhelming, physically painful emotion. In spite of my feelings I'm not running back just yet. I asked for a week and I'm going to take the entire week.

Today I plan to see my mother. Not sure why I need to give her the truth about what happened with my father, but it's become a nagging voice in the back of my head I have to deal with before it drives me insane.

Leaving the car, I saddle up and ride the fifty odd miles to her house.

The curtains are twitching as I pull into the drive and dismount. As I lift my helmet off, the door flies open, and she screams at me, "What the hell are you doing on that death machine? Just like your father! I told you to stay away from all things biker!"

I sigh. Here we go. This isn't gonna be a straightforward conversation.

Her continuous ranting grates on my nerves as I make both of us a cup of coffee. So far, I haven't even managed to get a hello in.

Maybe I should lace hers with valium? Or brandy?

Taking a seat opposite her in the kitchen, I wait for her to finish, knowing it could take a while. Finally, I can't stand it any longer.

"Are you done?" I ask, sounding harsh, making me feel the tiniest bit guilty.

To my surprise, she shuts up and stares at me wide-eyed. She's not used to me talking back like that. Normally, it's a case of me smiling and nodding to calm her. Not this time, though. This is too important for both of us. I need a relationship with my father and don't want to hide it.

"Mom, you really need to stop. I have something to tell you. Please let me finish before you comment, don't interrupt. Just sit and listen. It might actually clear some things up for you." No comment from her yet, so far so good.

"I met my father," I start. Her mouth opens and her facial features contort in rage.

"No-no! Shut up and listen!" I raise my voice this time to snap her out of her rant mode. Knowing I'm about to hurt her, my heart goes out to her, but this has to be done.

"Mom, he's a good man. Rusty set you both up. Dad really loved you."

"The fuck he did!" my mother bursts out.

"Shhh," I hush her. Her mouth sets into a thin line and her eyes are shooting daggers.

265

"Mom, do you remember that night? And do you remember Rusty?" I ask her. She nods, lips curling in disgust.

"How could I forget?" Venom tainting her voice, hands shaking.

"Helen, you remember her?" I carry on.

"Yes, Derek's wife. She used to be a good friend." Now she's a little curious.

"She still is," I continue. "Helen told me the entire story. Rusty more or less confirmed it by things he said to me. Also, Dad told me literally the same things Helen did without knowing that she had filled me in already. It's worth hearing, Mom."

I look at her, keeping my face soft and voice calm and persuasive. She looks doubtful, but motions for me to carry on.

Since she's sitting down opposite me, I lean forward, grab her hand and start telling her the whole disgusting story. Everything. From Clusseaud's denial to Raven's interventions—leaving out the details, obviously. She doesn't need to know about my sex life. That'd be a step too far. I explain Rusty's role, Helen's talk to me, and how I've since reconciled with Clusseaud, including his version of the story, which I stress matches Helen's. When I look up, I see a war of emotions on her face. Surprise, shock, anger, deep sadness, and disbelief.

I understand them all. By the time I finish, tears are streaming down her face. I know she cries for herself, for Clusseaud, for me, for Helen, and the whole fucked-up situation. It's a lot to take in. Giving her chance to collect herself and say something, I sit and wait. Only for her soft sobs to break the silence.

When she finally calms down, I brace myself for a flurry of questions, but she doesn't ask any. For the first time in my life, I find my otherwise very vocal mother speechless.

266

"I can't believe it," she whispers. "All these years filled with pain, sorrow, and bitterness, and he deserved none of it." When she looks up at me, her eyes are full of regret.

"I kinda knew something was fishy, but it was easier to hate than to fight. How could I have opposed Rusty? The club was so hard. Stone was evil, and no one would have listened. I never even gave him a chance to explain. Nor would I have believed it, if I had. So, Rusty followed me for a while? Knew about you?"

I nod. The whole situation is so unbelievably twisted, you couldn't make it up.

"Rusty is… gone, no longer part of the club."

Bile flushes my mouth as I mouth the words.

"They forced him to leave and won't be playing a role in the club anymore." I look at her, trying to give her a bit of reassurance without throwing up in my mouth.

"Mom, I'm not asking you to talk to Clusseaud, be part of club life or any such thing. But I love Raven with all my heart. I want to be with him, by his side, be his old lady and not worry about you having a fit every time I mention him. He'll be part of my life… hopefully, if I can put things right, and I don't want to hide that from you," I say to her.

"The club will be part of my life, but I want you to be, too. I've quit my job. It was eating me alive, Mom. I'll find something else to do, but I can't go back into nursing. I need to be happy, Mom. That includes being an old lady to Jamie, the President's old lady, who's nothing like his father," I explain to her as gently as I can.

"The club is nothing like it was then. I need you to understand that." I finish, praying she will be okay with this. Because I'm convinced, I'll chase Jamie to the ends of the earth and make it up to him. He's mine and I'll be damned if I don't lock that down.

I'd hate to lose my mom, but I have to live my own life, find my happiness and that means being with Jamie, no ifs, no buts, no coconuts.

Mom gets up and comes over to me. I'm surprised when she embraces me in an enormous hug.

"I'm so proud of you, Chloe bear."

She uses my old childhood pet name.

"Don't make my mistakes. Embrace life without bitterness and live it. It's not a dress rehearsal. We only get one chance, as far as we know. So go out, live it to the full and for God's sake, go get that man of yours. But if he doesn't make you happy, I'll kick his ass all over Minnesota state," she finishes with a giggle.

It's so infectious. We both stand in the kitchen, heads thrown back, laughing so hard we are literally crying.

"What the hell is going on? Have you both gone crazy?" a dark growly voice freezes us both to the spot.

Uh-oh. Dad? What the fuck? I whirl around.

"What the hell are you doing here?" I ask. My mom is frozen to the spot, mouth gaping, face pale.

"Figured you'd eventually see your mom and try to talk sense into her. It's what I should have done years ago. I don't want you fighting my battles, darlin'. I can speak for myself, and I will." He looks at me, his eyes more serious than I've ever seen them.

"How did you know where I was?" I ask.

"Well…," at least he has the good grace to look sheepish, "I asked Ferret to track your phone. I realized Terrie wouldn't have moved too far, despite you never telling me where she was, and Ferret found her for me through your phone.

"Before you say anything, no, I'm not sorry. I'd do it again in a heartbeat. To keep you safe and to get a chance to speak to your mother. Something that should have happened over thirty years ago," he says with conviction.

Now it's my turn to be silent. I understand why he did it, but don't enjoy being tracked.

"I'm pissed at you right now, Clusseaud!" I raise my voice, letting him know just how serious I am. "You could have called me and asked. I'd have given you her address." I turn to look at my mother.

"Sorry, Mom."

I would have eventually given him her address.

"I don't like being tracked. I am a grown-ass woman. I don't need your, or anyone else's, protection. Years of self-defense classes and gun training made sure of that." I'm on a roll, now shouting at my father, who looks at me with a smirk, making me madder than hell. Until I hear my mom say, "She's got your temper, Bob," with a giggle of her own. I look from one to the other, disbelieving, and throw my hands up in the air in defeat.

"That's it, I'm leaving! Before I say something I'll regret!" I shout like a petulant child as I stomp to the front door and throw it shut behind me so hard it rattles the frame. Fully aware of my childish tantrum, I stand there on the porch for a moment, as a big smile creeps over my face which quickly turns into roaring laughter.

By the time I reach my bike, I'm bent over on the seat, laughing so hard, my sides hurt. I stand, look at the house, shaking my head with a big grin and get geared up.

269

When I throw my leg over my bike, I feel lighter and more positive than I have felt in years. I start the engine, let the vibrations sink into my bones and soul, and pull out of the driveway, pointing her towards the cabin, taking the scenic route.

◊◊◊

Three days later, I ride down to Ally's, where Ashley and Caroline are waiting in a booth.

"Finally!" Ashley jumps up, shouting in my ear. My grimace tells of my fresh hearing loss through her screech. Her voice took on a tone only dogs can hear.

"Are you really going to do this?" she asks me in a slightly more normal register.

"Yes, ma'am, I've got every intention of following through," I confirm.

Ashley bursts into tears. "Damn hormones," she sobs. Ally and Caroline roll their eyes.

I grab the package Ally hands me.

"Thanks, girl, you are the best," I tell her, smacking a kiss on her cheek.

"Good luck." She winks at me, while Caroline is trying to calm Ashley, shoving carrot cake towards her. Tears insta dry and instead Ash leers at the piece of vegetable confection.

Ally sighs. "Best get her some chamomile tea before World War III breaks out. I hate pregnant women."

Caroline looks over to me and mouths a silent "good luck." God knows I'll need it if I want to bring my plan to fruition.

I've stayed in touch with Jamie. We've talked or messaged every day. It's given us the chance to talk about things we never took time to before, now that the sex component is on ice. Have I fantasized about him? Sure. Did B.O.B come out? Certainly. No self-appreciating girl goes away for a week without taking B.O.B. In my mind, I can picture every hard muscle, every ridge of his abs and shoulders, every tattoo, every bulging vein. I miss the feel of his skin, his warmth, his mind, his strength, everything about him.

Tomorrow is D-day, so I need to prepare.

First, I send a message.

Me: Hi, honey, how's your day?

Raven: Hello, gorgeous, was wondering when you'd text. My day is fine, would be better with you here!

Me: Jamie, I want to ask for a favor.

Raven: Anything, as long as you're back tomorrow. Miss you, gorgeous!

Me: Miss you too, so much!

Me: Can you meet me tomorrow? Out by Rice Lake? Eagles Nest Resort? I can meet you in the parking lot by the bar at 10 a.m.?

Raven: That where you are hiding? ;)

Me: Yup, it is. I'll explain everything tomorrow. Just be there at ten, k?

Raven: Sure, gorgeous, can't wait. Wanna go for a ride?

Me: That'd be fantastic! See you tomorrow, babe xoxoxox :)

I'm smirking as I finish my texts to him. He's still in the dark about my bike purchase. He'll expect me to climb on the back of his, but no-uh, not gonna happen. I'm taking the lead here. I grin, fasten my helmet and ride out, scouting the area.

◊◊◊

After hardly sleeping a wink, my nerves getting the better of me, I get up and am ready by six, taking extra care with my appearance. I make a few phone calls, ensuring all the details are right, before I have breakfast at nine. My stomach is churning, and I feel I'm gonna be sick.

271

Grabbing my gear, I get ready and mount up. Slowly, I roll down the gravel path to the resort's bar area, only a five minute walk away from my cabin.

I can hear him before I see him. The growl of the big bike is like music to my ears. I lean against my Sportster; my knees are shaking, and my legs feel like jelly. If I didn't lean, I'd topple over. My heart is pounding like a drum, and butterflies seem to crawl all over my skin and in my tummy. He gets off, removes his helmet, and takes me all in. In long strides, he closes the distance and rips me away from the bike, into his arms.

"Jesus, Chloe, I missed you so much." His voice sounds rough, then he peppers my face with kisses before crashing his lips to mine, kissing me senseless.

"Love you so much, never disappear on me again." His eyes show the pain he's gone through, and I feel rotten for having put it there.

"I won't," I promise between kisses when we come up for air.

"Love you so much too, Jamie. Missed you like crazy," I whisper against him. He's holding me so close that his long, hard erection is no secret. I can feel it pressing into me. If we don't leave now, I'll rip his jeans open and go down on my knees right here in the parking lot. I step back, taking all of him in.

Tight jeans clinging to his sexy-as-hell ass. Club shirt under the cut, wraparound sunglasses on top of his head, his long dark wavy mane wind tussled, bulging biceps; I have to squeeze my thighs together to get some relief of my throbbing, dripping pussy. That man is sex on legs!

His eyes are full of heat, as are mine, but we need to get this show on the road.

"Come on, slowpoke, follow me!" I smirk as I call to him. This could go amazing, or horribly wrong. I'm ready to deal with either.

I don't wait for him to mount his bike. He stares at me with surprise as I start mine, pull my helmet and gloves on, and roll out.

I know he'll be right behind me. He'll have no trouble catching up.

30 — RAVEN

What the fuck! My heart nearly stops when I see her leaning against a Sportster, I'm sure I recognize. Painted on black jeans, a cold shoulder club top with our insignia stretched tight over her ample tits, a black leather jacket left open and knee-high biker boots. She's a biker's wet dream! Mirrored sunglasses sitting high on her head. My cock wants to ride in that rodeo and bucks out of my already too-tight jeans. Fuck me, she's gonna kill me!

I almost forget to put the kickstand down in my hurry to get to her. Her smile is blinding, and my long legs eat the distance between us.

"Jesus, Chloe, I missed you so much." My voice is just short of breaking, and it's hard to hide my worry and angst that this might be the last time I'll see her.

Fuck that! I hold her face in my hand and pepper it with kisses before kissing her senseless. It's like a mad thirst I have to sate, and only her mouth will do it. My tongue wars with hers for domination and I can feel her sinking closer into me. My boner is by now digging its way into her and if I don't stop, I'll come in my pants like a thirteen-year-old schoolboy.

"Love you so much, never disappear on me again.".

"I won't." Her voice is raspy, and her eyes burn with need between kisses when we come up for air.

"Love you so much too, Jamie. Missed you like crazy," she whispers against me.

I know I should, but I can't find it in me to loosen my grip on her. The last week was hell, and I need to have her close. In fact, I could just bend her over that bike and fuck her into next week, parking lot, or no parking lot.

Hopefully, she forgot about the ride. I'm ready to ride *her* within the next twenty seconds. We need to get away from here and into her cabin, or I won't be held responsible for my actions.

"Come on, slowpoke, follow me!" She steps back and smirks as she calls me out. I can only stare as she zips up her jacket, plants her helmet on her head, puts sunglasses and gloves in place, starts the Sportster and rolls out of the parking lot, while I gawk like an idiot, wondering what the hell just happened.

I take about two seconds to reach my bike, get my helmet on, sunglasses on my face and the bike started, following her direction. Her Sportster is no match for me, so I catch up within a minute.

Watching her ride the corners turns me the fuck on, and riding with a hard-as-stone dick is no joke. Watching her ass move with the machine, her body shifting as she sets herself up. Hell, if I wasn't in love before, I am now.

Following her around Rice Lake is an absolute pleasure. She pulls up in the middle of nowhere, a lake to the left, fields as far as the eye can see to the right. What is she up to?

With the bikes parked by the side of the road—well, more like a track—we remove our protective gear. The sun is shining, and it's a warm June day. She smiles at me sweetly, grabs my hand and starts walking towards the field, picking a few wildflowers that are blooming early. It makes my heart soar, to see my woman carefree and relaxed. More relaxed than I've ever seen her before. She looks at her watch and drops onto the longer grass, pulling me down with her,

"For you." She nods, the hunger and desire in her eyes obvious. I crash my lips to hers, invade her mouth until we're both breathless and panting. I lift her and lovingly place her in the center of our bed. She watches as I shrug out of my clothes until only my boxers are left. Pulling them down, my cock springs up and hits my hard stomach. The sensation of the weeping head hitting me makes me hiss. Chloe spreads her legs for me and the dark spot where her thong just covers her sweet pussy shows me just how drenched she is.

"Please, Jamie, I need you inside me. Hurry!" she begs.

Ripping her bra and thong off, I push into her in one long stroke, close to losing it as her heat surrounds me. I won't last, but her fluttering pussy enveloping me tells me neither will she. So, quick and hard it is. I fuck her with all I've got, sweat running down my chest, dripping onto her tits. She groans, running her finger through it, licking it. What can I say? My wife is a little freak in bed, and I love it.

She looks at me and tightens her muscles, making me shout with the sensation of her squeezing me. I change the angle, lifting her knees up higher, which takes me deeper into her, and my dick hits her sweet spot on every pass.

"Come for me, baby. I need you with me, now!" I tell her, as I slam into her hard, unable to hold on any longer and fill her with ream after ream of my hot cum. The pulsing of my cock sets her off with a scream.

"Jamie!" She throws her head from side to side, her back bowing. She's the most beautiful thing when she orgasms.

We pass out in each other's arms, at peace, sated and the two happiest people on God's earth.

THE END

290

Printed in Great Britain
by Amazon

43836592R00165

places her flower bunch to the side, pushes me over and straddles me. The heat in her eyes scorches me, as does the love that burns equally hot in them.

She takes my breath away as she's staring into my eyes the way she's doing just now. Leaning down, she places the sweetest kiss on my lips while shifting, rubbing herself against my steel shaft, making me hiss.

I grind my teeth and think of my to-do list, my schedule, the bar renovation bill, anything but what she's doing to me, to stop myself from exploding.

"Chloe," I growl in warning. She just giggles and places her hand over my mouth.

"My turn," she says and smiles at me.

"Jamie, I missed you so much and love you more than anything. I'm sorry I just ran out on you. I needed to clear my head, make sure that this life, hopefully with you, is really what I want. That I can deal with the good and the bad that comes with it."

Her eyes glow with love but also a hint of nerves.

"Jamie, I needed to digest. What happened with Rusty, and, more so, my reaction to it. So much has happened in the last few weeks. It overwhelmed me. So, I ran without even trying to talk to you. For that, I am really sorry. I promise you on all that's holy, I won't ever do that again."

"Thank you, gorgeous. It nearly killed me to find you gone. We can talk about everything, anything. I'll always listen and be there for you," I get out before she shushes me. Damn woman, just shushed me! I try hard not to laugh.

"Not finished, big man. Listen up and hold your horses," she admonishes me.

I manage to get, "Yes, ma'am," out without snorting. It's a miracle.

"Jamie, I realized I want, no, I need, to be with you. I could, but don't want to do this life without you. You are the most important person in my life, and I want to share mine with you. Want you to be mine and mine alone, and I want to be yours and yours alone."

My breath catches as she gets up and pulls me up. When she sinks onto one knee, reaching into her pocket, drawing out the coolest ring, with the club insignia and our initials intertwined, holding it towards me.

"Jamie—Raven—pain in my ass and love of my life, will you please make an honest woman out of me and marry me?" she asks. Yes, she asks me to marry her.

I swallow hard a few times, not because I don't want to marry her. Fuck, I do, but because tears are threatening to burst loose. Yes, I'm an emotional wreck right now. Here is the woman I love more than life itself, doing my job. I can think of something else to do for her while she is down on her knee.

"Er... Raven?" Her eyes seek mine and I can see the nerves and a touch of panic rising in them.

In one move, I draw her up and plaster her against me. "Absolutely gorgeous. Try to stop me." I silence her squeak with my lips, and we sink down onto the ground.

Multiple orgasms later, we hunt down the clothes we ripped off and threw around.

She sits cross-legged on the grass, smiling at me with so much love and adoration, it weakens my knees.

"Come on, let's get dressed. I need to show you something. I promise you won't regret this, nor will you ever forget." She winks at me.

I sigh, unable to say no to her. I'd rather go back to the cabin and make sweet love to her, instead of fucking her into oblivion. But hell, what my woman wants, my woman gets.

I get up, dust off my jeans, and hold out my hand. We return to the bikes, and with her leading, ride further around the lake to a small clearing. I can hear soft and slow music, made for us at this moment.

We walk to the edge of the lake. The scenery is stunning, she's right, I'm sure I'll never forget this. As we walk around the corner, I stand stock still.

There by the edge of the lake is a marquee, a fire is burning on the shore, all our friends and family are there, even Fury, Masher, Ghoul, with Meghan, and Tanya. A blonde woman holding Clusseaud's arm drags him towards us.

"Mom, this is Jamie, aka Raven, the club president, and my old man, hopefully husband, by the end of the evening." I hear her, but I don't quite comprehend.

What is going on?

Clusseaud slaps me on the back and draws me into a hug.

"Come here, son, welcome to the family!" His eyes twinkling with mirth, while I remain stunned into silence.

"Hi, Raven. I'm Terrie, Chloe's mom and…" she looks from Chloe to Clusseaud and back, slightly nervous, "…his old lady," she breathes, pointing at Clusseaud. Chloe yelps and throws her arm around her mother, hugging her tight. The rest of the brothers break into raucous laughter.

Chloe holds out my ring to me, smiling wide as I stick my hand out to her. She pushes it on, and it feels one hundred percent right.

Ally, standing at the entrance of the marquee, wearing a dress. Wait, hold on a dress?

I shake my head.

Ally shouts, "Come on, you four, let's get this show on the road, places to be, food to eat."

Chloe turns on her heel and stares at Clusseaud and her mom, who's wearing tight dark jeans and a white flowy top.

"Four?" she gasps. Terrie and Clusseaud smile at her. Clusseaud looks happier than I've ever seen him. Relaxed even.

"If that's alright with you, Chloe? We don't want to crash your wedding, but we thought we'd finally do what we should have done years ago," he tells Chloe, who hugs both of them tight.

Hang on, crash your wedding? Did I hear that right? I can no longer contain my laughter. Tears are rolling down my face as I laugh and double over with my hands on my knees. I can't breathe and my stomach hurts like hell, but I can't stop laughing. The little minx organized all of this behind my back. That woman! She's the most precious and amazing thing that ever happened to me.

"Well, father-in-law dear, it looks as though they have caught us. Hook, line, and sinker!" I wheeze out between bursts of laughter.

"Better get on with it before the ladies change their mind!"

"Right, son, let's do this. You hurt my little girl and I'll shoot you." Clusseaud's reply does nothing to calm my laughter.

Sparks and Vegas appear out of nowhere and drag Clusseaud and me off to the marquee. I gasp as I see they've decorated it with wildflowers, similar to the ones Chloe picked earlier, and now shares with her mother. The interior looks fantastic, with Ally standing at the end of the makeshift aisle. White fabric hangs from the end of chairs lining the aisle, decorated with hearts, made from bike chains. How did they manage all this? The Restless Slayer congregation comes to meet and congratulate me. Fury looks me straight in the eye.

"I hope we can put the last few weeks behind us, and it never has to be spoken of again. Done and dusted!" I nod and shake his hand.

"Done and dusted," I agree.

The marquee is packed to the rafters with our friends and family. Clusseaud stands next to me, as nervous as I am. Spen comes forward and hands both of us our old ladies' cuts, which we will give them instead of rings for now.

I have to repeat, the women have thought of everything.

Everyone stands and Adele's *"Make you feel my love"* floats through the space. Clusseaud and I turn, watching Chloe and Terrie, each holding a small wildflower bouquet in one hand and having their other arms linked, walk slowly down the aisle towards us.

Clusseaud hands me a tissue, as I can't stop my eyes from tearing up. Chloe is the most beautiful thing I've ever seen. Clusseaud wipes his eyes and clears his throat. When they reach us, Chloe passes Terrie's hand to Clusseaud while Terrie passes Chloe's into mine.

Chloe smiles at me and all I can do is whisper, "You are so beautiful, Chloe, you knock me to my knees."

She replies, "Thank you. You are the most handsome biker I've ever seen. I can't wait to be tied to you every way I can."

Ally shushes us and makes us turn around as she hollers, "Dearly beloved and rest of you degenerates. Keep your traps shut or I'll smack you upside the head!" Laughter follows her introduction.

During the hilarious Ally-style ceremony, my mind keeps straying to the beautiful woman by my side, and the only thing I can think constantly is MINE. Ally's words flow over me as my eyes are glued to Chloe. So beautiful, smart, and strong. God, I am a lucky bastard.

Chloe elbows me in the ribs, shocking me out of my trance.

"Hello? Earth to Raven, anybody in there?" Ally teases me.

"Once again, for those who I bored to sleep, like this precious one here," Ally exclaims, pointing at me, causing the congregation to burst into heckling and fits of giggles.

"Now, pay attention, no sleeping on the job," she admonishes me with a wink.

"Do you, Chloe and Terrie, take the Robert and Jamie, aka big trouble," more laughter, "to be your lawfully wedded pain in the asses? To have and to hold, for richer or poorer, in sickness and in health, keep them on a tight leash and spank them when they are trouble, as long as you all shall live?" Terrie and Chloe look at each other, start laughing, and take a moment before they can answer.

"We do."

"Do you promise to never touch their bikes unless asked to and shove anyone else off their pillion seat and scratch their eyes out?" She winks at the women.

"We do!" they reply as one.

"See me after church for hair pulling lessons," Ally adds, which has everyone roaring with laughter and Clusseaud looking worried.

Then she turns to us.

"Do you hoodlums going by the names of Robert and Jamie, aka big trouble, take the Chloe and Terrie to be your lawfully wedded treasures?" Wolf whistles sound from the back row, and Chloe and Terrie are sputtering, trying not to laugh.

"To have and to hold, for richer or poorer, in sickness and in health, revere them and satisfy them every night, and during the day when opportunity knocks."

More wolf whistles pierce the air, and Chloe's cheeks turn a pretty shade of pink.

"Love and honor them as long as you all shall live?" Easiest answer I ever gave in my life.

"We do." Clusseaud and my voice ring out.

"Do you promise to love and protect them, be honest and true as long as you all shall live?"

"We do." We agree as one.

"You better, or else!" Ally shakes her fist at us mockingly, drawing chuckles from Clusseaud and I.

"Then by the power invested in me by the state of Minnesota and the unministry.org, I now declare you legally ball and chain, old lady and old man, husband, and wife. You may now kiss the brides! No hanky panky though, don't wanna have to bleach my eyeballs."

The last bit I almost don't catch as I grab Chloe, bend her over my arm and kiss her as though the world is ending.

Ally clears her throat after a few minutes, making us pull apart. She hands us the Property of Raven and Property of Clusseaud cuts, and we put them on our women. The entire congregation is cheering and hollering, throwing rice, paper bits, and beer bottle caps, as we make our way out of the marquee. The sun is setting and provides us with a nature spectacle like no other. We spend the rest of the evening eating, laughing, dancing, spending time with our family and friends.

Clusseaud and Terrie are the first to disappear.

282

Chloe grabs my hand and holds on tight.

"Let's get out of here. I need to be inside you," I whisper to her. She nods and we steal away to our bikes, gear up and start rolling. The most awful rattling and clunking noise brings us to a sharp stop. Our friends and family point and laugh at us, trying to sneak away unnoticed. We get off, inspect the bikes, only to find a load of bean cans tied to the back. Laughing, we remove them and throw them towards our family while giving them the bird.

Assholes! But we love them for it.

Finally, we pull into the parking lot of Chloe's cabin. We park right outside, and she walks ahead of me to the door. I grab her, lift her into my arms, and carry her over the threshold like a romantic fool. She laughs at me, her eyes happy, shining bright with happiness.

"I love you, Mrs. Saunders," I whisper in her ear as I push her against the closed door.

"Love you too, Mr. Saunders, aka big trouble. Now stop messing around and fuck me already." Her wish is my command.

EPILOGUE

Five Months Later

The last few months have flown by. I can honestly say I'm the happiest I've ever been. Married life suits us both, and luckily, my reluctance to have children was no issue for Chloe. We will just be aunt and uncle to our nephew or niece. Vegas is driving himself mad with thoughts and worries about having a girl. They chose not to know the sex of the baby.

Of course, we have a pool going.

Today is a special day. Ashley and Vegas's wedding, held here at the clubhouse. The old ladies spent ages, with some help of the brothers, decorating, and it's unrecognizable. They did an amazing job. It's perfect.

Chloe wraps her arms around me as we stand there looking at the finished project.

"You know, I love this, but I loved our setting more," she whispers in my ear as she squeezes me. I couldn't agree more. This is more ceremonial. It's what Ashley wanted.

She didn't make us guys dress up to the nines, but new black jeans and white button ups under the cuts and carnations as buttonholes, was her requirement.

"Come on, husband, let's give your sister her present." Chloe smiles at me. We make our way to Ashley's door and knock.

"Come in!" a voice shouts, not sure who.

When I open the door, all breath leaves me. My sister is in a flowy white gown, not hiding but showing off her considerable bump, in full makeup, trying to suppress tears. Ally steps back, looking at the garter she's placed on Ashley's thigh. Clearing the lump in my throat, I wipe a tear from my eye. I wish her mom could have seen her.

"It's not too late, Sis, you can still back out," I joke, watching her shake her head, laughing. Stepping closer, I take the box out of my cut pocket and place it in her hand.

She opens it, gasps, and her mouth drops open at the sight of her mother's diamond studs.

"Raven, where did you find them?" she asks.

"We found them after the fire when the old house was demolished. A workman handed them in. I kept them for you, knowing you'd want a part of her with you," I reply, my voice breaking. Chloe is standing behind me. She smiles and steps around me to hug Ashley.

"Don't mind him, he's just a soppy big brother today," Chloe tells her.

"Time to go," I remind her gently after Caroline fusses about Ashley's makeup. We walk to the clubhouse door side by side. The parking lot is crammed full of bikes and cars of all shapes and sizes. Chloe leaves us outside the door to take her place in the clubhouse.

I take Ashley's hand, ready to walk her down the aisle.

"Ready?" I ask. When she nods, I open the door and lead her inside. She gasps, taking in the space's transformation.

John Legend's "*All of You*" softly sounds through the speakers. Chairs rustle as everyone inside the main room stands. We step forward, her hand on my arm, as I lead her down the aisle toward the man she loves. He's my VP, brother, friend, but I'll still bury him if he hurts my sister.

"I, Ashley Saunders, take thee, Vincent Albright, to be my lawfully wedded husband. To love and to cherish, to honor and obey, in sickness and in health, 'til death do us part. Take this ring as a token of my love and unbreakable bond." Ashley's clear voice resonates through the room. Chloe clings to my hand for dear life, tears tracking down her cheeks.

Happy tears.

I hand her a tissue, which I stuffed into my cut pocket, fully expecting the waterworks. It takes me back to our own wedding. Less ceremony, but just as much happiness. I'm the luckiest son of a bitch alive to have her, and I know it.

We spend the night eating, drinking, dancing, and enjoying time with our crazy, but loving, family. Vegas and Ashley have long left. Greg walks up to me.

"Alright if I swap with Caleb, Prez?" I nod at him. Caleb, being our newest prospect, started his time with us about four months ago, and, so far, has proven himself to be solid brother material.

The bar has reopened and is a successful earner for the club. I should thank Karen and Rusty. Because of those two fucktards, it showed us the bar had so much more potential than we realized. Granted, their actions took us to hell and back, but we came out better for it. Zippy opened his tattoo studio and is always fully booked. He's thinking about taking on an apprentice soon. The last few months have been calmer, and Rusty is a fading bad memory.

Chloe nudges me out of my musings.

"Let's go home, old man. I've got a gift for you." She winks at me. Hopefully, it's her, with nothing on but a bow.

I can't wait to get her home, so throw her over my shoulder to her hooting and laughing, storming up to the house, smacking her glorious ass while I'm at it. The need to be inside my wife is staggering and hasn't waned one bit. What can I say? My dick loves her as much as my heart does.

Setting her down in our bedroom, she slaps my arm and giggles.

"Turn around," she requests.

I raise my eyebrows.

"Seriously? Since when are you shy? Don't tease me, woman. I need to be inside you within the next minute, or I won't be held accountable for what I do!"

She laughs at me, and repeats, "Turn around."

So, I do as I'm told, making a show out of sighing as though I'm hard done by. Clothes rustle behind me, shoes hit the floor, and after a few more seconds, she commands me, "Turn around, Jamie."

My breath leaves my body in a huff, my mouth falls open, my tongue hangs out, and my dick is threatening to break through my jeans. Have mercy! She stands before me in nothing but a deep dark red lace thong and matching bra.

Then I see it.

"Jesus!" I croak out as I step towards her, running my hand gently from her hand up to her left shoulder, where a beautiful branch of a tree of life meanders its way up her arm.

The leaves are a dulled green, butterflies and bees everywhere, orchid blossoms adorning it, and on the top of her shoulder, a large black raven sits guard over a much smaller bird of paradise. I can't take it all in. When I look closer, I see the beaks of the two birds are touching, and R & C is showing in their plumage. Lifting her wrist to my mouth, kissing it, I see my name spanning the inside of her wrists. How did I miss that? The tattoos are beautiful. I am floored.

"You did this? For me?" My voice is rough and my cock throbs in pain.